BAD DAY BREAKING

BAD DAY BREAKING

A BAD AXE COUNTY NOVEL

JOHN GALLIGAN

ATRIA PAPERBACK

NEW YORK   LONDON   TORONTO   SYDNEY   NEW DELHI

ATRIA
PAPERBACK

An Imprint of Simon & Schuster, Inc.
1230 Avenue of the Americas
New York, NY 10020

First Atria Paperback edition August 2022

ATRIA PAPERBACK and colophon are trademarks of Simon & Schuster, Inc.

For information about special discounts for bulk purchases, please contact Simon & Schuster Special Sales at 1-866-506-1949 or business@simonandschuster.com.

The Simon & Schuster Speakers Bureau can bring authors to your live event. For more information or to book an event, contact the Simon & Schuster Speakers Bureau at 1-866-248-3049 or visit our website at www.simonspeakers.com.

Interior design by Erika R. Genova

Manufactured in the United States of America

1 3 5 7 9 10 8 6 4 2

Library of Congress Cataloging-in-Publication Data has been applied for.

ISBN 978-1-9821-6656-4
ISBN 978-1-9821-6658-8 (ebook)

The prince of darkness is a gentleman.

—William Shakespeare, *King Lear*

Roman Pieter Vanderhoof #1553499

Wisconsin Secure Program Facility

It is written in the Bible: Let he who is without sin among you cast the first stone.

Or she. Am I right?

You know what this means because like me you have been wronged. We've all made questionable decisions in our lives. So who are they to judge us and take away our lives?

I know you are the kind of special person who will now make the best decision of your life because I am honest, non-judgmental, very good looking (so I'm told, but you decide), and above all a GENTLEMAN who will treat you like the precious LADY that you are.

Some people never pay for what they do. Or so they think. But we all deserve another chance.

Believe in yourself. Believe in me. Trust God. This is all I ask.

Race: White
Date of Birth: 1/30/75
Height: 6'2"
Earliest Release Date: 4/15/2020
Maximum Release Date: 4/15/2025
Would you like letters from both sexes? Women only (white only, no overweight)

Education: College
Occupation before prison: Construction engineer; contractor; developer
Activities in prison: Weightlifting, Art, Sobriety (AA, NA), Bible Study
Can you receive and send emails? Yes; also letters and photos

meet-an-inmate.com posted 6/1/2014
jpay.com last reply record 4/13/2020

PROLOGUE

I: July

There were plenty of witnesses.

At 11:13 on the scorching morning after the Fourth, with USA-themed inflatable yard goods, flags and pennants, barbecue aprons, pet accessories, and other items of patriotic decor at half price, a dozen or so shoppers had been making their way into or out of the Walmart in Farmstead, Wisconsin, when a Bad Axe County Sheriff's Department deputy named Mikayla Stonebreaker sprang in a red sweat from her cruiser.

A former junior high school gym teacher, Deputy Stonebreaker strode largely and purposefully along a row of parked sedans and pickups. Her pace tracked the outbound progress of a tall, soft, comfortably handsome man with a long gray braid, wearing an earth-toned peasant robe and Teva sandals. The man carried a small white pharmacy sack and moved sedately, while his wife, a foot shorter in a pale blue robe, steered him from the elbow. Their intention was to enter the vehicle they had arrived in and return home. To all watching, these two were known as the Prophet-Father Euodoo Koresh and his First-Wife Ruth, leaders of a prosperity-theology church that had appeared in May to occupy the former U-Stash-It Mini-Storage compound in outer Farmstead. Bad Axers had been calling them a cult. They called themselves the House of Shalah.

From a slot between an F-250 Super Duty pickup and a cart corral, Deputy Stonebreaker launched. She ripped the prophet-father from the grip of his wife and slammed him into a chain of nested shopping carts. She screamed at him, "What's in the bag, freak!" She tore away the little white sack, leaving its shredded top in the prophet-father's trembling hands.

The final report would list the contents of the sack: the sedative Halcion, .5 mg, 60 count; and the painkiller Opana, 20 mg, 60 count. The scrip was legally written by a Dr. Gregory Ho, a general practitioner in Reno, Nevada, to a patient named Jerome W. Pearl.

Deputy Stonebreaker kept the prophet-father folded back over a shopping cart and continued to command the situation while the horrified first-wife looked on. It was noted in the report that some of those watching had flashbacks from gym class.

"Let me see some ID! Now!"

The final report would confirm that the ID given was a valid Texas driver's license assigned to Jerome William Pearl, sixty-three. A plethora of documentation from the follow-up investigation would prove that Jerome William Pearl and the Prophet-Father Euodoo Koresh were one and the same person, that the medications were properly his, and that he had broken no laws, nor intended to. The report made clear that no legal standard whatsoever justified the parking lot attack on the prophet-father by Deputy Mikayla Stonebreaker.

The report would also state, accurately, that witnesses to the attack had whistled and applauded.

II: September

"The Bad Axe County Police and Fire Commission hereby unanimously recommends to the full county board for approval the retirement, with honor and with our heartfelt gratitude, of Interim Chief Deputy Richard Bender."

Marge Joss struck her gavel. She covered her mic and leaned toward Bender, who slouched, gray and frail, in the first row of audience seating.

"We love you, Dick," she rasped under the eruption of clapping hands. "You helped us keep some guardrails on your boss. Get well and catch some fish."

Bender's girlfriend, Irene, helped him up to leave. "We got two dozen minnows getting hot in the car," she explained. "Actually, they're black-tail chubs."

Shuffling out of the courthouse basement meeting room on Irene's arm, ex-Deputy Bender made teary eye contact with the broad-shouldered, red-haired, uniformed young woman in the back row of chairs. Though her green eyes glistened back, Sheriff Heidi Kick sent Bender the same lovely deep smile that as a seventeen-year-old had made her Dairy Queen in the next county south. The sheriff felt real joy in this fact: As her deputy, Bender had been an obstacle—a crank, he admitted—that she had turned into an ally. It had taken well into her second full term—1,084 days, not that she was counting—but from this moment forward she and Bender could upgrade from allies to friends. Last week he had given the sheriff's daughter an accordion. Lessons had been scheduled. Ripe tomatoes from the Kick family garden were agreed to be the price.

Bender's second glance at his ex-boss was fierce with meaning: *I'm sorry about what's going to happen next. I'd a hung in there if I could.*

Sheriff Kick nodded.

Marge Joss gaveled again.

"The commission now moves to closed session to discuss a personnel matter."

That matter was the evolving mess of Sheriff Kick's suspension of Deputy Mikayla Stonebreaker over the Walmart incident, followed by Deputy Stonebreaker's appeal of said suspension, followed by Stonebreaker's subsequent reinstatement by the commission while her appeal was processed, followed by Sheriff Kick's reassignment of the deputy to desk duty—meaning the jail, the evidence room, tours of the Public Safety Building—followed by Deputy Stonebreaker's gender-discrimination lawsuit against Bad Axe County and the sheriff herself. In the meantime, Dennis Stonebreaker, the deputy's unemployable husband, had formed an organization to defend the Bad Axe from the House of Shalah because the sheriff would not . . . though what she would not do to defend home ground was undefined aside from one thing: she refused to use the word *cult*.

"Clear the room, please."

Obeying the orders of Police and Fire Chairperson Joss, the larger-than-normal contingent of spectators withdrew. That left Sheriff Kick alone with Ms. Joss and the five male members of the commission, all farmers whose latest beef with the sheriff concerned her enforcement of traffic and safety laws with respect to on-road use of off-road vehicles. *Doors and seat belts*, she was saying, *if you want to use a public road. No*, she was saying, *your unsafe habits will not be "grandfathered in."* Her commissioners also shared the general dismay, Sheriff Kick knew, at her refusal to call the House of Shalah a cult.

After the room cleared there followed a short recess. The vending machine was worked for cans of Sun Drop while the moisture level of the corn crop was discussed. In an overall dry year, that half inch yesterday was a drop in the bucket, and what the doctor ordered was three or four good soaks in September.

Left out of this conversation, the former farm-girl sheriff retrieved her phone from behind her badge and took a moment to follow up on a different personnel matter, one that the commission didn't know about yet.

She moved to the meeting room window. From there she could see a thousand acres of field corn turning brown too quickly under a hot blue sky. Between cornfields she could see Bender's girlfriend's red car heading out Courthouse Road and passing between two great prairie oaks before disappearing down into Spring Coulee. When Sheriff Kick said she loved this landscape, she always felt like *love* was too weak a word. Among its many other graces, the coulee region was modest in the way that a view from ridge level concealed its intimate beauty: the narrow coulees carved by spring-fed watersheds through sea-bottom limestone, the densely forested hillsides, rugged and wild, that flanked fertile bottomlands spotted with family dairy farms and threaded with trout streams that meandered through embroidered sleeves of orange jewelweed, purple aster, and dusty-pink joe-pye. In the sheriff's mind, this sense of *so much more than meets the eye* defined the land and the people who went with it. The untrained eye looked from the state highway across the cornfield skin of the Bad Axe and missed the depth, the heart and soul—and honestly, from Sheriff Kick's point of view, most of the darkness and trouble.

The call connected. She asked Denise Halverson, her dispatcher, "So do we have a warrant?"

"The judge is skittish, Heidi. Jpay.com, prison mail, that's federal stuff. He wants more cause."

"But we're sure about the IP address."

"Right. It's ours. Oops, hang on."

Denise clicked over to take a different incoming call.

"You've reached the Bad Axe County Sheriff's Department. Whose bull is on which road? Thank you. I'll send a deputy."

She came back.

"It's our IP for sure, Heidi, the laptop in the squad room. But so far, the judge sees a policy breach more than a crime."

The sheriff sighed. "So far. It's just so disturbing that she would use one of our computers. Why?"

"Well," Denise said, "because she's more afraid to get caught doing weird shit at home than at work?"

"I don't know . . ."

The sheriff watched a gust rustle the corn. "She" was young Deputy Lyndsey Luck, apparently going through some personal struggles in her second year. On principle, faced with turnover midway through her first term, the sheriff had demanded more female deputies. But actually having them? Managing Lyndsey Luck and then Mikayla Stonebreaker had been another story.

"The meeting's back on, Denise. I gotta go."

I'm sorry about what's going to happen next.

Bender's look had referred to rumors that the matter of Deputy Stonebreaker's status had been secretly discussed and already decided—and linked to the now-vacant chief deputy position.

"Sheriff . . ." began Marge Joss. Peering over black half-glasses, she followed this with a preemptive sigh of exasperation, that of a massive God-fearing farm woman with a crew cut and sun-scorched cleavage. "The members of this commission fully expect that when you hear our decision you're going to kick and scream and stomp your feet . . ."

Kicking and screaming meant the sheriff speaking her mind thoughtfully.

"Nevertheless . . ."

III: October

Alexis Schmidt—who at age seventeen had begun to consider a career in law enforcement—had only one thin hour between milking twenty-three black-and-white Holsteins and the arrival of the bus that would take her to Blackhawk High School.

"Mom," the girl called, rushing out the door in barn clothes, with uncombed hair and wet hands, "I gotta get some pumpkins from the Amish. For a . . . Halloween school thing."

The Amish lived a half mile away on gravel. She took her Grandpa Ed's four-wheeler and goosed it.

She ripped past the Amish place, the Hochstetlers', and out of cold coulee shadows up to the ridge, where combines spewed chaff and dust into the bright sun.

She was riding illegally now, driving a four-wheeler where Schmidt Road crossed U.S. Highway 14 and became Fog Hollow Road.

Different township, different rules. Five-hundred-dollar ticket.

First there had been Sheriff Heidi Kick, then Deputy Lyndsey Luck—and recently her old gym teacher, Ms. Stonebreaker, had been promoted to chief deputy. With these examples, a girl began to see her world differently.

Understanding herself as a scofflaw at the moment, Alexis waited for an ambulance, a milk tanker, and a corn hauler, then nipped across the highway at full throttle and aimed the machine down the steep grade alongside Fog Hollow Creek.

In the shadows she was cold again. She did not wear a wristwatch and had left her phone at home. How long was this taking? Side by side, the winding road and winding creek screwed themselves deeper into the Fog Hollow coulee until at last the creek backed up behind the earthen dam that formed little Lake Susan.

Alexis parked the four-wheeler where a one-bar gate kept kids from driving out onto the dam.

Because otherwise they would, she understood now.

Drunk. Showing off. And sooner or later Sheriff Kick would find somebody's truck upside down in Lake Susan, with maybe someone drowned inside it.

That's why the gate was here.

The rising sun had just struck the fog along the dam's grassy eastern face. But it was still chilly. Alexis eyed the dusty work shirt wadded into her Grandpa Ed's dash console. She shook the shirt out and put it on, then stepped off the four-wheeler and into the dew-wet opening blooms of hawkweed and chicory.

Ahead of her, a loaf of soil five hundred feet wide held back Lake Susan and let the creek back out through a corrugated pipe on the downstream side of the dam.

Alexis hurried out along the spine of the dam, hearing the water spew out and crash into the pool below the pipe. *You want to see a miracle?* Win Carpenter had asked a few days ago. Win Carpenter was this quiet older guy from the cult who did farm work for her dad and grandpa. *You have to go see it,* he had urged her. And, though she couldn't say exactly why, here she was.

Alexis's long shadow hurried with her out along the dam, gliding blackly down the western slope and touching murky Lake Susan. Something made her stop and scan the shore, a grid of muddy bathtub rings left as the reservoir filled and emptied.

Nothing to see, no idea why she was looking, she moved on.

The sound of water crashing below the dam grew louder as Alexis neared its center, where Win Carpenter had said a trail cut back and forth between tall asters and joe-pye weed down to the top of the pipe.

There she found it. She descended excitedly through the tall wet flowers, sometimes skidding, until she stood upon the concrete housing for the pipe.

Arms spread for balance, heart thumping, she took tiny steps out onto the housing and then out upon the ribbed pipe. She reached the lip and froze. Beneath her, little Fog Hollow Creek poured out in force, fell and smashed mightily, splashed and foamed and spread, swirled and gathered, then tumbled on downstream, once again its simple, modest self.

She brought her eyes back and stared exactly where Lake Susan poured out, a smooth and solid curl of faintly mud-tinted water.

Stared and stared.

And, *yes!*

A trout as long as her forearm leapt up from the tumult.

For two breathtaking seconds, the creature hung before Alexis in the morning sun, a gorgeous gleaming ornament, golden brown with red spots, quivering in its effort to land inside the mouth of the pipe. *A miracle . . .*

To her dad and grandpa, Win Carpenter was a religious weirdo. But Alexis saw what he meant. The thick fish hung as a jewel in the sun . . . and hung . . . squirmed for more height . . . stopped Alexis's heart with its desire to land upon that fast lip of water, somehow grip it, and squiggle upstream into the pipe. It was a miracle of aspiration and will, of breaking boundaries, and she needed it.

"Oh, no!" she cried when the plunging current caught the fish by the tail and flicked it cartwheeling back into the pool.

"Try again!" she cried. "You can do it!"

The next trout, a slightly smaller one, caught the lip, held, and squirted up into the pipe toward Lake Susan.

"Oh, my God!"

The next one, an even bigger trout than the first, achieved enough writhing height, flashed spectacularly in the sun, but missed the pipe entirely, landed in the weeds below, and flopped itself back into the water.

Another make.

Another make.

A miss.

It went on.

"Oh-my-freaking-God-this-is-so-cool!"

Alexis lay facedown on the pipe, smiling, her unkempt frizzy blond hair hanging over, and she forgot time. She forgot her grandpa's four-wheeler. She forgot her lie about the pumpkins and the schedule of the school bus.

She forgot who she was, and where she was, until out of the pipe, inching along, emerged two white human hands, palms up.

Next came forearms.

Then elbows.

Next, thinning gray-brown hair and a long pale forehead, trout slapping off and falling back.

Then a man's half-familiar face: his open eyes, his mud-packed nose, his purple twisted lips, crawfish clinging to the white-pink meat of a deep slash across his throat.

Her joy replaced by frozen horror, Alexis at last roused herself and ran to the top of the dam.

She was surprised and relieved to see a sheriff's cruiser already idling beside her grandpa's four-wheeler.

She waved both arms, hollered, "Help!" at the top of her lungs.

Chief Deputy Mikayla Stonebreaker emerged from the cruiser.

Alexis waved, saw Deputy Stonebreaker begin to move in response. Then, with her breakfast loosening in her stomach, she ran back across the dam and down the trail.

Just as Alexis re-arrived woozily at the end of the pipe, the disemboweled remainder of Win Carpenter slid out and crashed into the pool.

BLACKOUT WEDNESDAY

Robert Kenneth Henderson #353714
Wisconsin Secure Program Facility

Wassup girl? Name is Robbie but my boys call me Skip. I thank you from the bottom of my heart for taking time out your busy day to check my profile. I promise you will not be sorry.

They tell me I'm the life of the party, always positive, but also very reflectional. My color is all the colors. I do enhance. Also I am every kind of gentleman that you need me to be. Let me see you. I like what I see and somebody bothering you, it will be my pleasure to take care of that.

Race: White
Date of Birth: 1/3/1988
Height: 5' 7"
Earliest Release Date: 5/15/2020
Maximum Release Date: 12/15/2020
Would you like letters from both sexes? Women
Education: Some high school
Occupation before prison: Sales, security
Activities in prison: HSED, Music, Prayer, Iron
Can you receive and send emails? Yes, also letters and pictures

meet-an-inmate.com posted 7/5/2019
jpay.com reply record 3/1/2020

CHAPTER 1

Wanna drink ketchup?

Midmorning on the day before Thanksgiving, Bad Axe County Sheriff Heidi Kick glanced at this text message and dropped her phone back behind her badge.

At just that moment the first snow of the year dropped decisively upon the impromptu circus of media, rubberneckers, and protesters that lately assembled each morning along U-Stash-It Road.

"Yes, that is true," Sheriff Kick confirmed, tucking the eviction order inside her duty jacket to keep it dry. "They are all named Carpenter. Twenty-three adults and nine children. Thirty-two Carpenters."

With no wasted motion, the reporter, a stylish young man about her age, mid-thirties, handsome in a brainy way, popped up what was possibly the only umbrella in the entire Bad Axe. The sheriff noted heads turning as wet flakes thumped the wide black fabric. Beyond, the sudden snow fell silently upon the green-brown expanse of Blackhawk Pines, the municipal golf course that bordered the north side of U-Stash-It Road. Blackhawk Pines security cameras caught the action on the road and inside the U-Stash-It fence from tall poles planted behind the thirteenth green and fourteenth tee. Those cameras, the sheriff knew, had been toggled to wider angles to keep tabs on the course's weird new neighbors.

"Except the prophet and his wife," the sheriff clarified. "Thirty-two Carpenters plus those two."

She felt like Markus Sullivan from the *New York Times* knew more than he was letting on, thought he was probing her for signs of ignorance as he reported on groups like House of Shalah across the country. She tried to check her impatience. She had official paper to deliver.

"But, yes, because all new members change their names to Carpenter when they join, we still don't know Win Carpenter's real name. No one inside that fence does either. Brother Win is all they know. So they say. Mostly, they won't talk to us at all."

She watched Sullivan raise his neatly bearded chin one-half centimeter. Were Carpenters talking to *him*? The sheriff's freckled features tightened to a frown. This was exactly what she didn't need . . .

"This among other things has made it tough to solve his murder."

"Sure. Of course." He scrawled a note with a stylus on his phone. "So, Sheriff, in order to join the cult—"

"I don't call it a cult."

"What do you call it?"

She stared past his umbrella, trying to gather herself at the end of what she felt had been the most difficult month of her life, at least since the bad old days. Her husband had been sick. Her kids—Ophelia, Taylor, and Dylan—had been out of school. Her mother-in-law, Belle, had lost her latest café waitressing job and moved in with the Kick family at their hobby farm ten miles out of Farmstead on Pederson Road. There, the sheriff and her husband, Harley, conducted homeschool with no internet and dealt with an extra seventy-four-year-old child who smoked and drank and knew a better way to do everything.

And that was just the personal stuff. Over the sheriff's "kicking and screaming," the PFC had replaced Bender with Mikayla Stonebreaker as her chief deputy. Signaling intolerance, the PFC's decision had emboldened Stonebreaker's husband, Dennis, to re-name his vigilante organization "Kill the Cult." Lately the group posted armed "observers" 24-7 on U-Stash-It Road. All this time, the Win Carpenter case had spun its wheels under a cloud of rumors about drug dealing in the House of Shalah and whispers of a cover-up related to the sheriff's substance abuse in her troubled years after high school down in Crawford County. She was protecting someone. Stupid as this was, it was the hot gossip.

There was more.

Still unanswered was the disturbing internal-affairs question of whether the sheriff's promising young protégé, Deputy Lyndsey Luck, had been using department computers to carry on romantic pen pal relationships with prison inmates. Deputy Luck denied this, and so far three judges, all citing First Amendment concerns and insufficient cause, had refused to sign a warrant granting access to the prison system's email service. The judges were probably right, but the sheriff couldn't shake the feeling that Deputy Luck and her department were heading for trouble.

And still more.

Ten days after Halloween, the House of Shalah had purchased the vacant 2.2-acre lot next to the U-Stash-It property. Immediately upon closing, they had pulled a permit and moved in heavy equipment, and Carpenters who obviously knew how had staked out the land and begun installing a residential sewer. Laying big concrete pipes had become proof of Kill the Cult's claim that the Carpenters planned to build houses, stay in Farmstead, and—here was the threat—take over the Bad Axe by populating the schools with its children and electing its members into county government.

Try and argue with a rumor, Sheriff Kick thought as the brim of her cap began to drip. Glancing through quickening snowfall at the reporter, she felt the urge to holler bad words.

"I call it what it is," she finally replied. "A religious community."

He nodded. "It seems that calling it that has made you unpopular."

"I'm not concerned about my popularity. The word *cult* is inflammatory, inaccurate, and not helpful."

She pointed behind Sullivan at Dancing Jesus. A local Christian protest group had somehow acquired the kind of advertising balloon that kinked and flailed crazily outside used car lots, except their balloon had Christ-like features.

"Why aren't those folks a cult? How is what they believe more legitimate? How are they more deserving of the protections afforded by the law?"

The reporter smiled and flinched as Dancing Jesus reeled away. His gaze led the sheriff's up and beyond to the Blackhawk Pines security cameras. "Defending the sanctity of golf?"

"Or just rubbernecking in the clubhouse."

"Circling back," he said, "to your unresolved homicide. All across the country, both illegal drug use and homicide are way up. I'm hearing Win Carpenter may have been murdered during a drug deal involving his religious community."

She had recited her answer to local news outlets already: "The Bad Axe County Sheriff's Department has no evidence that the House of Shalah is involved in dealing drugs."

"But wasn't there a backpack found where the body was dumped? With evidence of a drug deal? Why do I hear people saying that there *is* evidence, but it has been suppressed?"

Sheriff Kick's lips flattened together as she scowled in open frustration across the U-Stash-It fence. Her problem with the House of Shalah consisted solely of this: thirty-two people violating local zoning code by living in mini-storage units, which were unwired, unplumbed, uninsulated, windowless, etc.; two more people, the prophet and his wife, camping illegally on the U-Stash-It property in their luxury mobile coach; and finally, the three unpermitted portable toilets the Carpenters were using. That was it. The group had caused no problems otherwise. Nor had they committed crimes during previous stops in Texas, Nevada, and Colorado, according to law enforcement colleagues she had checked with in those states.

As for the backpack, her problem was that Chief Deputy Stonebreaker claimed she had recovered it—containing a pipe with methamphetamine residue, cash, and a fresh burner phone—at the muddy edge of Lake Susan, where Alexis Schmidt should have seen it but was sure she had not. In the sheriff's public statements after the body was found, she had withheld the cause of death and the existence of the backpack. Yet within a day or two it was considered common knowledge that a cult member had been knifed in a drug deal, and Sheriff Kick was covering it up because she was hiding something from her past. Her personal history, its details buried but its basic facts never a secret, had been making the rounds and acquiring brand-new fictional particulars.

Grimly she told Sullivan, "I can't comment on an ongoing investigation."

"Sure. But is it true that back in your late teens you caught some drug possession charges?"

"Expunged," she said. "Because I went into treatment. Therefore, no. No charges. It is true that I regularly used alcohol, tobacco, marijuana, and cocaine over a two-and-a-half-year period after I lost my parents. Those particular problems ended four thousand four hundred and eighty-nine days ago."

"Your mom and dad were shot, yes? In your barn? By a guy trying to steal equipment?"

"Right."

"You were away at a Dairy Queen event?"

"Now your story is about me?"

He smiled and his eyes drifted to the snow gathering on her hat and shoulders and in the creases of her brown-on-tan uniform.

"Back to the religious community," he said at last. "The House of Shalah. The Carpenters. What about the rumor that they shoot horses?"

She was startled. "What?"

"It's some kind of a ritual thing."

"Shooting horses? Says who?"

"I've just heard."

"Well, we have not. The Bad Axe County Sheriff's Department has received no reports of anyone, House of Shalah or otherwise, shooting horses."

"Okay. Then what about people saying that your religious community is harboring felons?"

"No basis," she said. But she felt a stirring of her Lyndsey Luck meet-an-inmate problem. "And no further comment."

"Understood. Moving on to the language in the name 'Kill the Cult.' Speech that advocates criminal violence is not protected speech."

"I'm aware."

"And?"

"Maybe you can educate my district attorney," the sheriff said, unable to level her tone. "He finds it catchy."

She aimed her frustration toward the sewer project beyond the western fence of the mini-storage compound. If they were building houses and taking over, the "cult" had a long way to go. The Carpenters had first sunk a new manhole through the freshly asphalted extension of Tee Road where it curved away from the golf course and became obscured among the remnants of an abandoned Christmas tree farm. From below the manhole, the Carpenters had connected two hundred yards of wide-bore concrete pipe into an existing storm-water line that drained the golf course into a ravine to the south of the U-Stash-It property. Halfway along this stretch of freshly buried pipe was an open pit inside of which hunkered an unconnected concrete junction box for undug lateral lines. There the project seemed to have stalled. *A long way from houses*, the sheriff thought—and winter would be suddenly upon them.

The Dancing Jesus people had begun a hymn. Quickly, across the fence, a storage unit door rattled up. From the doorway of the unit that served as their school, the Carpenter children and their teachers sang their own hymn back. This little battle was a daily thing, on and off. From somewhere along U-Stash-It Road a man bellowed the phrase in question: "Kill the cult!" As if in response, a gunshot cracked from inside the fence. The Carpenters, like everyone else in the Bad Axe, owned firearms, and all of the adults practiced regularly on a range along their back fence.

As if triggered by the gunshot, the sky let loose—fast and big as cornflakes—and the sheriff felt a surge of naked hope, as if a layer of fluffy white snow might make everything better.

"Sheriff, I have to be honest."

With this, Markus Sullivan interrupted her mental drift.

"Given the pressures here, the rumors, the whole power-keg feel, my mind goes back thirty years ago to the catastrophe at Waco . . ."

"No," she snapped.

She had educated herself on the notorious 1993 disaster in Waco, Texas. An ill-conceived government response to a dubious threat. A long and brutal standoff. Rumor, spin, prophecies, and lies. Then helicopters, tanks, snipers, CS gas, the complex exploding into flames that consumed eighty Branch Davidians, including twenty-five children.

"No way. Never."

With the shocking Waco footage looping in her head, she began to walk away from Sullivan, still protecting under her jacket the *Order of Eviction for Violation of Village of Farmstead Ordinance 34.46.ii.*

As soon as she handed over the document, the House of Shalah had five days—until Monday noon—to *cease illegal domicile and evacuate the property*.

The order didn't say where the Carpenters should go, or what the sheriff was supposed to do if they refused.

"But," Sullivan persisted, keeping up, his sneakers squishing in the fresh snow, "and respectfully, Sheriff, nobody in Waco thought that Waco would happen. That whole thing went from zero to infinity in six months. Mistakes, misinformation, ATF and FBI ignorance and bungling—"

Sheriff Kick stopped him there. It was not her style, but she jabbed a finger in his face.

"Not here. Never."

The reporter blinked at her through plunging snow. For a moment it felt like they glimpsed the same deadly inferno in one another's eyes.

"How are you so sure?"

Feeling pinned without an answer, she fished up her phone to buy time. Another text had just buzzed in.

Huh, Mighty Heidi? It's a holiday. Dont you wanna drink ketchup?

Missy Grooms was a high school friend from the bad old days in Crawford County. *Drink ketchup* was their old code for *catch up over drinks.* In the old days this meant they'd get bombed and misbehave.

Before she could stash the phone, another text arrived.

Dont forget cool whip.

For several seconds she no idea what her husband meant.

Then it came to her.

For the pies, she reminded herself.

That you promised to make with the kids.

Pumpkin, apple, pecan.

For Thanksgiving.

Tomorrow.

Life just would not stop.

She resumed her progress toward the U-Stash-It gate. "You can print my words," she told Markus Sullivan as he tagged along. "I will solve this Win Carpenter case. And there will not be another Waco in Bad Axe County, not on my watch."

On cue, more gunshots erupted from the House of Shalah practice range.

Sheriff Kick took her next several steps with her eyes closed—big cold snowflakes landing on her flushed face, triggering an intense desire for solitude and calm—until she had to open her eyes again to stop herself from falling.

CHAPTER 2

Whoa, granny-girl, she thinks as the booze hits. *Easy, now.*

A pair of Blackout Wednesday Bloody Brunch drink specials sit half-finished between them on the bar as Belle Kick's brand-new gentleman friend eases from his stool, tickles the small of her back, and tells her, "Sweet lady, a life like yours, you should write a book."

As he threads away through a noisy crowd to the little boys' room, Belle rests her strained voice, feels the buzz settle, and thinks: *Damn right.*

A life like mine, I should write a book.

So, Chapter One—right?—starts as she wakes up to hollering and screaming, the earliest moment she remembers with sound and color, as if everything before age seven doesn't matter. She knows the fight is different this time—for one thing, three voices—so she staggers half-asleep down the hallway toward her mom and dad's bedroom.

That house was really tilted. Marbles in that hallway veered straight to the wall. And the paneling warped in waves beneath her skimming fingertips. But probably, Belle decides, those things don't belong in a book.

The point of Chapter One would be that when the seven-year-old girl opens her mom and dad's bedroom door there is a loud bang and a bright hot flash and there before her stands the most impressive man she's ever seen: black-haired with silver eyes and a mustache, wearing a white bedsheet like a cape.

Does she include the detail that the bang-and-flash was a gunshot?

Maybe not, because the little girl doesn't see the gun yet. She looks at her mom, who is on the bed with a blue blanket to her throat, her face very red and very upset. Next she looks at her dad in his gray cooler-repair uniform, facedown like a rag doll on the floor at the end of the bed.

At some point, but maybe not yet, she should explain that her dad fixes the coolers on dairy farms that refrigerate the milk until the trucks take it to the dairy, and because he covers three counties, 24-7, he is not supposed to be home. She would have to explain later that her dad had come home by surprise and now he was dead, because she doesn't understand that yet.

Also, her seven-year-old self still has not seen the gun. When should she say so? She doesn't see the gun until a sheriff's deputy shows it to her asks her did she see it in her dad's hand. No. Except the gun is her dad's gun—so she says, yes, she did, but she means she saw it in his hand before, a different time.

But back to the scene. What happens next when she's standing in the doorway is that the man with the mustache and the bedsheet tells her everything is okay now, she and her mom are safe now, he is here, Jim is his name, and Jim is here with them now. Jim looks at Belle's mom. Belle's mom in gulps repeats every word that Jim has just said. So would this be the end of Chapter One?

▲ ▼ ▲ ▼

Her gentleman returns to the barstool next to hers.

"Sweet lady, another Bloody?"

"It's not even noon."

"Come on, you have to do the family thing tomorrow. You told me. All day in family hell. Today is the fun day. Drink up."

"I'm fine for now. Thank you."

But such a thoughtful man is hard to find, she thinks, and it's a shame to disappoint him. She has explained the family situation she has endured since the café closed. She has told him how her son and daughter-in-law really don't want her around—but of course they won't say so. What they say is they are thankful they can support her until—and they stop on *until*.

Her gentleman barks, "Barkeep!"

Jenny, at the other end, can't hear.

"I'm fine for now."

Belle has explained how her three grandkids are so goddamn smart about you-name-it, go ahead, name one thing they don't know better than she does. And they get every little thing they want too, which these days is called love, apparently. They use innocent voices when they talk to her, then spy through the curtains and tattle to her son, Harley, or her daughter-in-law, Queen Heidi, when she goes outside to smoke. She has mentioned how her twin seven-year-old grandsons grow these giant spoiled sissy rabbits that cost hundreds of dollars and win ribbons, but the damn things just ought to be eaten, and only their bad grandma will say so.

"Young lady! Barkeep!"

"Really, no. I'm supposed to be home making the stuffing. I'm told I make the best stuffing. I'm supposed to fall for that."

Although, you watch, she now resumes: at the table tomorrow, her oldest grandchild, nine-year-old tomboy professor of everything, will wrinkle her nose at the meal, probably her grandma's stuffing in particular, and speak in lecture form about *the one thing that nobody understands*, and only bad grandma will say, *May I ask who the hell is nobody?* and then be scolded by her son.

"Uh-huh," her gentleman says.

"Go ahead and mark my words."

"That's why I'm saying drink up," her gentleman says.

Then at some point during this, Belle continues, her daughter-in-law will have waltzed in late like a celebrity guest, and then in the middle of dinner, guaranteed, that woman will start fiddling with her phone and decide she has to waltz right off again. These people. And she can't just slap them, Belle says. Can she?

"Uh-huh." Her gentleman rattles his ice. "Like I said, you should write a book."

"Oh, I am. Chapter One is done."

"Call it 'What Doesn't Kill You Makes You Sweeter.' "

"Ha. Whatever."

"Ready for another, sweet lady?"

"I gotta tinkle," she says. "Then I gotta go."

This is at the Ease Inn on the edge of Farmstead, two-for-one rail drinks with free popcorn, the Blackout Wednesday Special.

Coming back from the little girls' room, Belle finds another round of Bloody Marys waiting.

CHAPTER 3

Today the House of Shalah gate was manned by a young white Carpenter with a hard limp and tattoos that snaked and flamed out the cuffs of his black hoodie and up beneath his chin. Cowled like a dark monk inside his hood over his KC Royals ball cap, he hitched away from the warmth of the illegal trash fire he had lit inside an oil barrel.

"What we gonna do today, Sheriff? More paperwork?"

Like they knew each other. They did not.

"Correct. More paperwork."

The sheriff rolled up her *Order of Eviction* and passed it to him through the chain-link. He hitched back to his fire and dropped in the document. He watched patiently as orange flames leapt above the barrel rim. When black ash fluttered up into the snowflakes, he came back to the gate.

"So, y'all got any fun plans for the holiday?"

"Tell your prophet-father it's time to go."

Snow melted on the hot back of her neck. The Carpenters had stopped singing. The Dancing Jesus people kept on, their voices twining with the new sound of muttering thunder. Beyond the storage units, Carpenter target-shooters banged away.

"Before somebody gets hurt."

"Yo, no offense, lady," said this Carpenter with his chin ticking up, "ain't but only God tells the prophet-father what to do."

"It's not legal to live on this property. Burning another piece of paper doesn't make the problem go away. This is Wednesday. Gone by Monday noon."

"That be all sounding like a threat."

She studied him. The roster of the House of Shalah was fluid, she understood. Some might leave. Others might find the website or hear by word-of-mouth and appear from anywhere in the country, or even the world, to hitch their star to the prophet-father's prosperity promise. She had met many Carpenters out in the community at their jobs, generally farms, construction and road crews, and restaurants, where they worked for cash. Over the past weeks, she had questioned several at this gate about the murder of Win Carpenter. To a person they were vague but perfectly polite. As for the prophet-father and mother, back in June the sheriff had provided law enforcement presence at a meeting in Farmstead City Hall where the couple had been officially informed that it was not legal to live in the storage facility. Though cagey and a bit smug, the leader and his wife were also faultlessly polite. This guy at the gate—his smirk and sass, his street style—didn't seem to fit.

"Which Carpenter are you?"

"They call me Brother Skip."

From an alley between storage units, several long-haired children in bare feet dashed into the snow, liberated from their lessons and hymns, celebrating. They were dressed in clothing from the collection the sheriff's department had organized. She recognized an outgrown Packers number 4 jersey that had belonged to one of her twin boys. She counted five kids and guessed they ranged from five to ten years old. Somewhere else there were four smaller ones.

"Where are you from, Brother Skip?"

"Here and there."

"You're kind of new to religion?"

"I been always tight with the Lord."

"I see. Well, it's not a threat," she said. "It's the law. People want to see the law enforced. I've bought you time, but I can't keep you safe anymore."

Brother Skip's chin went higher, his head tilted to the side, and his hand drifted down to grab the loose denim fabric over his crotch.

"Sheriff, we all good, yo."

"You're leaving."

For a moment they both watched the romping children.

"Tell the prophet-father that his time is up, Brother Skip. And tell him not to shoot the messenger."

▲ ▼ ▲ ▼

Back inside her cruiser, Sheriff Kick sat with her hands in her lap, letting her wipers slap the fluffy snow back and forth.

She lifted out her phone, looked at the text from her friend.

Wanna drink ketchup?

She typed back, *Hmmm . . .*

But she didn't hit send.

She stared into the wet early storm, musing that for every season there came that one day when it all turned: one season was over, and the next one had crept up to surprise you. It seemed that way in life too.

She deleted *Hmmm . . .*

As she had informed the *New York Times* reporter, 4,489 days ago today she had gotten sober, and when that happened, she and Missy Grooms had uncomfortably parted ways. But recently Missy had reached out to be friends again. They had met twice to *drink ketchup* over coffee, though both times Missy had let her actual coffee grow cold while she nursed herself on a Red Bull and a vape cartridge.

Pondering Missy's offer, the sheriff gazed across the U-Stash-It grounds at the tree line above the ravine beyond. Each black limb was now outlined with perfect white.

What was she thinking about?

About snowfall in the woods, that's what.

A place so deep in the woods that she could hear each snowflake land.

As if reading her mind, Missy sent another text.

Remember that old deer stand on Blackberry Ridge? We never even looked for deer? Just watched the snow fall?

They had been a couple of damaged country girls, hiding out, getting stoned and drunk. Missy had awful parents and a shitty home life. Dairy Queen Heidi White had been a girl with everything, most of all loving parents, but she had abruptly lost it all.

The sheriff texted back: *I do!*

But now someone was knocking on the cruiser's window.

She ran it down and was surprised to see the high school girl who had found Win Carpenter's body.

Alexis Schmidt was red-cheeked and out of breath. A rind of snow rode her frizzy curls.

"Sorry! They said you were here. I ran over from the high school. I'm supposed to be in some kind of online training, but we don't even have a computer at home. Can I talk to you?"

The sheriff popped her locks. Alexis sat on the cruiser's passenger seat and blurted a statement out of left field, the way high school girls often seemed to do.

"I don't know why I wore the pants!"

"They look okay to me."

"I mean the ones I wore the day I found the body."

The sheriff waited.

"I mean, I thought I'd never wear them again. I didn't mean to. But this morning I was late getting up, and in the dark I just threw on whatever and went out to milk."

"I know how that goes."

"I'm dripping on your car."

"Don't worry. Just tell me what's up."

"Well . . . I have to tell you something. Three somethings. One old. And two new."

"Go ahead."

Again the sheriff waited. Interviewed multiple times, Alexis had sworn she had seen no backpack on the banks of Lake Susan. Chief Deputy Stonebreaker maintained that because the backpack was in plain sight, the girl had to be lying. As in, what kind of high school kid makes a special trip at seven in the morning to see trout jump up a pipe? How could this be the truth? Clearly, Stonebreaker maintained, Alexis Schmidt had gone to Lake Susan to buy drugs from Win Carpenter and found him dead. Alexis said no way, and Stonebreaker's theory didn't square with the medical examiner's determination that Win Carpenter had been knifed and dumped in the lake approximately forty-eight hours before he had slid out of the pipe—making it highly unlikely that Alexis, a girl who couldn't even pronounce *methamphetamine*, had set up a meeting with Brother Win to buy some that morning. With these contradictions, and without the grounding of Win Carpenter's true identity, the murder investigation had scuffled along under building clouds of innuendo and rumor.

Alexis began.

"First, I'm totally sure there was no backpack."

"Okay."

"I stopped on the dam. For some reason I felt weird and I looked around. The picture you showed me, where the backpack supposedly was found? I looked right there. No backpack."

"I believed you a month ago, Alexis. That's old. What's new?"

"Well, I remembered something, and I asked some people. This kid at school had a backpack exactly like that, a couple years ago, sophomore year, I think. Some kid that just moved here and right away he got in trouble with you guys for drugs."

The sheriff tried for a moment to remember the arrest but gave up. Going back two years, she and her deputies had made at least a hundred mostly small-time drug busts, more than one a week, so common, sadly, that the cases blurred together.

"Do you remember his name?"

"Um, all anybody can remember is Shawn something. I could ask a teacher. They can probably look it up."

"No. Shawn somebody. High school age. We can do that at the sheriff's office. Thanks."

"Okay, and now the really new thing," Alexis said, "which is about my pants."

She opened her palm to reveal a tiny plastic case, bright orange, no bigger than her thumb.

"What is it?"

"Some weird thing I totally forgot that I found."

The sheriff waited. Alexis sighed.

"Okay, so I was laying on the pipe watching the fish jump up. Before the body came out. I saw this orange thing floating at the edge of the pool. My grandpa wears earplugs when he drives his four-wheeler, and it looked like the orange case he keeps his earplugs in, and since I was cold I had put on his shirt that was in his four-wheeler. So that's what I thought this thing was, his earplug case that fell out of his shirt that I was wearing. So I climbed down and got it and put it in my pants pocket. I didn't even look inside it. Then I went back to watching the fish."

The sheriff opened the case. Inside was something she had never seen before: two tiny disks of thin, opaque plastic, each the size of her thumbnail, spiked on their outward curves. That was all. A pair of spiked . . . spined? . . . shell-like? . . . what? The case snapped together and had a blue-dot sticker on the bottom, like the price tag at a yard sale.

Alexis said, "Then everything happened and I freaked and I forgot about it until I put those same pants on to milk this morning. But I thought maybe it was something Win Carpenter had, that came out the pipe before he did."

"Thank you. You might be right. I'm glad you found me."

"I gotta go. I'm supposed to be learning, like, online safety, even though most kids know way more than the teacher."

▲ ▼ ▲ ▼

When the girl was gone, the sheriff focused on the blue-dot sticker.

Yard sales, flea markets, antiques-on-consignment shops . . .

Some seller might remember Win Carpenter—or at least know what the disks were for. She might catch a loose thread, something she could pull.

Her phone alarm went off. She sighed. It was already noon. The Carpenter children frolicked barefoot in the snow. Dancing Jesus kinked beneath the dumping sky. Some new agitator, probably a Kill the Cult guy doing some Blackout Wednesday drinking, walked along the front fence dragging something like a crowbar along the chain-link, making a racket and hollering filthy ultimatums. When the guy got to the fence corner, he turned and came back the other way. Shit, did the asshole have a sword?

The sheriff shouldered open her door.

She shut it again and closed her eyes. It had been 106 days since her last day off.

"Drunk guy," she said when Denise answered the dispatch line, "possibly with a sword, here on U-Stash-It Road. But it's noon and I'm off until Monday."

"And good for you. It's about time."

"Okay, I just got a better look. And yeah. Dude has a sword."

"Ten-four, my queen. You get home to your lovelies and have a happy Thanksgiving. I'll send someone to scoop the asshole up."

Sheriff Kick put her cruiser into DRIVE. But before she rolled, she looked again at Missy's question.

Wanna drink ketchup?

She touched her finger to the reply space.

Did she want to sit for an hour or two in the middle of nowhere and watch the snow fall?

Yeah.

Yeah, as a matter of fact, she did.

CHAPTER 4

Because Sheriff Kick had to change out of her uniform into winter wear and then find her dad's old deer rifle—the one she used to bring to the party with Missy—and because after finding the Deerslayer she made a snowman with her twin seven-year-old boys, Dylan and Taylor—and because when the snowman was done she returned inside to confess to her husband her failure to get Cool Whip, and to discuss how this would be remedied (the Piggly Wiggly in Farmstead, on her way back from hunting)—and then because ten-year-old Ophelia, reading constantly these days, somehow heard just that one word, hunting, through her earbuds, which she promptly tugged out to make way for an ongoing dialog with her mother about how humans treated animals (the sixteen-pound turkey taking up half the refrigerator, turning pink and yellow as it thawed, was "obscene," Opie said)—and then because at this point the sheriff noticed someone missing and said to her husband, "Where's your mom?" and Harley said, "Brunch," and she, somewhat shrilly, it was true, said, "Brunch? Harley, seriously?" and they had a spat about supervision

of their seventy-four-year-old teenager—and then because she had
to stop in Zion and put gas in Harley's truck—and then because she
aimed a little too far across the Crawford County line and wandered
through the wrong remote coulee before she found Blackberry Ridge
Road—and then because Blackberry Ridge Road was trackless and
drifted, requiring her to drive very slowly across deserted high ground
that seemed to pitch like a whitecap on an ocean of ridgetops—
because of all this she finally arrived at the turnout with the rusty field
gate at 2:23, twenty-three minutes late.

But there were no other tire tracks in the deepening snow to suggest that the sheriff's old friend had come and gone, meaning Missy
was even more behind schedule.

This was normal. Late was Missy's middle name. Or one of them.

The sheriff let the truck idle, the heater blow, and the wipers slap.
She watched the storm and waited, thinking of her and Missy's initial
reunion a few weeks ago, after twelve years of estrangement.

They had met at Traeger's Café in Zion, an old haunt. The sheriff
had waited forty minutes. *I'm sorry, Heidi. My worthless car . . .* Missy had
been muddled and restless, yawning and biting her fingernails, sniffing
Traeger's thin coffee but putting it aside for her Red Bull. They were
both bad at chitchat and had mostly just sat in their soiled-white Lucite
booth fiddling with the shakers and sweetener packets and getting stared
at by old-timers in the café, some of whom knew their story. They had
steered widely around their lurid past, especially the topic of the dangerous older man who had come between them. Asked about her current
living situation—was Missy still in the little white house on Mill Coulee
Road?—she had answered vaguely that her parents had passed away
and she had been staying with "some friends across the river"—which
translated as couch-surfing in Iowa. When it was time to go, the sheriff
had given Missy what she had meant to be a simple gift: a photo taken
just days before—Harley, Heidi, Opie, and Grammy Belle surrounding
the twins and the glowing cake commemorating their seventh birthday.

She had known the gift was off target from the moment that she showed it. Missy had grimaced, then broken into sobs. As they hugged goodbye, Missy had squeezed harder than appropriate and whispered across her ear, "Mighty Heidi, next time let's get fuckin' high."

Now, after waiting at the farm gate until 2:40, the sheriff shut down her husband's truck. From there, the deer stand was across several acres of corn stubble and down the steep slope beyond, where it looked out over a swampy expanse through which flowed the lower Bad Axe River. She would rather wait there.

▲ ▼ ▲ ▼

With her dad's old Deerslayer rifle on a strap across her back, Sheriff Kick climbed the stand's welded ladder, swiping a neat four-inch stack of snow off each rung. Inside she found the same old wood desk, warped into a twist, and the same pair of swivel-style office chairs, their foam padding shredded by rodents and their wheels stuck with rust. She and Missy, right here, used to snort coke and slam twelve-packs of Old Milwaukee. Beer cans still littered the floor. They never knew or cared who the stand belonged to—Missy couldn't remember how she found it, just that she knew where it was—and they had never met anyone in it or near it.

· The sheriff sat in the more-stable-looking chair and looked over the swamp. She was glad to be here now. Here was the raw and simple beauty she was looking for: the slow scrawl of snow across open space, how it clung to the reeds and the cattail heads. Here was the hush that she craved: so silent she could hear individual snowflakes landing on her coat sleeve. A tree squeaked, crows called, an early owl tried one soft hoot.

Then she heard, ever so faintly, a snapping branch.

Was someone coming across the hillside?

Missy?

Then a snort.

A deer?

She and Missy used to joke that if Roman Vanderhoof ever found them here—Hoof was his nickname, perfect if you imagined that horny-hairy-handsome creature that was half man, half horse—that if Hoof ever found them here, they would shoot their drug source and mutual boyfriend dead and claim they thought he was a deer. Exactly such an accident happened in the coulees at least once a year anyway. They had gotten into intoxicated arguments, sometimes hilarious, sometimes gut-wrenchingly real, about who would get to pull the trigger and put the fucker down.

Eventually one of them, the ruined Dairy Queen and future sheriff, had pulled a different kind of trigger. At the edge of her abyss, Mighty Heidi White had walked into the Crawford County Sheriff's Department and laid out everything she knew about coke and about the new thing, meth, and about burglary and assault, regular and statutory rape, embezzlement, arson, and insurance fraud, and she had even shared Hoof's consistent threats to kill her—not Missy, just her—in various sick and graphic ways. This was the end for Hoof, who went to prison for a twenty-year term. This was the end too for Heidi White and Missy Grooms as friends. But it was the beginning of Sheriff Heidi Kick—the start of here, and now.

On their second *drink ketchup* coffee visit, Missy had surprised her with the news that Hoof was out of prison on early release. Of course the news had darkened her. Overcrowding. Concerns about disease.

So where is he?

I don't know. I just know he's out.

How do you know?

I just heard.

Another branch snapped.

Then a hard, non-human snort.

A deer, the sheriff thought with relief.

Probably a buck, she heard her dad add excitedly.

A big buck.

Because now she felt him with her, she loaded five shells into her dad's precious old rifle. She chambered one, pushed the safety through, rested the barrel on the windowless sill, and made herself quiet—like he had taught her—except now her heart thundered and the snowflakes crashed against her coat sleeve. She moved her eyes corner to corner, seeing nothing yet but black tree trunks and streaming clots of suddenly heavier snow. Her dad's voice expanded in her head. *This is big-buck weather, Heidi-girl. This is trophy time.* Like he had done, she peeled her hat off her ears and turned her head by centimeters, hoping to carve some telltale sound from the hiss of the wind. *But do you really want to shoot a deer?* This background thought registered but then receded, like treetop branches squeaking higher and higher overhead.

She was sharply focused when from her right some large creature stepped into partial view, a shaggy brown tone amid the blacks and whites.

Another step, antlers rattling understory.

Yes.

A buck.

He stepped clear—big—his black nose lifted and steaming, his tail flicking, his ears on swivels.

That's a trophy, Heidi-girl.

The one we all dream about.

She scoped him. In fact he was a bull buck, a real old-timer, stiff gait and leaky tarsal glands, thinned by the rut but still close to three hundred pounds, a huge and complicated rack with splintered points. She could smell his rankling musk.

As her dad had taught her, she found his shoulder, gateway for a bullet to his lungs and heart and liver.

But, Heidi, why?

You don't even want to shoot a deer.

He looked directly at her.

Her breath stopped.

Trophy of a lifetime, Heidi-girl.

He looked away. Looked back. Gathered his haunches to bolt—

She fired.

▲ ▼ ▲ ▼

She searched a hundred yards across the hillside before she found where the buck had collapsed and then struggled back to his feet, leaving compacted bloody snow. From there he had fled into the swamp.

As she followed, a firm new wind threw crisper snow in slants and swirls that made the landscape toss and spin. Her face burned and her heart ran fast. She never should have pulled the trigger. A good hunter never let a creature suffer. She stopped beside a hoof drag and a red hole melted in the snow. The injured buck was moving toward the river.

She trailed over snow-hidden pits and hummocks, pockets of slush, muskrat trenches, gasping and sweating and stumbling, connecting blood dots until she lost him in the tangle of box elders that lined the lower Bad Axe.

Where would he go from here?

She bushwhacked through a thicket of willow scrub to the riverbank, where she stood catching her breath above the current, raising a glove to shield her eyes from the pelting snow, squinting up and down the near bank, squinting across.

There.

His blood on the opposite bank.

▲ ▼ ▲ ▼

She made her mistake so quickly—in three moments—that it was done before she understood she was making it.

One moment she was following the injured buck across the river, up to her knees and sidestepping cautiously, feeling cold shock as the current seeped through her boots and insulated coveralls.

The next moment she was raising her dad's rifle overhead as loose limestone cobble shifted and her footing was suddenly in question.

In the third moment, she had decided that the current was too deep and too fast, the bottom was too loose, and her eyes had strayed downstream to a sandy-bottomed spot that looked slower and shallower.

She had only half decided. She had only half turned, half shifted her weight, when the current picked her up, swept her ten yards, and set her down exactly where she had been looking.

She gasped as she sank.

It was as if she had been fed into the river's hungry mouth, the silty bottom eagerly devouring her.

Before she could gasp again, the river bottom was chewing past her boots and up her legs, sucking at her pants and then her coat hem.

She heard her dad's voice. *You're okay. Just stop. Stop moving.* She could not. She thrashed in place against the muck, tried to lunge toward the bank, sank herself another inch.

And another.

Heidi!

He was alarmed.

Stop moving!

She stopped.

But then what?

Damn it, this is why you never hunt alone!

She released a single angry shriek. Then she struggled more and sank until the icy flow touched her crotch.

Did you at least tell someone where you are?

You died! she raged back. She pawed through coat pockets for her phone. No trace of a signal.

She twisted, yanked up from the hips. Her feet lifted inside her boots, which did not come along but received her returning feet and sank a fraction deeper, finally touching something solid.

She raised the rifle with two hands into the slashing snow.

"Missy!"

She had four rounds left.

Would Missy follow her tracks in the snow?

Would Missy hear her shooting?

But what if Missy had never come in the first place?

How near was . . . anything?

"Help! Help me! Missy? Anyone?"

Wasn't three shots—fired evenly—wasn't that SOS?

As if anyone would know.

As if anyone in deer season would pay attention to three rifle shots.

"Help me!"

As if anyone would even hear.

CHAPTER 5

Stepping outside Barn 2 at Ernhardt Pig Feeder, Fernanda Carpenter zipped her thin hand-me-down coat against the wet white gust. A Texas native, nine years in the House of Shalah, she viewed the ridge-top scene with grim astonishment.

Before her shift began at dawn, the world had been a somewhat familiar dry gray-brown. Then, inside the disorienting hog barn, she had forgotten where she was. Escaping the barn eight hours later, she had expected one of the mild low-desert landscapes—Texas, Nevada, California, southern Colorado—where the House had been since she became a Carpenter.

But no.

The Carpenters were suddenly facing winter.

Huddling in unheated, uninsulated mini-storage units.

Something wasn't right.

Fernanda surveyed the parking lot, wincing as fat snowflakes struck her face. Her awful new husband wasn't out there revving his smashed-up silver Honda and flashing headlights to make her giddyup. He wasn't late, tearing inbound past the manure pond along the farm driveway. He wasn't coming at all, she guessed. How had so much changed so fast? How were they going to keep warm?

Behind Fernanda, snowflakes tatted down on the corrugated barn roof, instantly melting from the heat of three thousand hogs and running off in a curtain of perfectly strung drips that glittered as they raced to splash down. She stepped through the drips and huddled against the warm side of the barn, watching the parking lot empty, tire tracks filling with snow.

Not that she wanted him to come.

Not that she wanted him, period.

She wanted Roy back. Everybody did. Hosanna wanted her Papa Roy. The babies wanted their Papa Roy. Roy's Carpenter brothers and sisters wanted their calm, thoughtful, sweet-singing Brother Roy back.

The last car left the lot. The sky flickered, then lowered with an audible grunt of compression.

Fernanda whispered into the flurry, "Where are you, Brother Milk? *Who* are you?"

Even her new husband's name felt sickening and wrong. Milk should be a good thing, a comfort, reliable—whereas he was everything else. But "Milk" was what the three other men he came with called him. Skip, Spooner, Peep . . . and Milk.

At the end of summer, he and the other three had appeared together, surrendered their meager possessions, and been welcomed as new Carpenters by the prophet-father. Since exactly then, the House had begun its tilt toward upside down. Within days, kindhearted Brother Tom, who taught Bible to the children, had been expelled for some unknown apostasy, and Brother Tom's wife, Sister Cora, had been married by the prophet-father to new Brother Skip, half her age, gangbangy and crude. Overnight, lovely Sister Cora had wilted into bent-necked silence.

In an equally strange turn after this first remarriage, Brother Rasheed, Fernanda and Roy's neighbor in Unit 13, a sensitive soul who wrestled with anxiety and guilt, had begged the prophet-father for annulment. No one understood why, given how Brother Rasheed doted on and clung to Sister Maryellen. But the brother's wish had been granted. Immediately new Brother Peep, a lumbering mass with a soft voice and buried eyes, had assumed husbandry of bewildered and grief-stricken Sister Maryellen. "He's just very quiet, that's all," she had told Fernanda numerous times about her creepy new husband. Brother Rasheed had moved into an eight-by-ten unit alone.

Fernanda frowned through racing drips and pelting snowflakes at the empty lot and waning afternoon, reminding herself that at three P.M. in Wisconsin in November, darkness was hardly more than one hour away.

The House of Shalah remarriages had not ended there, of course. There were still Brothers Spooner and Milk. At the end of October, skittish and quiet Brother Win had been found murdered in a lake, his neck and belly sliced open with a knife. Within a few nervous days, glinty-eyed Brother Spooner, with his ancient brown suit and half-gone ear, was wed to Brother Win's young jewel, Sister Soon-Yin.

Fernanda shivered in her thin coat, scrounged from a donation box dropped off last week by the lady sheriff of this cold place. Next had come Fernanda's own loss. By the time of Brother Win's death, she knew her marriage to Roy was marked. By then, the sweet and devout man she had gladly called husband had been missing for six days. There had been no news of an apostasy, an annulment, or a death. Roy was simply there one day and gone the next. The prophet-father had stopped Fernanda from talking to a sheriff's deputy who came asking, and after Brother Win's body was found, he had denounced Roy as a runaway, a defector back to Babylon, and bestowed weepy Fernanda upon waiting Brother Milk.

I pronounce thee man and wife . . .

▲ ▼ ▲ ▼

Her boss's son interrupted.

"Well, winter's here."

"I guess."

Tyson Ernhardt Jr. put an envelope into Fernanda's hands.

"Thanks for coming in today."

"You're welcome."

Seeing cash inside the envelope, she felt her pulse speed.

"It's not payday."

"It's a holiday bonus. To spend on yourself. Put it toward your own car, maybe? And you forget you saw Ramon kick that sow, right? That's just Ramon."

He smiled leadingly. They called him E.J. The Carpenters worked for cash only, surrendered every penny at the House of Shalah gate, and trusted their prosperity to the prophet-father, who made their wealth multiply like loaves and fishes. This was as much as E.J. knew. He could not know how the prophet-father preached that it was wickedness to possess money for personal use.

"I can't accept this."

He drew his hands back, now grinning more than smiling. They said E.J. was a charmer who played on his wife. He could not know how it was for the women in the House, in how many ways, and how quickly, they could feel the ground give way beneath them.

"Sure you can. You can do it. Keep it for yourself. And how about a ride home?"

She plunged her hand into her coat and showed her phone.

"My husband is on his way. Thank you."

"Okay, well, you have a wonderful Thanksgiving."

"You as well. Thank you."

He went back inside the hog-farm office. Fernanda watched his head and shoulders through the window as he looked at security

screens. She vacantly listened to her phone ring, staring at the thickening snow. Hosanna and the babies were going to need mittens and
hats and boots and thicker clothes. Taking the money for herself
would be a sin, for sure. It could be earthly trouble too. But she
would keep her children warm. And she would get home to them.
She worked the envelope of cash into the torn lining of her coat,
feeling nothing catch her as she fell.

▲ ▼ ▲ ▼

After Tyson Ernhardt Jr. dropped her off, Fernanda picked up her
babies, Rachel and Josiah, from the day-care unit, and her big girl,
Hosanna, from the school unit. Her little family hurried home under
thickening snow. Inside chilly Unit 14, she flipped her phone to
selfie and touched up her face. She spritzed a little perfume beneath
her chin against any lingering hog-barn aromas. The prophet-father
might choose any minute.

Rachel, nearing three, and Josiah, eighteen months, focused on
rice crackers from the Village of Farmstead food pantry. Hosanna,
nine nearing ten, observed her mother's every move through deep
mahogany eyes.

"Take a picture, girl."

Hosanna said back, "You always look pretty."

"I smell like pigs."

"Jesus loves you."

"Yes."

"The prophet-father loves you."

"Yes. Thank you for reminding me."

Fernanda rushed on clean sequined jeans and the clingy pink
sweater that the prophet-father favored. She brushed her hair. The
cloudy mirror that leaned against the corrugated steel wall had a fun-
house effect. Her legs were not quite *that* short, thanks be to God.
Her actual head was normal size, muchas gracias. Her long hair, on

the other hand, truly was that glossy black and spectacular. Seeing it
made her sassy. *She perceiveth that her merchandise is good: her candle
goeth not out by night.*

Now it was hurry up and wait. With Hosanna still watching,
Fernanda opened her laptop and performed her ritual search for Roy.

She googled *Roy Carpenter.*

Nothing new.

She googled *missing persons in Wisconsin.*

Still no.

She searched *Inmate Locater.*

Thank God, no.

Then, as she checked email, her hopes surged. In her in-box was
an email forwarded from an address she didn't recognize. The subject
was "FYI" and there was no message, just a zipped attachment. She
clicked UNZIP and the leap of tawny skin stopped her stiff.

Hosanna.

Standing naked in the washtub.

A dozen or more photographs, Hosanna unaware, washing
herself.

In a hot flash Fernanda deleted the email, emptied the trash,
closed the laptop, and looked at the thin steel wall between Unit 14
and Unit 13, home of Brother Peep and Sister Maryellen.

This whole time Hosanna had been watching.

"Sweetheart, you have homework, I'm sure."

Mother and daughter locked eyes.

"Get busy."

▲ ▼ ▲ ▼

A blank stretch later Fernanda still trembled as she prayed with all
her might to be unchosen.

Merciful Christ, spare me today.

Let me breathe.

God in Heaven, guide me.

But the gossip among the other wives was true. Fernanda was the prophet-father's favorite, and sure enough there came a familiar rattle at the Unit 14 door. Old Mother Ruth, the first-wife, sang out.

"Fernanda! Lucky lady!"

Hosanna watched her mother flinch and scowl.

"Lovely, lucky Fernanda! He's in love with you today, and you're in love with him!"

CHAPTER 6

With the current of the Bad Axe River rushing around her, Sheriff Kick held her fire.

No matter how she discharged them, three rifle shots in deer season communicated nothing more than some flatlander missing his yearling doe but still banging away.

Except maybe Missy had arrived. She would hear the shots.

But then the sheriff couldn't picture Missy crossing that swamp to reach the river. Missy would be in the mindset for drinking ketchup, not for slogging blindly through snow-buried muck. She was the kind of country girl who despised the country, refused to cave to it by driving safely on gravel or dressing for the weather. Probably Missy wasn't even wearing socks.

Sheriff Kick looked up and down the river that had half swallowed her. She now felt rooted on the bottom, probably standing on a slab of limestone under three feet of mucky sand. What if she—

No. Not yet.

Because if she gave up her balance, lunged and tried to grab

a fistful of the dead nettles on the nearest bank—six feet away?
eight?—or the red snarl of submerged willow roots in the cutback
beneath, and if it turned out she couldn't reach, or if she did reach
but the nettle stalks or the root tendrils broke off in her grip, then she
was underwater grasping nothing, her phone ruined and maybe also
the rifle, no leverage to pull or pry her head back above water. And
if she didn't drown—if she could surface—she would be completely
wet, that much closer to hypothermia.

She shuddered as a fragment of the twins' recent birthday party
flashed involuntarily across her brain, the dining room dark and
Taylor's and Dylan's air-filled cheeks pushing into the light of candles
on the white-frosted sheet cake their big sister Opie had baked and
decorated with a thirty-piece set of mini–jungle animals.

But didn't this riverbank have to be somebody's private property?

Didn't every square inch of land belong to someone?

Not that she and Missy had ever cared, but wasn't NO TRESPASS-
ING the unofficial motto of the Bad Axe?

What if someone lived nearby in a house she couldn't see? And
what if inside that house there were people playing euchre and they
heard shots on their property, and though the women tried—*Let
it go! It's Thanksgiving eve!*—the men of course were drunk and so
naturally they loaded shotguns and fired up four-wheelers and came
looking?

And just like that she was saved?

Or maybe they just called the sheriff. Then, if she was lucky,
Rhino would dispatch someone other than Chief Deputy Stonebreaker, who might find a long stick and shove her under. If it all
broke right, Deputy Luck would be her rescuer, and then Luck, she
imagined, might feel secure enough to come clean about her creepy
meet-an-inmates thing . . .

She fired one shot up into the sailing snow.

Waited.

She remembered Missy saying, *Mighty Heidi, next time let's get fuckin' high . . .*

Realized that even if Missy eventually showed up at the gate on Blackberry Ridge—underdressed, of course—most likely she would be wasted.

Understood that even so, Missy was her best chance.

A hard shiver jolted the sheriff's bones. She focused on her right foot, which felt looser inside its boot than the left.

Could she pull her foot out of the boot?

From her right hip, she wrenched up with all her strength. The effort nearly tipped her and when her arms wheeled for balance she barely hung on to the rifle. When she was steady again, her right heel had slipped fractionally up inside the boot, whereas her entire left side felt driven down another inch.

Fire the next shot?

Wait longer?

She tried to holler—"Missy!"—but it came out a croak and then she saw her husband turn from paring pie apples at the sink.

Don't forget Cool Whip . . .

New idea: What if she shoved her arm down through the current, pushed her whole shoulder under, maybe even her head . . . then clawed down through the soft river bottom . . . and untied her boots?

Then—could she just slip out?

Float or swim to solid ground and come ashore in her socks?

The cold was in her spine.

It was in her brain.

That was dumb.

Or not.

She only knew she never should have trusted Missy. She only knew she should be making pies.

She fired a second shot.

She listened for one eternal minute. Her hips had locked. Her coat had wicked the river to her chin. The whooshing wind and creaking trees and rushing current were all she heard.

She slurred a thought at herself—*Don't waste rounds, don't shoot again until you count one hundred*—then stopped at twenty because she was counting the wrong thing. She should be counting bullets.

One in the shoulder of the buck.

Two in the air.

Three gone, total.

Two left.

One was in the breech.

The last one was in the magazine.

The cold was in her lungs and heart. It would be dark in minutes.

Her thoughts slowed down and began to sail away.

Oh, Harley . . .

Oh, my babies . . .

I'm so sorry . . .

I never should have . . .

Then she heard one shot back.

CHAPTER 7

Lovely, lucky Fernanda! He's in love with you today, and you're in love with him!

She truly did love him.

Fernanda truly did love the man God had chosen to be the Prophet-Father Euodoo Koresh, creator of prosperity.

She did.

She had loved him since she first laid eyes on him.

She had walked straight up to him—in a shopping mall in Texas, when she was sixteen—to a fifty-four-year-old man with a weathered face and a gray gossamer ponytail, sitting in an unplugged massage chair under an indoor palm with his turquoise eyes serenely staring, a glossy white suitcase full of House of Shalah pamphlets at his feet, his high, clear voice calling out to every passerby, "God loves you! And He wants you to be wealthy! Yes, you!"

Fernanda Maria Cervantes, out shoplifting and just that moment finished with the trashy, scary everyday struggle of her old life, had walked right up and laid her troubled head upon his lap.

Her girlfriends had gasped.

The boy who believed he was her boyfriend had turned red and tried to smirk.

Fernanda hadn't even noticed.

Euodoo rhymed with voodoo: *to assist one on a prosperous journey*.

Koresh was Cyrus in Hebrew: a liberating king.

Shalah rhymed with *aha!*

A place of rest and prosperity.

She was moving on.

▲ ▼ ▲ ▼

Now a twenty-five-year-old mother of three—the first two were from her prophet-father's seed for sure, the youngest was possibly Roy's— Fernanda followed along a snowy path between storage units behind the first-wife, Ruth, who had been there at the mall that day in Texas, watching from the next massage chair over. Mother Ruth kept track of things. Mother Ruth counted pills and tallied miles between oil changes on the mobile coach, made sure there were bank deposits, internet connections, PayPal links, and website updates.

"Otherwise," she now continued, briefing Fernanda for her connubial visit, "he is over-agitated by the legal pressures, the local harassment, a rough day on the Nikkei, the phoniness of the Babylonian Thanksgiving . . . and of course he is deeply disturbed by the carryings-on of Babylon in general."

As the prophet-father's long-haired, blue-gowned first-wife hustled ahead on a bad hip, one wet moccasin slapping down harder than the other, Fernanda felt even more troubled by the sudden snowfall. What was the prophet-father's plan? Why wasn't Mother Ruth steering him to the next stop? How would the Carpenters survive a winter in storage lockers?

Under plunging snow, Brother Skip watched from beside his barrel fire. He tipped his chin up to show the murky tattoos thrashing at his throat, and he smirked at Fernanda. Feeling a flash of her teenage mall-rat self, Fernanda showed him her brown middle finger, its sharp pink nail inset with a rhinestone heart charm.

Mother Ruth continued, "The European markets also closed down today. Plus that lady sheriff was back with more threats. Meanwhile, the IRS is asking for documentation to validate his religious tax exemption, which they want to take away. He took a Halcion."

Fernanda hardly heard this. Unlike usual, she was distracted by the Babylonian circus on the other side of the fence: the inflatable Jesus gyrating in the streaking snow, the tent-sheltered "true Christians" singing counter-hymns, the guy selling KILL THE CULT T-shirts, the procession of the curious in their vehicles creeping in and out along U-Stash-It Road. For the first time, Fernanda wondered what the House of Shalah truly looked like from outside, for example in the objective view of the cameras aimed from the tall poles across the golf course. Who were the Carpenters, really? How far on their road to prosperity? As for the ever-present armed man in the pickup, the rotating member of the hostile group that watched them 24-7, Fernanda once more listed her middle finger.

Where is Roy?

She ought to march right out there and ask him.

Did you kill Brother Win? And Roy too?

As she glared that way, a different man in dirty coveralls hooked his heavy paws through the fence and bellowed at her, "You're not welcome here!" He rattled the chain-link and bellowed again.

"Prophet, my ass! Get out while you can! Kill the cult!"

"Or maybe your father took two Halcions," Mother Ruth told Fernanda.

▲ ▽ ▲ ▽

Out of eyes that had recently faded from turquoise to a water-thin blue, the prophet-father watched Fernanda sit on the edge of his king-sized bed, strewn with his laptops and scratch pads, his sippy cups with three kinds of macrobiotic smoothies, his medication bottles, the remains of a pepperoni pizza.

"Oh, Fernanda," he said with a sigh, almost slurring. "How I do love thee."

" 'I loveth Thee too,' " she replied as he had taught her, " 'as whoever liveth in love, liveth in God, and God in them.' "

"Yes, yes."

The second came out *yeth*.

So two Halcions, she thought, for sure.

"Sow's life," he said.

It took her a second. *Sow's life?* The hog farm? Her? Did she smell bad?

No: *So how is life?*

"Life is good, as God is good."

Amoebic on the bed, the prophet-father shifted inside his white bathrobe with a soft grunt and pulled himself into focus. Lately and quickly, his prosperity efforts had caught up with him. Rising at three every morning to prepare for the overseas markets, coping with the roller-coaster economies, getting hounded out of Nevada and then Colorado . . . the stimulants and depressants, the weight gain and hypertension . . . his general darkening mood and creeping anxiety since settling in Wisconsin . . . this was etched upon his once-sweet face, stored in the bloating tissues of his once-trim body, seeping from the corners of his leeched-out eyes.

"God is good," he agreed. He added, "He is good to the good, and woe to the rest."

She stiffened. He had expelled Brother Tom with language like this.

"God in His wisdom provides everything we need. We do not want."

"Yes," she agreed.

"Then why is it, Fernanda, that I'm hearing you've been with a man not your husband?"

"I have not."

"Brother Skip tells me otherwise."

"I got a ride home from work."

"Alone, with a man who wasn't your husband."

"My boss's son."

"Why?"

"My husband never picked me up."

"Why not?"

"I wouldn't know."

"Where is he?"

"I wouldn't have any idea."

"You seem angry."

She gulped. Because God was good, she was not allowed to be angry.

He insisted. "Are you angry?"

"Of course not."

"Are you unhappy with the new husband I've given you?"

Because this would be *her* weakness, not the man who stranded her after work. The weakness of Sisters Cora, Maryellen, and Soon-Yin, for suffering with their new husbands. She shook her head to say no: *I am not unhappy.*

"Dear Fernanda," her prophet-father now said sternly, " 'the unbelieving husband is made holy by his wife.' "

She gulped again and dropped her head to hide the frown.

"Tell me what troubles you, child."

"Where is Roy?"

She had blurted it without meaning to, causing him to gaze at her through ripples of disturbed feeling, as if she had dropped a stone in his Halcion waters.

Well, it was out.

"Prophet-Father, please, what happened to Roy?"

She waited. *And to Brother Thomas, Brother Rasheed, and Brother Win?* Something like a bulldozer rumbled close behind the mobile coach, in the open field where the House of Shalah was laying sewer pipes for the actual houses they had been promised.

"Fernanda . . ."

He had made her name into a weary sigh.

". . . who knoweth not. Roy resisted his prosperity, just as other men have embraced theirs. God is good to the good. It's really as simple as that."

He yawned.

"Let go of all resistance, my dear child, and everything you deserve will come to you naturally."

Then, at a flick of her prophet-father's soft, thin finger, Fernanda lowered her head and began to undress.

CHAPTER 8

The returning gunshot seemed nearby.

Should she wait? Fire back?

Was someone trying to locate her?

She croaked, "Missy?"

Or maybe she had heard lightning? Or a branch cracking?

Between one stiff eye-blink and the next, Sheriff Kick felt her rush of adrenaline give way to a rapid metabolic slowdown that felt like drunkenness.

"Missy! I'm in the river!"

She had been severely hypothermic once before. The dreamlike sensations had inverted the danger she was in, and she had learned later that certain processes controlled by her brain stem—the paradoxical undressing, the terminal burrowing—had already begun when she was rescued.

Then in dull dread she was replaying that night in January when she was nineteen, when she and Missy had been across the Mississippi on the Iowa bluffs cleaning a new home that Roman Vanderhoof Inc.

had built and was about to list for sale. The painters had finished just hours before. She and Missy were wiping down countertops and baseboards, detailing fixtures, mopping floors, playing music, and staying on a weed high while the outside air dropped into the teens.

Around midnight, Hoof had shown up to pay them in booze and blow. In the midst of the ensuing party, after something she had said, or had refused to say, or had refused to do, Hoof had picked her up by the ankles and hurled her through the front window, the one with the money view of the Mississippi. Bleeding, wearing just her bra, Levi's, and underwear, she had crawled away into deep snow while Hoof screamed that if he ever saw her queen-ass face again he would shoot her like a stray dog. Later, when she was found by a farmer—burrowing into his silage tube, her jeans and bra gone—she had been dreaming of springtime on her family's pastures, green grass and dandelions, new calves romping . . .

▲ ▼ ▲ ▼

Another gunshot brought her shuddering back to the Bad Axe River.

Then another, just upstream, so close that moments later bits of branches spun past her on the current.

"Help!"

She could hardly hear her weak call over the river and the wind.

"Help! In the water!"

Stream-bank willows thrashed, their limber tips flinging captured snow. Then a man's head and shoulders shoved through, cascading more snow over the black balaclava that covered his face.

Her slow brain said: *Heidi, something's wrong.*

The man was facing her but didn't see her right away. He was following the buck's blood, or he was following her tracks as she followed the buck's blood. He was seeing the pink smear where the buck had climbed the opposite bank.

What she saw wasn't making sense. A long-sleeved T-shirt and no coat? Ripped jeans and bare feet in Crocs, like he'd just stepped outside for a smoke? But where did he step outside from? With a rifle strapped on his back and a balaclava covering his whole head and face? As this confusing figure turned away to look upstream, she saw the weapon was a fully accessorized M16: bump stock, forward pistol grip, flash suppressor, high-capacity magazine. The whole package was a few different kinds of illegal. Dressed like this, with this weapon, he was not out hunting. Unless . . .

Heidi, something's really wrong.

Snow scrolled between them, melting on the current. He turned toward downstream and saw her.

"Aha," he said, vapor escaping the mask. "There you are."

"Please help me."

He swung the gun around and fixed his hands on its grips and stared at her for several seconds. He was musclebound, hairy, and murkily tattooed. His inadequate clothes were soaked from the snow. If this man wasn't cold, the sheriff knew dully—and he showed no signs of being cold—then he was high as hell. Probably meth.

"Help you?" he said finally. "Whatcha needing help with?"

"I'm stuck. I can't get out."

"How the fuck'd you do that?"

"Can you help me?"

"Can I?" he said. "*Can* I?"

"I'm Bad Axe County Sheriff Heidi Kick."

He replied, "And mighty is the work of the Lord," in a tone that told her, *I know who you are.*

"Who are you?" she said.

"This is such a sight," he answered. "Such a trip."

She ground her teeth to stop her jaw from trembling. He was high, the way he acted, the way he was dressed. He had hunted her. In a snowstorm. With an outlawed military assault rifle. Wearing Crocs and a T-shirt.

"You have to help me."

"Is that so?"

"You have to render aid."

"I do?"

"If you don't, it's a crime."

Wisconsin had no Bad Samaritan law, but she hoped he would believe her lie. Again he stared a long time, two glittering eyeholes, lips pressed in what she knew was a grin.

"Okay, it's a crime. But who's calling it in?"

She nipped a glove off in her teeth and shoved her numb finger through the Deerslayer's trigger guard. As she leveled the rifle at him—"Help me now"—she knew it was a cold-brained thing to do.

He laughed.

"Or else what?"

In a few quick motions, the M16 was on full auto. He squirted a burst of bullets into the current just ahead of her. On brain-stem instinct she tried to run and pitched herself off balance. She thrust her left arm to catch herself, touched nothing but water, plunged until her face was under. The current sucked the glove from her teeth, swept off her hat and filled her coat. When she recovered, she had gone nowhere. Now her phone was ruined. Her rifle dripped. The grainy snow stung. His mouth hole had widened with silent glee.

"You followed me."

He nodded.

"You understand that I'm the sheriff."

And nodded more eagerly.

"Please. I'm the mother of three children."

He shrugged.

She felt a warm sensation on her cheeks. Tears. Fiercely, she blinked them away.

"Let me pray for my family."

He shrugged again. "Knock yourself out."

But language fell into a heavy tangle and she could not form prayer. Then in a surreal surge that racked her whole body she saw their grief-hollowed faces. The image made her try to run away again, and again she plunged under.

When she thrashed back up, he was laughing. Why did he sound so familiar?

Through chattering teeth, she managed to say: "If you're going to shoot me, shoot me."

"Like a stray dog, huh?"

He kept grinning through a hard swirl of pinprick snow. But he lowered the weapon and fingered up the hem of wet black fabric at his neck.

"Nah."

As he peeled off the balaclava, at last she understood.

This whole time—*Wanna drink ketchup?*—Missy had been setting her up. Roman Vanderhoof, twelve years of prison clotting his still-handsome face, leered at her like old times.

"Nah, don't think I'm gonna shoot you, Mighty Heidi. This is so much better."

CHAPTER 9

Fernanda's sex with the prophet-father lasted four and a half minutes and ended with a once-mighty, once-much-admired roar that of late just faintly escaped the containment of the mobile coach.

Then his two Halcions dropped him like a downer hog.

Fernanda peeled away and dressed quickly, desperate to get back to Hosanna. The girl had been so contained since her Papa Roy had disappeared. She had hardly said one word from the moment she had been told it was now "Papa Milk."

Fernanda was fastening her bra when the words came back: *Roy resisted his prosperity, just as other men have found theirs.*

She didn't believe it. Roy was a devout and patient practitioner of the Prosperity Gospel, often chosen by the prophet-father to recite at recruitment seminars when the House had offered those in Nevada and Colorado. And if by *other men* the prophet-father meant Brother Milk and his three friends, she didn't believe that either. Not one of those creeps—God forgive her—could recite a single line from any gospel, prosperity or otherwise. They didn't work for wages either, like the other Carpenters. They hung around "supervising projects" and "providing security."

As Fernanda yanked on her jeans, her angry thoughts compounded. Projects? With all the supervision, and with winter coming, why was there so little progress on the new houses they were going to build on the lot beyond the fence? The other project? A bunker! To hide in! Why suddenly did they fear attack so much that they were digging a bunker? Security against what? Or who? Sometime in September a rumor had been sent rippling through the House that one Carpenter among them was a government informant. One among them had been approached by the feds and was talking.

Really? What was there to talk about?

Fernanda found one sock on the carpet and, hopping irately, yanked it on. *Approached?* Seriously, who among them could not be approached? By anyone? From anywhere? Except for the new "security team," they all had outside jobs. That was where the prosperity came from. If someone had approached Roy—if this was the hint beneath the rumor—what was he supposed to do? Turn invisible? Run into the corn?

She couldn't find her other sock. She stopped looking and jerked the pink sweater over her head.

If someone "federal" talked to her, then what?

Poof?

She disappeared?

Her children lost their mother?

As her head emerged from the sweater neck, her glossy black hair crackled with static and the other sock fell away, landing on the carpet by the bed skirt. As Fernanda picked up the sock, she saw a MacBook Pro that seemed hastily shoved under the bed.

She put the sock on first, slowly. Her prophet-father snored, journeying toward the Tokyo and Hong Kong markets.

She was in no mood to stop herself.

She opened the laptop and a photograph leapt to fill the screen: Hosanna standing naked in the washtub.

She stared until disbelief dissolved.

She touched the arrow key.

More Hosanna.

And more.

A folder.

Folders.

▲ ▼ ▲ ▼

Back inside Unit 14, Fernanda found the hole in the wall to Unit 13 and fiercely slapped tape over it. Then she dug through the shoebox of stray stuff she had been collecting in the weeks since Roy had disappeared: his coins and keys and business cards, notes of scripture to himself, candies he meant to give to the children, nuts and bolts.

Hosanna watched. Her daddy Roy had worked for an agricultural implement dealer called McKormick's. He had detailed the new tractors and other machines for sale, kept them radiantly clean where they were lined up on a berm above the highway north of town. The day when Roy had not returned from work, he had gone for lunch in a company truck that McKormick's had traced to a wayside fifty miles south and across the Mississippi River in Iowa. His worried employer had already contacted the Clayton County Sheriff's Department, and when an Iowa deputy asked to speak to Fernanda through the House of Shalah gate, their only exchange had been, "Ma'am, what is your husband's last name?"

"Carpenter."

"No, ma'am, his actual last name."

She had had no idea. Just then the prophet-father himself had appeared, to shoo her back to her children and assure the deputy that Roy had simply exercised his freedom to leave the House. That had been the end of Roy. But suddenly she hoped the rumors were true and he had secretly been talking to someone.

"Mommy?"

Hosanna's sharp little finger marked a page in the family Bible. Fernanda had to squint to see what her watchful daughter had found: in handwritten ink, between verses 6 and 7 of the Lamentations of Jeremiah, Roy had written a phone number.

Fernanda touched the number into her phone.

A man's voice answered, "Roy?" Waited. Said, "Go ahead."

"I'm the wife of . . ."

Nerves had closed her throat.

"Who is this?"

"I'm the *former* wife, the ex-wife, of Roy."

A long silence. Heavy snowflakes splatted against the unit door. How were they supposed to keep warm?

Then she heard something like the clicking of a pen.

"Mrs. Carpenter, I'm glad you got in touch."

She waited to hear who it was.

CHAPTER 10

"Who?"

Chapter Two, Belle Kick has just explained, as neon-red snow falls through early darkness at the tavern window, begins at age nine, when they get married.

"Who?"

"When they get married! At age nine!"

"When who gets married?"

The Ease Inn is packed with people yelling, four TVs blaring four different sports programs, games of shuffleboard, bar darts, blackjack, bridge, and euchre, a petition going around to run off the cult. The band loudly tuning up is Belle's favorite, the Coulee Cats.

"My mom and Gentleman Jim!"

"At age nine?"

"No! I'm nine!"

"Well, sugarplum, you are quite mature for nine!"

"Chapter Two! I just said! I turn nine! I get buds! They get married! Now he's my father!"

"Who is?"

Belle's elbows feel sticky. Her new gentleman has been toying with her long silver braid, laying it this way and that way over the hump of her back, tickling her cheek and ear with the split ends beyond the rubber band. Suddenly she is sinking.

He yells, "Anybody ever tell you you oughta write a book?"

She grabs his coarse brown suit coat sleeve because suddenly something tastes like rubber and there is backward spin to the planet. She tries chewing celery to eat something, but she's not exactly sure if that's why the tavern is narrowing down to a tunnel because

CHAPTER 11

She watched Hoof review her desperation with dark glee.

"Seeing Sheriff High-and-Mighty Heidi Kick stuck in her own Bad Axe River—her own fault—drowning in slow-mo—day before Thanksgiving—I bet your phone don't work, huh?—I bet your family wonders where you are—the shock, the grief—the poor kiddies—the poor baseball-hero-dickhead husband—if only someone could have saved the bitch. Shoot you? Nah, this is so much better than I ever dreamed. So much better."

His breath streamed away on a gust of gritty snow. As she understood the full cruelty of what he meant, full presence came into focus. He was the same, but not. He would always be a jolt to look at: dark eyes, heavy brows, square chin, great teeth, sly grin. But a lumpy pink scar ringing his neck made it look as if his familiar handsome head had been attached to a new body. His booze-bloated torso from years ago had been replaced as if by a piece from a toy set, his T-shirt plastered to a freakish package of muscles decorated with obscurely violent tattoos. Then beneath the belt he was the same again—the same "buttless wonder," Missy's term, balanced on the thin legs pinned back together after shattering in a car crash.

"And I did dream, Mighty Heidi. For twelve long years, oh, did I dream."

Suddenly shaking too hard to see him anymore, the sheriff drifted back to Crossing Waters Hospital and her day of decision. As she recovered from frostbite and hypothermia, deputies from both sides of the river had cautioned her: When charges were pressed in a case like hers—allegations of violent abuse—revenge against the woman was an ongoing concern. Did she understand the risks? Did she have a way to be safe? Would her story stand up to investigation and trial with a jury?

Yes.

Maybe.

Fuck it.

Six months later, she was on probation in drug-and-alcohol treatment. Missy, the subject of multiple warrants, was hiding out with friends in Minnesota. Disgraced, stripped of his family and his business, Hoof was re-dressed in orange and beginning his term at the Supermax in Boscobel, never dreaming, like he said, that he would have revenge this good.

His grin blurred. Her mind slipped. Out of rehab with her criminal record expunged, she had left the coulees for college, then law enforcement academy, and by the time she returned in 2014 as a Bad Axe County rookie deputy, she had imagined the nightmare was behind her.

She had never told Harley about Missy and Hoof, and to the extent that she had allowed herself to think about that part of her past, the narrative had been wishful and naïve. *Missy will move on and forget me. And sitting there in prison all this time, Hoof will admit to his sins. He will feel lucky that I didn't say more—*

"No . . ."

His delight brought her back.

"No, there is nothing here I can improve on. You're gonna cry and beg and shit yourself. After that you're gonna try and gnaw your legs off like a coyote in a trap. Eventually you're gonna see my new friend Jesus. Then you're gonna lay down and go under. I'll watch for the news. You'll be bones and jelly when they find you. You'll be dental records. But as you know"—the wind paused, Hoof's breath crawled out—"I always am a gentleman."

As he watched her jerk with hard shivers, he nodded slowly, agreeing with himself.

"Always. And as a gentleman," he said, "I won't watch."

He slung the M16 on its strap around his back.

He gave her a final grin.

"You have a perfect evening, Sheriff Heidi Kick."

CHAPTER 12

As he turned to go, she raised the Deerslayer.

Not anymore was she a sheriff. Not anymore was she a mother or a wife, not Heidi Kick anymore, nothing but a brain stem flashing, *Shoot the fucker*, and tracking movement down a shaky rifle sight.

Her target grew distant quickly.

Willow stems thrashed.

She pulled the trigger.

The muzzle flared.

The air cracked.

Roman Vanderhoof flew forward. In a reciprocal instant, as if broken backward at the waist, the sheriff was driven underwater, and the river closed over.

▲ ▼ ▲ ▼

Bubbles streamed.

Bits of sticks tumbled through.

A dead leaf sailed across her own reflection, a strange dead face trapped within layers of water and sky.

Then her billowing coat became a black horizon riding up and over her chin, pulling at her armpits, racking her spine in a wave. Then a lock of pressure broke, cold water rushed into her sinuses, and this shock restarted her thoughts.

Had she held on to the rifle?

Yes. She felt it wobbling in her numb fist.

She stabbed the barrel at the river bottom, hoping to connect with a rock or a log, pry herself back up.

But as she probed, she twisted, and as she twisted, the current got a better grip, and it screwed her deeper underwater while the rifle groped through an empty cloud of silt.

Abandoning that plan, she streamlined her arms behind her with the current. With her lungs about to burst, she flattened out. With her half-stripped coat acting like a sail, she slowly rose—but not quite to the surface.

So . . . drop the rifle?

No.

Unzip the coat?

Yes.

Get it off.

She was skimming anaerobic darkness as she tried to shuck the coat. Her stiff fingers fumbled blindly at the zipper, kept on task by a piercing chorus: *I am drowning! I am drowning! This is drowning!*

At last, the slider caught the bottom stop.

She yanked the zipper and the coat swept open behind her, caught inside out at her wrists.

When her face popped up, she wasn't ready.

She gasped late, inhaled mostly river.

Again she was a wave.

The current drove her down, up, down.

She spewed water, caught a snip of air, sealed her lips.

Under again.

Up again.

This time more air.

Next time more.

A clear thought arrived: she shrank her left hand and let the current strip the coat sleeve. Now she traded hands with the rifle and felt the whole coat peel away off her right wrist.

She felt much lighter. She caught the rifle in both fists and jerked hard with her stomach muscles.

She was upright suddenly, breathing, but as stuck as she had been before, dying in the original way all over again.

On the right-hand bank, Hoof was a dark lump in the snow, his Croc heels facing her.

Was he moving?

Or was it her?

Or was it an illusion caused by the scrawling, swirling snow?

A strange fact shocked her: she had shot him.

She was the sheriff—and she had shot a man in the back.

But it didn't matter.

But could she at least go peacefully, with her dying mind flush with green grass and yellow dandelions? Her heart alive with visions of her loved ones?

Could she at least fall asleep and dream happy dreams as she drowned?

She heard a snort and thought it was an answer: *No.* She had shot a man in the back.

She had left her family in shame and grief.

Then another snort, harsh and furious. She strained to see up-river. A black shape loomed along the left bank.

Hoof?

The fucker was on his feet.

Somehow, impossible what she was seeing, he was now on both banks of the river.

She raised the rifle—one round left—no idea if it would fire again. She sighted on the black shape, growing larger as it neared, taking on detail, articulating, rattling the streamside brush, snorting a third time explosively.

No.

This was not Hoof.

This was a deer.

A big buck.

This was the buck she had shot, wanting to recross the river, go back where he had come from.

The wounded creature stared at her. He blew another snort, low and dismissive. Then he limped to the edge of the steep bank, haunched back, and began the process of descending. Each stiff leg seeming to have a different idea of how to proceed—and then, losing control, he half slid, half leaped, and landed with a crash in the river.

He struggled explosively until he got his hooves beneath him. He looked at her again, blowing a harsh indignant shriek that cut through the wind.

Then he was crossing. She had one round left. Could he save her? His body?

Sluggishly, dizzily, she sighted-in his shoulder down the rifle barrel. Then she lost him completely—had to look up and find the entire animal all over again—her body shaking and pitching.

She lowered her eye back to the barrel. Fifty feet seemed like a quarter mile, her target massive, yet jumpy and elusive.

It has to be a kill shot.

She tracked him down the rifle sight, chasing his heart as he staggered across the rocky bottom. She nearly pulled the trigger but then he stumbled, crashed his chest into the current, struggled back up. She had to find his heart again. She looked down the barrel and saw only water. She gritted her teeth to stop her head from shaking. She bent her neck again and laid her cheek on the rifle stock. She re-found him, re-narrowed to his heart, but couldn't feel her hands. She could only guess that she was squeezing.

But the rifle fired.

The old buck took two more steps.

He sank to his knees.

His final snort sprayed blood. Then he toppled and crashed. The downstream wave washed over her ribs.

Now she waited, shivering so hard that her teeth cracked together.

For an eternity, the buck lay where he had fallen, the river gnashing and snarling around him as if enraged by the new obstacle. His back was toward her, blood trailing out beneath. The current broke around his heavy hindquarters, lifting and jittering his tail, flashing the white. At a slight angle upstream, the river broke around his skull and antlers—and as she watched she understood that several tines had embedded in the sticky bottom. Would they pull loose? As she waited, a strange hot grogginess swept through her, a profound weariness in her muscles and her mind. But sleep was death. Loss of pain was death. Feeling nothing . . . that was death.

Stay awake, Heidi.

She bit a finger, felt the bone in her teeth.

Awake.

At last, the power of the current prevailed. The buck's body inched toward her, inched, inched, then twisted slowly into deeper water and buoyed up. From there it drifted halfway to her before it caught bottom again.

Minutes passed into sudden dusk.

The air went still and silver.

Then some stalemate broke. Once more the river had control, sweeping three hundred pounds of dead animal straight at her.

Drop the rifle, Heidi.

As the antlers bobbed toward her face, picking up speed, she ducked and thrust her hands up, grabbing for tines—and as she caught them, she pulled down with her knees, ducking deeper. As the creature's massive bulk swept over and downstream, her shoulders nearly left their sockets—but she hung on—and his drifting weight pulled her free.

The body dragged her beneath as it spun downriver.

Then it struck a corner and tumbled and her face popped up.

She hung on across deep water, gasping, her numb legs dangling.

▲ ▼ ▲ ▼

Later, in darkness on a mud spit, Sheriff Kick lay against the dead buck, taking heat from his body.

When she could move again, she crawled, then stood, then forced herself back upstream along the brush-tangled riverbank until she found where she had shot Roman Vanderhoof.

The storm had quit, new weather under a cold black sky. By starlight she searched until she was sure.

He was alive.

He was gone.

Hoof had survived too.

THANKSGIVING DAY

Nelson Abernathy Woods #30749756
Wisconsin Secure Program Facility

Good day to you, Madam.

You have heard a picture tells a thousand words. As a man of few words, I am an Artist of the eye. As a caring Man of creation you know that comes with mistakes but you will find me a true gentleman who means no harm, only love and beauty of God's natural creation.

I have a dream to be my true self for my God and Life while I wait for my freedom from this wrongful conviction. Justice! I shall overcome! Love for all. Never say never. Everything is natural. A picture tells a thousand words. These are my mottos. I am an Artist of the eye.

If you have children of your Own that is not at all a problem with me, as I assure you I am wrongfully convicted.

All Love,
Nelson

Race: White
Date of Birth: 2/17/1979
Height: 6' 3"
Earliest Release Date: 4/23/18
Maximum Release Date: 4/23/20
Would you like letters from both sexes? Female
Education: Bachelor of arts
Occupation before prison: IT consultant
Activities in prison: God, Author
Can you receive and send emails? Yes; also letters and photos

meet-an-inmate.com posted 3/6/2012
jpay.com reply record 4/4/2020

CHAPTER 13

Duke Hashimoto saw from the window of his Gulf Shores condo that his Uber had arrived in the form of a cute yellow car.

He locked up and pulled a pair of wheeled suitcases down the wooden steps. The twenty-something driver waited by her open trunk, lukewarm November gusts whipping beach sand across her face. She insisted on lifting his suitcases, sagging under the weight of the second one, his gear, the sixty-pounder.

"Jack Edwards, right?"

"Right."

"And which concourse today?"

"Straight to car rental, please."

She asked once they were under way, "Seeing family for the holidays?"

"Work trip."

Her eyes flashed over him in the mirror: red Renk seed cap, green-and-gold Packers sweatshirt, day-old stubble.

"Volunteer work," he said.

He added, "I'm retired."

In the curious way of her generation, she assured him that being a volunteer and retired was cool and not a problem. Or perhaps it was his stab at Wisconsin beer-me style that she was approving.

▲ ▼ ▲ ▼

At Jack Edwards Airport, his driver took Hashimoto on a tour of the rental car lot until he found a black Ford Ranger already camouflaged with Wisconsin plates. He completed the rental process with his own credit card, hefted his suitcases into the club cab, and slid behind the wheel of the truck to get set up for the seventeen-hour drive to meet Roy Carpenter's wife.

From the left outer pocket of his suit coat, the former ATF special agent produced his omamori amulet for safe driving, a small, embroidered rectangle, pink and green, with a loop on the top and a tassel off the bottom. He hung this on the mirror stem.

Next, from his right outer pocket, Hashimoto removed seven small magnetic pebbles that looked like beads of mercury. Using one pebble as his metal detector, he skimmed the dash until he felt a pull. There he stacked the pebbles, clicking them together, one on top of the other, pagoda-like. Since the twenty-five Branch Davidian children were lost in the inferno at Waco, he had kept this stack of pebbles near him to remember.

The pebbles stacked, he went back into his left-hand pocket for another charm—the red-and-silver yakuyoke: strength against evil—and hung this charm also from the pickup's mirror. Since Roy's disappearance, the House of Shalah had developed an ogre problem. Or so he chose to think of the bad news that he had heard from Roy's wife.

This was yesterday. Off he went.

▲ ▼ ▲ ▼

Funny then how Google Maps had sent him on yet a third route to Wisconsin, different than the routes he had taken in both July and August.

Those trips had been pieces of the last assignment of Special Agent Hashimoto's forty-year career, delivering unassembled gun parts to the follower of a cult that the beleaguered ATF had an interest in raiding, on behalf of the IRS, as a way of showing interagency synergy, for the purpose of bolstering the ATF's annual congressional budget request. The business-as-usual plan had been to get Hashimoto's inside-the-cult confidential informant—Roy Carpenter—to put a bump stock on an M16 automatic rifle, thus breaking federal law—*and in we go to confiscate financial records, just in time to tell our story on the House floor.*

As a traumatized bit player in the Waco debacle, later a key cog in the Wide Receiver and Fast and Furious gunwalking scandals, Hashimoto had gritted his teeth and followed orders while churning with internal dismay: *Gee whiz, what could go wrong?*

He found it interesting, this trip, how Google had routed him up Interstate 10 around Mobile. From there he had gone north on U.S. 45 to Tupelo, west on U.S. 78 to Memphis, then north again via Interstate 55 on a straight bead through the night toward rural southwestern Wisconsin—which, as the sun rose on Thanksgiving morning, was a winter wonderland.

The roads squeaked beneath his tires.

The fence posts wore little dunce caps of snow.

The dairy cows steamed where sunlight touched them.

▲ ▼ ▲ ▼

Later, as he arrived under a high blue sky in Farmstead, Hashimoto saw that since his last visit, the tavern attached to the Ease Inn Motel had acquired a new sign.

KILL THE CULT.

Ogres on both sides of the fence, then.

He parked beside a diesel pickup with smokestacks and four rear wheels. He straightened his pebbles and sent Fernanda Carpenter a text: *I'm here.*

CHAPTER 14

Fernanda truly did love her prophet-father.

Who had desired her, when she had believed herself unworthy of desire.

Who had said, *Turn your back on family and friends*, when this was exactly what she had wanted.

Who to a child of want had guaranteed abundance, and who upon a purposeless girl had bestowed the sacred work of a woman to bear children.

For all of this, she could not help but truly and deeply love Euodoo Koresh. But now she hated him too.

She rapped with cold knuckles and the Unit 13 door rolled up. Sister Maryellen, Fernanda's neighbor, shuddered at the outside air, her little Zachariah, sixteen months, riding red-nosed and sniffling on her hip bone. Fernanda spoke quickly and quietly.

"No!" protested the wife of Brother Peep. "I didn't send you pictures in an email! I knew nothing about it! And the prophet-father would never!"

"Oh, no, he seems fine with it. He made folders."

Fernanda's phone stirred.

I'm here.

When she looked up from the text message, she saw that tears had formed behind Sister Maryellen's smudgy round glasses. She hugged her little boy to her chest.

"Your husband made a hole in the wall," Fernanda said.

Sister Maryellen scowled sharply at the crooked pattern of ink-smudged sticky notes on the corrugated steel wall they shared. "I'm not allowed to touch those." Below the notes and six feet from the wall, Fernanda saw a strip of silver tape across the concrete floor. "I'm not allowed to cross that line," Sister Maryellen said. "He always makes me go outside." Then she dropped her face in shame.

"Yesterday afternoon," Fernanda said, seeing herself beyond the wall, "was he . . ."

But the moment she began her question, Fernanda knew she had been caught hiding the extra cash from Tyson Ernhardt Jr.

▲ ▼ ▲ ▼

Brother Skip, main security, gripping his pants at the crotch as he limped behind her, herding Fernanda across the grounds toward the mobile coach.

"I told y'all don't play, girl."

"Keep your hands off me."

"Ain't only one place for that lip you got."

"Shut your dirty mouth."

He shoved her.

"You gonna tell us what you playing, girl."

"I'm not playing."

Up on U-Stash-It Road, the Kill the Cult sentinel pickup, blue today, glinted in the sun. Fernanda's soul kept splitting deeper as she doubted God was watching. How could He allow this?

In another minute she stood inside the coach's crowded lounge area, surrounded by brothers Skip, Peep, and Spooner . . . their names striking her suddenly like proof that they were all in on one big, sick joke—and she had just understood one small part of it.

"Go on. Who you taking money from, sister?"

Her prophet-father watched dully as she flinched back from Brother Skip. Though it was still hours before his normal bedtime, he looked wet-eyed and groggy, his bathrobe slipping open, Mother Ruth behind his captain's chair discreetly tugging on his braid.

"It was a holiday bonus."

"Girl, don't play!"

"I'm not playing. It was a holiday bonus."

It had to be that Brother Peep was watching yesterday as she had withdrawn the envelope from the lining of her coat, counted one hundred dollars in twenties, and hidden the cash up the bottom of an empty baby powder shaker. She had been thinking she would buy some kind of snowsuit for Hosanna, and an electric blanket for the babies.

"I'll go get the money," she promised. "I'll tithe it. I'm sorry."

"Oh, we done ate that cake, girl."

Her breath stopped. They had been inside her unit.

"Question is, yo, where *you* got it."

"Tyson Ernhardt. My boss's son. He gave me a holiday bonus. I wanted to buy something warm for my children."

The prophet-father said, "Hmmm," and nodded with possible credulity. This seemed to stall Brother Skip. After a few silent moments, Mother Ruth leaned to whisper in the prophet-father's ear. Then she exchanged glances with Brother Spooner. Fernanda took the chance to glare at Brother Peep: *Does someone think your name is funny?* Brother Peep stared back from his buried eyes. Had he also reported her conversation with Duke Hashimoto? And now she would disappear like Roy?

Brother Skip broke his stall. "Where Milk at?"

"I don't know."

"Who that motherfucker dropped you off?"

"Tyson Ernhardt," she said. "My boss's son. They call him E.J. My husband didn't come to pick me up. There was a storm. I was standing there. E.J. came out. He gave me a holiday bonus. I started walking home, so he gave me a ride."

Brother Skip refreshed his crotch grab and stepped menacingly closer. "See, sister, you so precious to God and all, we here to protect you."

"Thank you."

"We all up in here to protect you."

"Thank you."

"Now where Milk and that chopper at?"

"He dropped me off at the pig farm. I haven't seen him since. I don't know what a chopper is."

"Bitch—"

But Brother Spooner had stepped forward, scowling. With a precise strike he swatted Brother Skip's hand off his crotch.

"Sister Fernanda," he said, "we worry that you're getting paid to talk."

"To who? About what?"

She held her breath.

"You tell us."

"I just did tell you. Tyson Ernhardt. About nothing. It was a holiday bonus."

"Did Brother Milk have a machine gun when he dropped you off yesterday?"

"I didn't see one."

Brother Spooner—what was *his* joke?—stepped in closer: his worn brown suit with silver hair leaking out the cuffs, his houndstooth hat over his half ear, his eyes lit too brightly blue inside his cavernously lined face.

"Where did Brother Milk get that car?"

"I don't know."

Now Brother Spooner stepped around behind her. She worried he would find her phone, shoved into her sock and covered with her pants cuff. Instead, he lifted her glossy hair and held it, held it—she shivered at his breath upon her neck—then let it fall back against her.

Fernanda glanced at the prophet-father, who stared back sleepily. Mother Ruth tugged his braid.

"We don't know where Brother Milk is," she said loudly into his ear. "One of our guns is gone. The security people have evidence Sister Fernanda has been talking to outside people and keeping money for herself. What do you want to do?"

The prophet-father yawned.

"She's a good girl."

Fernanda's soul split even more deeply. Her prophet-father yawned again.

"Anyway, the time has come, yes?"

Mother Ruth tugged his braid. "Bedtime, yes. Time for bed."

Although it wasn't. And he went on.

"Aren't we ready? Hasn't Brother Spooner found a match for Mother? Isn't the tunnel—"

Mother Ruth yanked so hard his eyebrows rose, stopping him in dopey surprise.

▲ ▼ ▲ ▼

Back in Unit 14, Fernanda reminded Hosanna how to lock the rolling door by putting a screwdriver through the hole at the curve in the track, which stopped the wheel from rising.

"Give the babies Cheerios if they fuss. I'll be back."

She paused before she rolled the door down.

"Hosanna, your mother loves you. More than any other love you can imagine."

The girl frowned.

"Keep this door locked until I'm back."

Fernanda sneaked around the far end of the storage units and behind the new chapel, where by now the untouched snow had drifted knee-deep. They should have been gone from here a month ago. *The time has come*, the prophet-father had said. Time to pack up and caravan to a warmer place, she had hoped. But that hadn't seemed to be the topic.

He had continued, *Hasn't Brother Spooner found a match for Mother?*

What did this mean?

▲ ▼ ▲ ▼

Fernanda plunged across the shooting range and reached the massive dirt pile against the back fence. All this dirt, she had learned, had not come from digging a bunker, like the Carpenters had been told. But instead . . . *a tunnel*?

To where? Why?

The pile had become so big that it had sloughed through the chain-link on the back side, consuming a section of the fence. Climbing was messy, snow on top of mud, but Fernanda was quickly over. She checked the time: she had two minutes left.

She looked at Duke Hashimoto's second text.

U-Stash-It to Robert W. Check Park

.29 miles

7 minutes on foot

CHAPTER 15

Hoof had survived too.

Her layered blankets, heavy as water, triggered panic. But when Sheriff Kick threw the layers off, she shivered in the warm bedroom air.

Bullet.

Rifle.

Ballistics.

An omission-heavy version of what happened.

And he was out there.

What did she do now?

"Try again," she told her dispatcher, Denise Halverson, through the landline phone receiver. "I didn't quite catch that."

Denise repeated, "A gun nut, a killer, and a liar."

The sheriff's heart sped. The numb fingers of her left hand nearly let slip a mug of chicken bouillon.

"Okay, got it. They all walk into a bar?"

"Right. A gun nut, a killer, and liar. Picture the Ease Inn. But Heidi, your voice sounds all shivery."

"I'm fine."

"Are you warm enough?"

"Denise"—more untruth—"I'm fine."

All she had admitted to was chasing a buck and falling in the river. The ER doctor had released her shortly before Thanksgiving Day noon with orders to rest, keep the warm fluids coming, and stay alert for signs of mental impairment. The kids and their very hungover Grammy Belle had come along with Harley to retrieve her from the hospital. Belle had shuttled Harley's truck back home while the sheriff, riding in the minivan, had been tested by the kids.

What was her middle name?

She said George.

How old were her children?

She said Opie, nine, was forty-two.

She said the twins, Taylor and Dylan, were twelve and twenty-one. Wasn't that how twins worked? Like a mirror?

No! Mommy! What county do we live in?

That's easy. Bad Apple County.

Though she had made them laugh and eased their minds, she had felt desperately eager to get off the roads. In the brutal glare of sun-on-snow, each oncoming vehicle had made her flinch, fearing that Roman Vanderhoof, alive and on the hunt, would swerve and murder them all.

Since getting home, just as Dr. Patel had predicted, she had battled extreme drowsiness. In her recurrent nightmares, she was underwater with lungs bulging, eyes bulging, searching the bottom for her dad's Deerslayer rifle. Then she would jerk awake, burned by the same thought over and over.

He survived . . . but if he dies later, it's still murder.

She gathered a shallow breath.

"Okay, Denise, so a gun nut, and killer, and liar all walk into a bar. And?"

"And the bartender says, 'What can I do for you, Officer?' "

"Ha."

"Moving on," her dispatcher said, "I'm happy to report that the Thunder Queen has been a good witch so far."

Thunder Queen was Denise's name for Chief Deputy Mikayla Stonebreaker, officer in charge during the sheriff's rare days off, and Stonebreaker would be the interim sheriff should the real sheriff happen to shoot someone, just for example, and get herself suspended—or worse.

"We'll see if it lasts," Denise went on. "She hasn't had to do much. Overnight we had a couple of car-on-snow mishaps, four domestics, and a bar fight. Overall kind of subpar for a Blackout Wednesday. Today has been super-quiet."

"Hangovers will do that."

"But Heidi, that shivery voice. How are *you* feeling?"

"I'm totally fine, Denise. I'm smarter. I survived my own stupidity."

"Okay, well. Jeez. But after all the hunter-education stuff we put out there, I think everyone's trying to figure out why the county's number-one safety officer went hunting by herself."

An awkward pause hung between them.

My friend Missy didn't show up.

This was what she had told Harley.

That's why I was alone. But please keep that to yourself.

"Like I said, stupidity."

"Maybe overwork?"

"I'm fine, Denise."

"Okay, still moving on," Denise continued, "another reason I called is to let you know that Deputy Luck is leaving here any second with your backup cell phone. Maybe you can ask her about displaced anger and aggression? Maybe you could ask how things are going in her private life? But not take her word for anything she tells you?"

"I'm sorry, Denise. What are we talking about?"

"I'm an internet psychologist now. Did you know that when women fall in love with inmates it's because the inmates symbolize the rage and defiance that they themselves can't act on? Honestly, it makes sense, doesn't it? I myself am well known to fall in love with know-it-alls and egotistical fuckups, being as I was brought up to feel stupid and worthless. See how this works?"

With tingling fingertips, the sheriff rubbed the dull ache in her forehead. Hoof was out there somewhere. Unless he had died later. What should she do?

"Let's keep moving on," she told Denise, pulling her laptop across the bedcovers. Distracted as she was, the possibility of movement on the Win Carpenter homicide had now pulled her into focus. "I need you to look into something for me."

"Hit me."

"Let's maybe not say 'hit me.' "

"Right."

"Yesterday Alexis Schmidt gave me this weird thing she found below the dam on Lake Susan. And I know you haunt the local antiques shops, so . . . I just emailed you a link to some photos."

In a moment they were both looking at objects similar to what Alexis had given the sheriff: pairs of dish-shaped plastic pieces the size of thumbnails, with spikes on their convex sides.

"I've figured out what they are. They're contact lenses with barbs on the eyelid side."

Denise said, "Weird. What for?"

"Morticians use them to keep dead people's eyelids closed."

"Holy shit."

"My exact thought. Alexis found them floating in the pool below the dam spout. They might have been in Win Carpenter's possession. If so, why would he have them? Where did he get them? They might help us find out who he really was. It seems like they're discolored, like they're old. And the case has a color-coded sticker that suggests a yard sale or a consignment shop. Can you think of any local shops that might sell something like a vintage undertaker's tool kit?"

"Sure. Crazy Frank's in Readstown sometimes has vintage medical equipment. Shall I call them and get back to you?"

"Yes. Thanks."

"Anything else I can do?"

Beneath the bedroom window, the front door had opened and closed.

"Hang on, Denise."

The sheriff parted the curtain to see her mother-in-law headed toward Harley's truck. Fear rose like cold water in her chest—*he's out there*—and she ran up the window.

"Mom, stop!"

Belle turned, her eyes slitted against the brightness, and hollered up, "Somebody didn't get Cool Whip!"

"No! Stay here! I mean it! Stop!"

"You said you'd get Cool Whip!"

"We can do without Cool Whip!"

"It's not Thanksgiving without Cool Whip! And we don't have Cool Whip!"

"Belle, please."

"Please what? Don't get Cool Whip? When the kids want Cool Whip?"

In her ear Denise said, "Heidi, is something wrong?"

"Not at all."

"But—"

"Everything is fine," the sheriff lied again.

But she could not just sit here sipping chicken broth. What, though? Below, her restless mother-in-law kicked snow and started a cigarette.

"Okey dokey," Denise said. "But Deputy Luck is just leaving now with your phone. Shall I have her pick up some Cool Whip on the way?"

"Denise," she answered, "can you call me back on your own phone?"

CHAPTER 16

In twenty minutes, Sheriff Kick was up and dressed for holiday pie-making with the kids, wearing her mom jeans from after the twins were born and her Blackhawk High Booster Club hooded sweatshirt, secretly Kevlar-vested and SIG-strapped beneath the baggy orange-on-black fabric. In strict confidence—Denise knew the truth now—her dispatcher and friend had helped dress the sheriff for safety and find a general approach forward. To facilitate, Denise was now making some calls.

Thanksgiving pies were made from scratch. That was the family rule, going back at least to the kids' great-great-grandmother Aurora, who according to family lore had lured rattlesnakes from beneath her summer kitchen by playing waltzes on her accordion—hence Opie's fascination with the instrument—then hacked them to bloody pieces with a hoe.

Per Aurora, a proper pie crust required hand-rendered lard, a six-hour process that the sheriff's misadventure yesterday had made impossible. Instead, dizzy and shivery and hiding her distraction, she got busy churning butter. With a pine fire crackling in the living room fireplace, the rest of the family followed tradition. Beginning pie number one, Opie was boiling chunks of homegrown pumpkin, Dylan and Taylor were baking the pumpkin seeds, Harley was grinding Einkorn wheat grains and sifting the flour, and Grammy Belle was on the front porch having a smoke and some hair of the dog. This was when Deputy Lyndsey Luck arrived with a cell phone and a sixteen-ounce tub of Cool Whip.

The sheriff met Luck on the porch.

"It's okay, boss," her young deputy said, handing over the phone. "I did that once too."

"You did what?"

"Had a brain fart and nearly got myself killed. Denise said—"

"Mom," the sheriff interrupted, turning to Belle, "how about you get this Cool Whip into the fridge?"

Her mother-in-law took the tub from Deputy Luck and sulked away.

"Denise said what?"

"Denise said to tell you the story. I'm not sure why. But I was thirteen. My uncle was chasing me. All I had to do was stop at the highway and stay there, because there were cars going by, and with people watching, he wouldn't have tried anything. But I tried to run across, and I—"

By the sheen on her eyes, she was thirteen again, in the middle of a busy highway, vehicles just missing her.

"Your uncle was chasing you?"

"Well," Deputy Luck backtracked, bucking up as if she just remembered she was in uniform, "he *called* himself my uncle. He was actually my stepmom's half brother, this guy Billy." Then she made air quotes. "After 'Uncle Billy' came to live with us, he—"

Again, Lyndsey Luck stopped herself. Harley had appeared in the front doorway—a handsome man in a flour-dusted apron—and he said, "Thanks, Lyndsey. You saved the day."

The young deputy's cheeks flushed.

"Not a problem!"

Harley had gone back inside but hadn't closed the door yet when Luck frowned at the sheriff's rigid bustline beneath the booster club sweatshirt and blurted, "Hey, don't you have your Kevlar on? Is that to keep you, like, extra-warm, or what?"

Harley was hearing this.

"And wait—are you strapped? Is something going on?"

▲ ▼ ▲ ▼

An anguished hour later, a cold wind shoved steadily and leaden clouds had closed the sky, trapping wood smoke and shadowy snow-light beneath. Inside their darkening bedroom, the sheriff had come close to crying, recovered angrily, and come to the edge again. Her husband had been pacing between the window and the closed door, muttering threats and clenching his fists.

"Don't," she said. "You can't tell anyone, Harley. Not one word. I fell in the river like a dumbass and I'm fine. Do you understand? Only you and Denise know I'm lying. Only you and Denise know what I did."

Harley seethed, "Let's hope the fucker's dead."

"Then I'm up for homicide. Second-degree if I'm lucky."

"It was self-defense!"

He wasn't getting it. His brain was stuck.

You've broken everything . . .

"Listen: I shot him in the back as he was walking away."

"And leaving you to die!"

"Which is not a crime. And that won't be how he tells the story. If I let him tell it."

Her husband nearly sobbed but caught himself and inhaled deeply. He reached like he wanted to hug her, but the air between them said no. He sat heavily on the bed.

"Shit, Heidi."

"Exactly," she snapped. "I've put myself in deep, deep shit."

"And Denise can't find him?"

"She's been trying. None of the surrounding counties has taken a call. He hasn't shown up at an emergency room anywhere. Or a pharmacy. None of the bartenders Denise talked to has seen him. Missy won't respond to her phone. That's pretty much all Denise can do without making a case out of it and involving the department. The only safe assumption is that he's out there and he's coming after me."

And I'm here: baking pies, Thanksgiving Day parade on TV.

Harley hung his head. Then he shook it.

"What?" she demanded. "Tell me."

"Forget it."

"Say it."

He looked up. His eyes flashed resentment. "So involve the department," he challenged her. "You have a whole team of deputies."

"One more time, Harley: A law enforcement officer shoots somebody, *any*body, for *any* reason, she gets herself suspended on the spot. Badge, weapon, keys. She is required to go home and stay there. She's a sitting duck. Do you want Roman Vanderhoof looking for me here?"

Below them, Belle left the TV room coughing and moved through the house. She opened the front door on her way to the porch.

"Then, as you know, the investigation into my conduct moves slowly. Days, weeks. And in the end, because I *will* tell the truth under oath, the fact remains that I shot a man in the back. I will face discipline at the very least, probably charges, maybe prison."

"You shot a man who hunted you!" he hissed through gritted teeth. His mother let the screen door slam. "Who was leaving you to die!"

Just like that, the sheriff was back in the river. Her breath shortened. Her pulse pounded. Her muscles froze and her bones locked.

The current pushed, her boots sank, the storm swirled. He was walking away. She found him in the rifle sight.

"Meanwhile," she pressed on, forcing herself deeper into what she had discussed with Denise, "because I'm suspended, the Thunder Queen becomes interim sheriff. Mikayla Stonebreaker handles my conduct investigation. She takes over the Win Carpenter homicide case. She determines policy with the House of Shalah, which goes down the Kill the Cult path because she'll want to please her husband. And as we all know, her husband is dangerous."

Harley grimaced at the mention of Dennis Stonebreaker. In August 2016, he had kicked his former high school teammate off the Bad Axe Rattlers—but not because Dennis was a hundred pounds overweight, drinking before games, hitting under .200, cussing out umpires, and dropping throws at first base. All this was "just Dennis." No, in violation of village ordinance and team rules, the unemployed former corrections officer had brought a loaded firearm into the dugout—for *the third time*.

"When you pulled Dennis Stonebreaker's plug, do you remember how that all played out?"

Because who could forget? Misquoting the Second Amendment with a semiautomatic pistol in his fist, Stonebreaker had hijacked someone's beer and occupied the pitcher's mound, and from there he had held forth on the subject of his wrongful dismissal by the Wisconsin Department of Corrections on a bogus charge of brutality, and he had clarified his right to protect himself from retaliation by released criminals.

As she gave her husband a few moments to recall, the sheriff thought of prison. She checked her fist against her teeth and looked away so Harley wouldn't see her face. She had spent her drunken nineteenth birthday in a Crawford County Jail cell with a schizophrenic woman who had driven her car through the window of a real estate brokerage in Gays Mills because she had been commanded to *begin the killing*. And compared to the jailer, that woman was a sweetheart. Prison would be like this, times a thousand. Meanwhile, her career would be obliterated, her husband and children would be ashamed and forced to move without her.

Heidi, why?

But she could not reconstruct her thinking in the moment yesterday because she hadn't been thinking at all. The act had come from her brain stem, her reptile. Without a shred of remorse, she had meant to end a man's life.

This is what the prisons are for.

This is the kind of crime that fills them.

"Do you remember, Harley? Dennis Stonebreaker hated you enough. Then I got involved."

Long story short, brand-new Interim Sheriff Heidi Kick had arrived and evacuated the baseball stadium down to the last truck in the parking lot—Stonebreaker's—and left him alone on the pitcher's mound with his loaded firearm and empty beer cup. When a tow truck arrived a short time later, Dennis had boiled off the mound to accost the driver, which had turned out to be her. She had Tasered him out the window, cuffed him on the asphalt, and impounded his truck and his weapon. In the aftermath, Stonebreaker had sued the village, the sheriff's department, Interim Sheriff Kick, the Bad Axe Rattlers Baseball Club, and Harley personally.

Her husband stood from the bed and headed for the window. From there he stared back at the sheriff like she had broken through, like he was remembering that the shit show hadn't ended there. One month after Stonebreaker's lawsuit was thrown out of court, his wife had quit her junior high gym-teaching job and enrolled in an out-of-state law enforcement academy. Fast-forward three years, Bad Axe County Deputy Mikayla Stonebreaker forearm-shivers the House of Shalah's leader into a train of Walmart shopping carts and thereby—over Sheriff Kick's "kicking and screaming"—earns herself the chief deputy's job.

Harley parted the curtains and stared down at his coatless mother. Looking marooned in the suddenly rushing early dusk, Belle pulled on a cigarette with her phone to her ear, a sharp new wind tearing her exhales away.

"She's talking to her new boyfriend," Harley muttered.

"What new boyfriend?"

"Some guy dropped her off at two this morning. She was so hammered I had to put her to bed. Does she usually not wear a bra?"

"She always wears a bra."

"Then she lost it somewhere. I called around. Her car is at the Ease Inn."

The sheriff sighed. She took up Harley's thick hand.

"And not to mention," she said, "if I'm suspended, Thunder Queen controls the hunt for Roman Vanderhoof. Or the non-hunt. We don't have a Bad Samaritan law in Wisconsin. It was no crime to leave me there. So does Interim Sheriff Stonebreaker conduct a manhunt to find a man who has committed no crime? Or does she kick back and let the man find me?"

In the pause, she felt Hoof moving. They heard thunder.

"Harley—I have to get to him first."

"If Denise can't find him, how?"

"I know some places, some people. I'll figure it out."

"He'll recognize my truck."

"I'll take Dad's."

"Heidi—"

"I'll fix it."

"Then what?"

"Please listen. If anyone but me finds him first, he gets to sell a lie, and if it's Stonebreaker, she's buying wholesale. If he finds me first, I'm dead. And if that asshole dies out there because I shot him, I'm a murderer, and you won't see me for a long, long time."

He looked at her, incredulous. "So you're going to save him?"

"I'm going to save myself, Harley."

He said nothing.

"Us."

He let go of the curtain. He took back his other hand. The rising air from downstairs smelled like pie crusts burning.

"Happy fucking Thanksgiving," he muttered.

CHAPTER 17

In the barn the sheriff pulled a dusty tarp specked with sparrow dung off the truck she had driven in the bad old days. New in 2001, hers as of the tragic events of July 9, 2004, her dad's red Ram 1500 had been her spaceship through the alien universe of loss and grief. For the better part of two years she had driven the Ram on dirty oil, low tire pressure, and stolen gas, had driven it with broken shocks and gravel stars in the windshield, had hit things and run over things and rolled it twice, had puked and bled and screwed in it, had even lost the candy-red, two-ton truck once for a full week, no idea where she had left it, and for a few months before that final winter, she had lived in it.

White script on both doors spelled out *Cress Springs Farms— Est. 1937—Ron, Darlene, and Heidi White.* She blew dust off with compressed air. "Sorry," she whispered beneath the rattle of the agitator bead as she shook a partial can of red Rustoleum. Then, gulping back a hot, bulging sadness, she sprayed over the words.

She was under the hood pulling plugs to clean them when her

new phone's text alert surprised her. She saw it was Denise and her
breath stopped.

Found him!

"No, sorry, I don't mean Roman Vanderhoof," Denise explained.
"No luck with him yet. And I snooped around in Iowa court records
to see if I could find out where your friend Missy is staying. No luck
there either. No, I'm calling because I talked to my bud Gary of Crazy
Frank's. Direct hit on the dead-eyeball thingies. There's a little story
that strangely enough might include Vanderhoof. Do you want to
hear?"

"Go on."

"Last month, a few days before Halloween, Gary filed a report
with the Vernon County sheriff because some guy bounced a check
for a batch of embalmer's tools from the 1960s. I have a call in to
Vernon County right now. They have the check. Meanwhile, Gary
said the buyer was bald, smallish, white, late middle age, nothing
about him really standing out . . ."

Denise paused because this was another part of the Win Carpenter problem: the only photo they had was taken after the victim had
been marinating with a slit throat in Lake Susan for at least two days.
If Alexis Schmidt hadn't known him as Win Carpenter, they might
still be guessing. But this description sounded right.

"The guy was skittish," Denise continued, "but Gary says he
seemed to know what he was looking for. He knew the undertaker's
trade. He pieced together a full tool kit, basically. But now," she went
on, "getting back to Vanderhoof, I wonder if your psycho friend
didn't go along to Crazy Frank's with this guy. Drove him there.
Loomed around like he was making sure the guy did as he was told.
I mean, it sure sounds like the way you described Vanderhoof to me.
Gary basically gave your description right back to me."

"Go on."

"Gary says it was two guys that came together. It seemed like the guy who drove, the muscled-up dude with the tats and the Frankenstein neck scar, with the bird legs, was telling the little guy who kited the check what to do. According to Gary, their relationship looked tense, weird, not friendly."

The sheriff exhaled. So . . . Hoof, fresh out of prison, had gotten involved with Win Carpenter and the House of Shalah? Was that what this meant? And for some reason they needed an undertaker's tool kit?

"Did Gary see a vehicle?"

"Small. Foreign. Silver. Pretty smashed up."

That description fit Hoof, too. When they had met to drink ketchup, Missy had shown up in a much-abused version of the silver Honda Accord she used to borrow from her dad when he was alive. Hoof could have been driving Missy's car.

She touched the paint on the Ram's door. It was tacky, leaving her fingertip red. Why, of all people, would Hoof be hanging out with a Carpenter from the House of Shalah?

She said it out loud.

"I don't know why Hoof would be interested in a religious community." A *cult*, she suddenly wanted to say. "He might be the least spiritual person on the planet."

"Well," Denise mused, "the father, the son, and the holy dollar bill? Plus dumb chicks? Could be all kinds of criminals inside that fence. But what do I know?"

The sheriff stared for a long moment at the erasure on the truck door.

"Okay, Denise, get back to me as soon as we have the name and address on that bounced check."

"Aha," her dispatcher responded. "Vernon County is calling back right now."

▲ ▼ ▲ ▼

Just like that, colliding with her need to find Hoof, the sheriff's stalled Win Carpenter homicide investigation began to lurch forward. Now she had to consider that Hoof, aside from Missy, might have other and possibly more dangerous connections. She had to consider that now, while she worried about Hoof, herself, and her family, she might be facing other, broader problems. Had Hoof killed Win Carpenter? Was any of this related to the House of Shalah?

▲ ▼ ▲ ▼

Back inside the house, working on her phone and laptop in the bedroom upstairs, she learned that Darwin John Fuss, the name on the bounced check, had been the owner of Fuss Funeral Home, in Rapid City, South Dakota. Online pictures of Darwin Fuss matched descriptions of Win Carpenter alive. Darwin Fuss looked just like the description of the man who had bounced a check for undertaker's tools, possibly with Hoof, at Crazy Frank's. Now the sheriff could initiate dental forensics and confirm. But she would bet the house right now that her murder victim was Darwin Fuss.

"Mommy?"

Her daughter, Opie, nine but going on nineteen, was in the bedroom doorway with a plate of Thanksgiving dinner: turkey, stuffing, mashed potatoes, gravy, buttered green peas, yam casserole, cranberry sauce, roll.

"Oh, sweetie, thank you. I'm sorry I have to work."

"You always have to work."

"I know. I'm sorry."

"Are your hands bleeding?"

"It's paint."

"Why are you wearing your gun?"

"Opie—"

"Something happened yesterday," her daughter said. "You're different. Daddy's upset. Grammy Belle has hamster breath again. The twins are kicking under the table because they need attention."

The girl stared evenly at her mother.

"But don't worry. I'll handle it."

▲ ▼ ▲ ▼

She couldn't touch the food. In mid-May, according to an article in the online *Rapid City Journal*, seven decomposing bodies had been discovered inside a nonfunctional refrigerated truck parked behind Fuss Funeral Home. Facing criminal prosecution and civil suits, Darwin Fuss had disappeared from Rapid City in July.

She called Rapid City PD. They could report no trace of him since. The likely explanation was that Darwin Fuss had run from trouble and become Win Carpenter, hiding out while seeking salvation and renewed prosperity in the House of Shalah. Eventually, possibly under duress, he had purchased an undertaker's tool kit. A few days later, someone had sliced him up and dumped him in a lake. Had some bereaved relative finally tracked down Fuss in Bad Axe County? Or was the killer Hoof? Or someone else in the House of Shalah?

At the window, surprised by how dark it was, she looked at the time: 4:32 P.M. Out on Pederson Road, a moving fan of yellow light indicated an approaching vehicle.

Hoof was out there . . .

Her phone startled her again. This time it was Rhino, splitting the holiday shift with Denise.

"I thought you should know," he began. "We just got a call about a suicide jumper off the County P bridge. But hang on. I've got Stonebreaker on the radio. I might have new information."

Waiting, the sheriff stared at the approaching fuzz of light. A suicide jumper. The holidays could do that. The County P bridge spanned a narrow sandstone gorge over the Kickapoo River in the far southeastern corner of the Bad Axe. Not so high, not very deep water underneath. Probably just convenient.

She watched the pale yellow gauze resolve into weak headlights that groped the snow-covered road.

"Okay," Rhino came back, "so the witness is telling Stonebreaker that a white female, thirty to fifty years old, long dark hair, was standing on the bridge rail. He pulled over and she jumped."

The sheriff's heart skipped.

Missy?

What were the chances?

"Okay. Alert River Search and Rescue."

"Done. I've got Zion VFD heading for the downstream bridges. Deputy Luck is with Stonebreaker on the scene."

"Okay. You're on it."

"But it's dark out there. And we're expecting more snow."

"Right."

The headlights approached too slowly. The sheriff wore her SIG pistol high on her right hip, underneath her sweatshirt, but still she measured her distance to the loaded twelve-gauge Mauser shotgun she had laid into the gun rack of her dad's truck in the barn. Meanwhile, Rhino, sounding hesitant, continued.

"But, um, Stonebreaker says there is no vehicle anywhere nearby. Someone must have dropped her off. And she left her purse by the bridge rail."

No, it can't be Missy.

The sheriff's old friend had had a thousand reasons to end her life, but she never had done it. Anyway, Missy knew enough to choose a better bridge.

But as the sheriff squinted at the creeping headlights, one brighter than the other, she admitted that Missy's old-friend *drink ketchup* invitations had been a setup for murder. Had Missy felt remorse?

Someone must have dropped her off.

Could those headlights be Hoof driving Missy's old silver Honda?

"Sheriff? Did I lose you?"

"No, I'm here. Thanks, Rhino. Sad story. Keep me posted."

"But, um . . ."

Something he didn't want to tell her.

"Go ahead."

"Well, um, in that purse, Deputy Luck found some stuff including a driver's license, renewed last month, for Melissa Abigail Grooms . . ."

It was Missy!

". . . thirty-seven years old, address on Mill Coulee Road."

So Missy had lied about her living situation: this was right where the sheriff's friend had always lived, the little white house too close to Mill Coulee Road that she had shared with her parents.

"I'll send a deputy there as soon as I can," Rhino said.

"Ten-four."

"But, um . . . well, Sheriff, does Melissa Grooms sound like anyone you might know?"

As the vehicle neared the Kick mailbox, she saw it was a neighbor on a tractor.

"No," she said.

Because she knew where Hoof was. It was time to go.

"Sorry, Rhino. But no, that name doesn't ring any bells."

CHAPTER 18

Fernanda Carpenter hurried into the Village of Farmstead's little Babylon: freshly plowed streets in early darkness, chimneys belching wood smoke into low sky, warm light and TV colors leaping through glass, gales of laughter and cheering, the wafting aromas of rich foods, the chiming of silverware and glassware . . .

What existed after betrayal?

How would she live?

She plunged on, praying.

When my child walks through fire, may she not be burned, may the flame not consume her . . .

▲ ▼ ▲ ▼

At Robert W. Check Park, she stopped, out of breath, blowing clouds of steam beside a black pickup with odd items hanging from its mirror. The glass came down and her heart nearly stopped: the jowly, dark-toned face, the stiff gray hair under a worn red cap, the drifting eye, the implacable grimace . . .

Since that day nine years ago at the mall when she had laid her head upon the lap of her prophet-father, Fernanda's recurring nightmare had featured the surprise appearance of Nestor Cervantes, her natural father, who would materialize out of dream air smelling like alcohol and farm chemicals and wink and leer and whisper like a bogeyman, *Te encontre.*

I found you.

"Mrs. Carpenter?"

She could not speak but she nodded.

"Duke Hashimoto. Retired ATF."

She saw past him to an odd thing on his dash: a tilting stack of silver pebbles.

"Come on in and sit down."

▲ ▽ ▲ ▽

As the ex-wife of Roy Carpenter settled on his passenger seat, Duke Hashimoto followed her eyes and noted his silver-pebble pagoda at a precarious tilt. A slide by the truck on a corner had nearly toppled them, the magnets barely hanging on. Feeling this tilt set the right tone for now—in position for ruin—he left the pebbles as they were.

"Ah, well, so," he began, "the confused place this country has come to, so many people seeking a spiritual wormhole. Yes?"

His bad habit: getting all pent up, unleashing sudden depth in conversation where it wasn't wanted. Very soon he would be lamenting Waco, a disaster from before she was born.

Confused, Roy's ex whispered, "Yes."

"Seeking an escape route, I believe, from the heartbreak and existential danger of this sinking ship. This is why we have Koresh after Koresh after Koresh—"

She stiffened at the name. Another bad habit: he fumbled out a cigarette that would tighten the wires of his mind.

"I mean no offense to your prophet-father, Mrs. Carpenter.

Koresh is just my way of speaking about a certain kind of spiritual leader, the first Koresh being the Old Testament King Cyrus—*Koresh* in Hebrew—who released the Jews from Babylon. Our Waco Koresh was not the first, nor will your own Koresh be the last. But do forgive. You know King Cyrus, yes?"

"Yes."

He gushed smoke out his lowering window. Here came Waco, as always from the beginning.

"Of course," he continued, "bringing King Cyrus up to modern history, we have Cyrus Teed, Koreshanity, Hollow Earth, blah-blah, the Shepherd's Rod, and so on. Eventually, and now we come to Waco, a mental patient named George Roden challenges a rock-and-roll guitarist named Vernon Wayne Howell to see which one of them can raise the dead, but it ends up in a gunfight . . ."

He was smoking in a rental. He tossed out the cigarette and put up the window. Ogres, all of these men. Insane. Sex-obsessed. Power-mad. A danger to children. Stories so twisted they had to be told in more than sound bites. In his grief after Waco, he had studied. He had marveled at the capacity for belief, and the facility for abuse—and almost equally at the determined ignorance and homicidal hatred of "normal" people on the outside. And he had marveled further at how government—his, the one he had served— had turned out to be all about optics and self-preservation. His point was to illuminate for the Carpenter woman her House of Shalah and her own Koresh, her situation today, with the same light that had helped Roy see his way clearly, by the light of the blaze that had consumed all on that day in 1993.

Hashimoto went on. "Our guitarist, Vernon Howell, believes that he can impregnate George Roden's sixty-seven-year-old widowed mother, Lois, and this will prove that he has special seed and is therefore divine. Right?"

The Carpenter woman nodded vaguely. Hashimoto looked away

across the park and understood that he was seeing the end of daylight in the leaks of pale yellow where clouds had stretched thin.

"But eventually, after many attempts at his divine miracle, Howell gives up on Lois Roden, marries a fourteen-year-old girl, takes her to Israel, and comes back calling himself David Koresh and claiming he's the Lamb of God."

Now Fernanda Carpenter stared into her lap.

"I mean no offense, Mrs. Carpenter. I'm simply explaining why I'm here, and perhaps what's at stake. It's after Koresh returns from Israel that we have the gunplay. The Lamb of God is charged with attempted murder but escapes on a hung jury. Roden kills one of Koresh's followers with an ax, gets the loony bin for life. This allows Koresh to take over Roden's Mount Carmel property in Waco. He gathers a following and starts working on his wormhole, collecting guns and spouting scripture and catching the attention of the ATF and the FBI. Dubious claims are made about illegal weapons. Meanwhile, the rumor everyone likes best is that Koresh is inside his compound humping any female tall enough for the teacup ride. Children in danger. We go from there to Sherman tanks, helicopter gunships, snipers, CS gas . . ."

She had closed her eyes. Hashimoto now closed his too. All twenty-five children in the compound had burned to death that day, twenty-seven if you counted the two in their mother's wombs.

"Which brings us, Mrs. Carpenter, to the whole problem of children caught up in this colossal mess that we've made of our world. It brings us to these unfortunate photographs that you have brought to show me, to what you and I can do about them, and how careful we must be."

▲ ▽ ▲ ▽

During his story, Farmstead had turned dark. Fernanda felt a chill shoot up her spine.

"But I don't have the photographs."

He had been anxiously rubbing his forehead. This stopped him.

"You don't have them . . . Mrs. Carpenter, meaning what?"

"I saw them," she stammered. "Someone sent them to me in an email and I freaked and I deleted the email."

He looked away across the snowbound little park and drummed short, square thumbs upon his steering wheel.

"Who sent—"

"Then I emptied the trash."

He reached and fiddled with the stack of silver pebbles on his dashboard.

"Mrs. Carpenter . . ."

He let the pebbles go and sighed deeply, fumbling for another cigarette.

"Mrs. Carpenter, in Japanese Buddhist lore, the souls of lost children are sent to purgatory, which is a riverbed at the entrance to hell."

She shuddered, felt tears pushing, wishing he would stop.

"This riverbed is called Sai no Kawara. In an effort to stay out of hell, the children stack little towers of pebbles, like pagodas. But every time, just as they finish, ogres rush out, chase the children away, and scatter the towers."

He lit the cigarette and tossed it out his window.

"The only hopeful part of this story," he continued, "is that a bodhisattva appears, a guardian, called Jizo, and Jizo stands by the children while they stack their pebbles all over again. Jizo keeps them out of hell. And this, Mrs. Carpenter, is why I have come here."

As if some terrible memory had just then gripped him, he winced in pain, checked his lips with the back of his hand, then went back to massaging his forehead.

"I have seen children burn in hell."

They were silent a long time then. With a trembling hand he made his pebble stack neatly vertical. The sky may have rumbled.

At last, Fernanda whispered, "Where is Roy?"

"Ah. So. Yes. It all connects. Roy and I were working on a project. Not about the children. The usual budget fight in Congress was the trigger for the project. Appropriations. The bureau needed a successful raid to impress the senators, that kind of thing. Then Roy stopped calling back."

"What project?"

"Putting gun parts together."

"We already have guns."

"Correct. Legal guns. The Carpenters practice. You are responsible. No one seems to be trigger-happy. This is why an illegal firearms warrant seemed quick and safe. I provided Roy with parts and instructions on how to put the parts together into one illegal firearm. Just one gun, Mrs. Carpenter, certain features of it breaking federal law. Not even any ammunition. Then Roy informs to the government. ATF agents descend with a warrant and confiscate financial records. A cult is vanquished long before we reach Waco levels of danger. Congress approves our budget request. But it never happened."

He paused. Her head spun with pictures of Hosanna nude in the washtub. She had deleted the email. Who was it from? Why had she deleted it? What else was going on in the House?

"What financial records?"

"Mrs. Carpenter, I'm sorry. The version of House of Shalah that you Carpenters belong to serves as petty-cash flow and a humble public storefront. It appears delusional—forgive me—but honest. However, parallel to this, Jerome and Ruth Pearl run an online prosperity church that is a pyramid scam, stealing from your virtual brothers and sisters. They hide illegal profits and don't pay taxes. The Pearls have been the subject of a criminal investigation since you folks were in Nevada. The IRS wants their hard drives. The delicate problem is the religious rights angle. But as I've suggested, the idea of children in danger could override everything else—and this is how children die. People want so badly to save them."

Tears blurred her vision again—anger, grief, disappointment in herself. She had been furious with Roy for suggesting trouble in the House. She had cursed him and turned her back.

"Anyway"—Duke Hashimoto sighed—"in September Roy stopped returning my calls. Then the government suddenly had bigger fish to fry. They lost interest, as they do. I retired . . ."

"But the photos still exist," she said.

His eyes slid to meet hers.

"Meaning what, Mrs. Carpenter?"

"I trashed them with the email on my own laptop. But then I saw them again on his."

"On his?"

"On the prophet-father's laptop. Then I called you."

"You have access to his laptop? To his files?"

Did she? Could she?

What existed after betrayal?

"Yes."

"Are you sure?"

"Yes."

Duke Hashimoto exited the pickup with a grunt. He opened the club cab behind her, unzipped a suitcase, rummaged for a few moments. When he returned, he held a tube of ChapStick on his palm beneath the dome light.

Where would she go?

How would she care for her children?

"This is a high-capacity thumb drive, Mrs. Carpenter. You know how to copy files, yes? Good. Take the photos first, then take everything else you can get."

He shook free a third cigarette and tossed it unlit directly into the snow.

"Then send a text and let me know."

CHAPTER 19

Outside in new darkness after Thanksgiving dinner, Belle Kick rasps into her phone, "Just like I predicted, off she waltzes."

Her cold feet in stiffening snow, her head soaring like a lost balloon, the rest of Belle Kick stretched thin to snapping, she hears from her new gentleman, "What chapter are we on?"

"I just said."

"Off who waltzes?"

"Did I not just say?"

In her right hand, her cigarette. In her left hand, her phone. In her forehead, her pain. In her heart, her stupid hope that he is real. Behind the curtain, her sneaky grandkids spying.

"Who do you think waltzes off?"

As she waits to hear who he thinks waltzed off, if he's been paying attention to her at all, a dim light goes on inside the blacked-out space in her brain. Last night they had negotiated over the question of up to what age should children be hated—yelling giddily over the Coulee Cats—and she had fought for hating up to eighteen years old, because once someone hit eighteen you had to respect a person old enough to go to war—and he had argued for up to twelve years old, because he said twelve is when girls become worthy of interest—and eventually they agreed, made a pact—touching one another's thighs—God, she was so plowed—to despise all human life-forms under the age of fifteen—and this was fair, because they had both been such shitty children themselves—

"Mom, who are you talking to?"

Her son is on the porch in a wet apron, since you-know-who has waltzed off to God-knows-where, leaving dirty dishes.

"I'm talking to my friend."

"What friend?"

Belle scowls. What friend? The sensitive gentleman friend who agrees that her son and daughter-in-law don't own her just because they have stepped in and paid off her liens, loans, back taxes, and IOUs, to the tune of forty thousand. The wise gentleman friend who tells her, *Sure, they say it's because they love and support you. But the truth is they just want free childcare.*

"Anyway, honeybunch," he now purrs into her ear, "all the big Black Friday sales are tomorrow, right? So if you're not too busy writing your book, how about I take you to the mall?"

"Mom," Harley demands to know, "what friend?"

Belle Kick returns a wobbly snarl.

"What am I, twelve years old?"

CHAPTER 20

The way darkness crashed down in late November was transformative in a disorienting way, turning daylight into something murkier and more ominous than simple oncoming night. Snow cover made the landscape even more unfamiliar.

Sheriff Kick slowed her dad's repainted Cress Springs Farm truck and turned its headlights off. The lack of contrast helped her see. Still, her brain played catch-up, sorting objects and space from the dense black-and-silver luster. It didn't help that she had not been down Mill Coulee Road in fifteen years. And never before, probably, had she come this way in a state of sobriety.

The three silos shouldered close together tipped her off. Once she had passed the silos on her left, the trackless road would hug a weepy limestone bluff—yes, here it was, hung with prehistoric ferns and drilled with cliff swallow holes—then turn sharply south and cross a rattly bridge over a forlorn little trickle that she and Missy had called Snot Creek . . . and there it was, the Grooms place, straight ahead.

She stopped her dad's truck several hundred yards away to plot her approach. The house stood alone and hugged the road too close. The Grooms family had never had any garage or shed, never any neighbors' lights across a field, never even any flowers planted inside truck tires or any accidental trees, just their slumping little vinyl box the color of skim milk, surrounded by pointless junk and marooned in open space.

Its windows were dark, but no doubt Missy still ran with the crowd that hung blankets to black out what went on inside.

No steam rose from the chimney, but even when Missy had parents, the fuel-oil tank was often empty. There was never a water heater, a woodstove, or a fireplace.

A small sedan faced the sheriff and tilted toward the house, its outer wheels on the road. She would have to get closer to see if it was Missy's Honda.

A text buzzed in. She fished the phone from her sweatshirt pouch and saw it was from Deputy Lyndsey Luck.

Are you sure you don't know Melissa Grooms?

Why was she asking?

The sheriff stalled her reply while she layered her soiled brown Carhartt barn coat over the sweatshirt, strapped on a headlamp, stepped down from the truck, lifted out the Mauser, clicked the door shut, and began to move stealthily toward the house. Was she hearing thunder? A distant snowplow?

Closer in, she saw the sedan was a stripped-out Ford, empty rims, just a husk of a car.

So had Hoof dumped out Missy at the County P bridge? Was he still out there in Missy's car, gunshot wound and all?

Closer yet, she saw trampled snow beyond the front door.

Had she guessed both right and wrong?

She retreated to the truck before she called. She tried to keep her voice calm. "Pack everyone a suitcase," she told Harley. "Denise is home. I'll give her a heads-up. Go to her place."

"Heidi, it's Thanksgiving—"

"Right. I ruined it. Go."

Before she started back toward the house, she tapped a lie back to Deputy Luck. Her denial wouldn't last. But she would deal with that later.

I don't know her. I'm sure.

▲ ▼ ▲ ▼

She approached through a shudder of memories. That she had once lived here was a perfect measure of how badly her life had shanked after her dad and mom had been murdered. Three months short of her eighteenth birthday, she had been physically carried off Cress Springs Farm by Crawford County Human Services and placed into foster care. To this day she could not recall the childless couple's name. To this day she could not recall when or how she had been stripped of her Dairy Queen title. But she remembered perfectly the first time she had gotten high with Missy Grooms.

Fifty yards out from the house, she left the road and crossed the ditch into the snow-buried cornfield that surrounded the cut-out little property. From sneaking in and out when Missy's dad was still alive, she knew how to approach the house from the northeast corner, where there were no sight lines. Even if Hoof was inside watching through blanketed windows with his M16, he wouldn't see her coming.

Right where she expected was the opening she and Missy had cut through the rusty barbed-wire fence Bob Grooms had strung to protect his property . . . from corn?

It made no sense now. Two pilled-up girls sneaking out of this shithole . . . emerging like zombies from the cellar doors that opened crypt-like off the surface of the backyard . . . once "free," they added alcohol, weed, whatever, dangerous car rides, petty theft, maybe fist-

fights, frequently sex . . . then faithfully—every time, racing sunrise—
they had *sneaked back in*!

What explains why captives can't escape? She and Missy had shared
Missy's bed. They had lived on junk food stolen from the gas stations where
they bought cigarettes and alcohol. Outside the bedroom, Missy's mother
nagged and wheedled, her father raged and sulked—while inside they
nursed hangovers and ate candy bars on Missy's bed, feeling successful.

Focus, Heidi.

She found the wood-plank cellar doors beneath the snow. She
kicked the snow away and lifted. The doors opened like rotting book
covers, letting up a black smell, faintly warm.

Get this done before Rhino sends a deputy here.

She turned her headlamp on, gathered a breath, and descended
the crumbling concrete steps. In the cellar, nothing had changed
except to become a darker version of what it used to be.

Seeping fieldstone walls.

Leaking toilet stack.

Cobwebs so wet and heavy they hung to the floor.

She cleared the webs with the Mauser barrel, recalling how Missy
had envied her eventual escape from this place, how Missy had
watched from inside these walls as Mighty Heidi White had crashed
at rock bottom, reawakened, then progressed slowly and steadily
through sobriety, training, career, family . . .

Let's drink ketchup, her old friend had offered.

Delivering her to Hoof.

Setting her up to die.

Then jumping off a bridge.

Did Missy have a rock bottom?

As the sheriff climbed the cellar steps toward the kitchen, she
paused on each rotten tread to listen through the floor. If Hoof was
here, he wasn't moving. If he was here, where was Missy's car? Could
there be others involved?

She turned her headlamp off before she touched the kitchen doorknob, pinched it softly in her fingertips, and turned it.

As the door squeaked open—the same exact sound as years ago—a hard truth shivered through her: she had never escaped.

Not completely.

Of course not.

She could no more escape Missy, nor Hoof, nor this house, nor anything from that brutal time, than she could escape her own bones. Loss, despair, self-abuse, emotional wilderness—these, as much as the safety and love her parents had provided, had created the flawed wife, mother, and sheriff that she was.

Following the Mauser and hearing her own heart pound, she stepped up.

The kitchen stank of stale cigarettes. She moved through. The hallway was clear. The master bedroom was first on her left. Packed with garbage. Clear. First on her right was the bathroom. A foul smell. Clear. Next on the right was Missy's room. Clear. Ahead was the living room. No Hoof.

That was it, the whole house.

She let her breath catch up.

She turned her headlamp back on and found herself surrounded by too much mess for even Missy to have made alone. The coils of an ancient space heater cast a dull orange glow across the littered surface of a coffee table where the sheriff noted a bloody hand towel and a plastic brick of blue ice.

She touched the blue brick: still cold.

She unplugged the heater. She texted Harley.

Left home yet?

Yes.

Relieved, she began to search the house for any clue to where Hoof might have gone.

Missy's room seemed frozen in time, just as she remembered it except for a fish tank with one pretty orange-and-black fish finning at the surface, hoping for food. She tipped in a few grains and watched the fish glide toward them.

In the bathroom she found Hoof's black balaclava. She kicked a gray-blue shirt wadded on the floor. Had Hoof's shirt been blue? She didn't think so. She lifted this shirt and shook it open, finding long sleeves and no bullet hole or blood. McKormick's Farm Supply was on the highway north of Farmstead. The name patch said Roy.

Yellowish crystals and something rusty-colored had crusted in the bottom of the bathtub. An empty pill bottle had fallen into the clogged sink. The prescription, *OxyContin, 50 mg*, was for *Roscoe*.

No last name?

Retrieving her phone to photograph the shirt and the pill bottle, she saw two reply texts from Deputy Luck.

First: *OK. You say you don't know Melissa Grooms. When can we meet in private?*

Four minutes later: *Can you meet me somewhere soon?*

Deciding not to reply, the sheriff headed back to the kitchen. Aiming her headlamp across the counter by the sink, she saw an old leather case. She turned it open and stared with her heart speeding. Neatly banded onto fleece halves were scalpels, scissors, knives, files, tweezers, hemostats, syringes . . . here, in Missy's house, where Hoof had been . . . this was the undertaker's tool kit purchased by Darwin Fuss . . . the man who had run away, joined the House of Shalah, and become Brother Win Carpenter . . . who had gone to Crazy Frank's with Hoof—it *was* Hoof—to bounce a check for this kit . . . and then been murdered.

What was the kit for? What was it doing here? Did this mean that Hoof had killed Darwin Fuss? Was Missy also involved? If, as the sheriff suddenly felt convinced, Deputy Mikayla Stonebreaker had obstructed the Darwin Fuss investigation by planting evidence of a drug deal—why? What was the deputy's connection? Did Stonebreaker know Missy? Did she have a connection with Hoof? Were all three of them entangled with the House of Shalah?

The sheriff took a long, shaky breath.

She took a photo.

Then she moved on. Also on the table was the stub of a paycheck to *Melissa A. Grooms* from *Old Friends Farm*. Over coffee, Missy had been vague about everything, mentioning "kind of a part-time job" where she "subbed for someone sometimes." Old Friends Farm was a convalescent home for old horses. It was in Bad Axe County, not far away. The pay stub was for $48.82.

As the sheriff photographed Missy's pay stub, a sequence came to her: *Roscoe* was an old horse in pain, Missy had stolen Roscoe's Oxy, and Hoof had eaten it.

Her phone buzzed in her hand.

Lyndsey Luck again: *It's really kind of urgent.*

But she put the phone away.

Her best guess: Hoof had gone to Old Friends for more.

CHAPTER 21

Waiting on Fernanda Carpenter—could she really get the prophet's files?—Duke Hashimoto killed time in the tavern attached to the Ease Inn Motel. Should he be surprised the tavern was open on Thanksgiving night? He was in Wisconsin, after all.

In his seed cap and Packers jersey, alone with a can of Keystone Light for additional camouflage, Hashimoto had a view out the window. To what he had seen in September, the snowfall had added a lurid touch. Under plaza lighting the hardening plow piles glowed yellow. Bulk quantities of ice melt had eaten through slush down to the pavement, leaving blue-rimmed black holes. Also new since September, a red steel kiosk outside the mini-mart door instructed someone to DEPOSIT TISSUE SAMPLE HERE!—a mystery for which Hashimoto lacked theories. He signaled for another glass of horse piss.

She brought a can and snapped it open for him, Jenny, nice kid he had met in September, hustling to take care of a behind-doors party in the back room.

Hashimoto sipped and looked out the window again. In the tavern window itself, out-facing but readable backward, the KILL THE CULT sign had a new partner: THIS LAND IS OUR LAND.

"Card game back there?" he asked Jenny.

A sheet of paper taped on the door to the BANQUET ROOM read PRIVATE.

"Yeah," she said, her expression unsettled. "Sure."

"Can anybody get in?"

"I don't think so."

"Can you ask?"

"Ummm . . ."

Her oven toaster pinged. With a huge knife she scored a greasy pizza into tiny squares and bustled it through PRIVATE. Hashimoto caught a glimpse: at least a dozen people in there.

The outside door gasped, letting cold air in. He turned as a young couple blustered in— stocky, apple-cheeked mom, bearded dad with ham-hock hands, their infant in a car seat. Hashimoto's trained eye went straight to the his-and-hers thigh holsters that he guessed held Glock 19s. The family looked him over mistrustfully, especially the baby, on their way into PRIVATE. Jenny then came back out, followed by an angry-looking man so large that his arms swung as he waddled.

He came right to Hashimoto.

"Do you have a problem?"

"Not that I know of."

"What do you want?"

"Not much. A couple beers. A card game if there is one."

"There isn't one."

"Well, then, Happy Thanksgiving. And thanks for coming out to let me know."

This guy bore down like he needed to break something.

"Where you from?"

"Alabama."

"*From* from."

"California."

With THIS LAND IS OUR LAND over his shoulder, Hashimoto extended his hand.

"Duke Hashimoto. U.S. Army veteran. Forty years in public service. Named after Duke Snider, John Wayne, and Duke Ellington."

He stopped on the *how-about-you?* beat, still offering to shake. His sister, a retired nurse, was named after Betty Boop, Betty Crocker, Betty Grable, and possibly other Bettys. His recently late father, Ken, who had watched *his* father lose a third-generation strawberry farm and die in grief at Manzanar, had been a fanatical assimilator. Learn the songs. Observe the holidays. Never criticize the president. Always put your hand over your heart. And do not bow. *Never* bow. Always shake—and shake *hard*.

But no deal. The man turned and lumbered ferociously back into PRIVATE.

"Sorry about that," Jenny said when she could get back to him.

"He doesn't have to like me."

"I guess. But don't feel too special," she said. "Dennis doesn't like anybody. Even Dennis, I'd say."

Hashimoto nodded. That kind of thing led to all sorts of problems.

"Can I ask Dennis who?"

"Stonebreaker."

"And who is Dennis Stonebreaker, to charge out here demanding answers from me?"

She shrugged. "I don't know. He used to be a prison guard until I guess he jammed an inmate's head into a toilet and broke his neck. At least that's one story. Then I think he drove a milk truck. I heard these days he's a DJ, which I think means the last step toward unemployable. Even *I'm* not a DJ. I guess I should say *not yet*."

She made a face and blew hair off her forehead.

"I wasn't supposed to tell anybody, but that group back there is against the cult. I guess Dennis thought you were snooping into that."

She twisted a rag, then tossed the rag as if that were not the actual body language she wanted. She sighed and looked toward PRIVATE.

Hashimoto asked, "'Against the cult' as in KILL THE CULT, the sign?"

"I think that's stupid," she said. "Saying it like that. But yeah." She had the rag again, wiping vigorously past Hashimoto's beer can. "No one deserves to be killed for believing something. But, I mean, what if they really do try to take over?"

"Take over what?"

"The schools, the county government, everything."

"Everything?"

Her cheeks had reddened. She moved on. "They shoot horses."

Hashimoto took a sip.

"Hmm. Shoot horses. Do they?"

"That's what people say."

"Why would they shoot horses?"

"I guess they're supposed to, or whatever. Like a ritual. I guess they did it in Colorado, or wherever."

She blundered back to safer ground.

"Anyway, they bought the property next door to the mini-storage place. They're putting in a sewer. People say that means they're staying. They get new members all the time. One of them got murdered, but they won't say anything. The other night the library showed this documentary about these psychos in Oregon that actually did try to take over. They poisoned a bunch of salad bars . . ."

Hashimoto nodded. The Rajneeshees. Antelope, Oregon. If the House of Shalah was drawing Rajneeshee comparisons, affairs had escalated since September.

"They have guns," Jenny added. "They have a shooting range. They practice shooting guns."

Hashimoto considered making a point or two. Everyone around here had guns. Practicing was a good idea. As an ex-ATF guy, he could speak at length on the topic of the American citizenry and its messy passion for firearms. But then for a second time the outside door opened, this time letting in a hulking female sheriff's deputy. She stomped snow off her boots.

"Diet Coke," she barked at Jenny.

She lumbered in and stopped at Hashimoto. He looked up from his stool at a plain, pale, middle-aged woman who was six-feet-something and went two hundred, maybe two-twenty, with deep-set blue eyes and mighty shoulders and wide-hanging arms.

She said, "Something I can help you with?"

"No, ma'am. Just a lodger at the motel."

"Care to state your business?"

Hashimoto pleasantly but evenly met the stare of CHIEF DEPUTY M. STONEBREAKER, according to her tag. With that name, she was tight with big-bad Dennis somehow. Hashimoto's initial orders to keep local law enforcement out of the loop still seemed like the right choice.

"Have I done something wrong? Otherwise, no, ma'am, other than I'm having a cold one, I don't care to state my business."

Now she glowered. Being who he was and having worked alongside a thousand cops in his career, Hashimoto recognized the flare of rage that was actually fear when unearned authority was resisted by a citizen whose life less-than-mattered. Then he caught another vibe. It looked like M. Stonebreaker was supposed to keep going into PRIVATE and join Dennis's Kill the Cult folks. But now, with Hashimoto as an unidentified witness, she was nervous.

"But you can have my card," he said.

It was an old one, but only by a month. The seal of the United States Department of the Treasury/Alcohol, Tobacco, and Firearms— blue-green-red and lots of gold—glowed in the dim tavern lighting.

M. Stonebreaker took a long squinting look, fit the card into her breast pocket, and turned tail, leaving in a whoosh of cold air. The dome light in her cruiser came on. She was on the phone.

"That's Dennis's wife," confirmed Jenny. "That's Mikayla."

Hashimoto sipped his Keystone.

"She roughed up the cult leader coming out of Walmart back in summer. I think that was wrong, but it made her real popular around here. She got suspended, but she sued the county and the Police and Fire Commission ended up making her chief deputy."

Again, Hashimoto suppressed a comment: botched leadership had set the stage for every disaster he had been part of.

Jenny went on. "Dennis has this crazy temper. People say he just about killed Ms. Stonebreaker—see, she was my P.E. teacher then—before she became a deputy packing a gun everywhere. Dennis ran her over with his truck in a parking lot of a different bar with people watching, but she didn't press charges, so nothing happened."

"Does anybody know what that means, 'Kill the Cult'?"

Jenny shrugged uncomfortably. "I heard they got a legal order to be out of the mini-storage by Monday. Meanwhile, they're digging a sewer next door, so people say that means they're not leaving. So I guess we'll find out what 'Kill the Cult' means."

The children stack their pebbles, Hashimoto thought. The ogres rush out. Over and over.

Headlights. Outside, Chief Deputy Stonebreaker backed her cruiser away from the window, her phone pressed to her ear.

Jenny took another round into PRIVATE.

Hashimoto laid a twenty on the bar.

CHAPTER 22

Sheriff Kick was right: Missy's battered silver Honda was parked outside the Old Friends Farm office. The front door was open. Shadows lunged inside. Instantly she knew Hoof was here.

She idled past without headlights and stopped her dad's truck behind a horse trailer. Not long ago, she and Deputy Luck had visited Old Friends on behalf of Operation Safe Supply, a public outreach campaign about the hazards of unsecured veterinary opiate stocks. All for naught here, apparently. Anybody who gave Missy Grooms a job and a key just wasn't getting the PSA.

The sheriff bumped her window down to listen as she took a moment to recall what she knew about the layout. The office was an old house, a simple roadside box like Missy's place. But this modest front served as the gateway to a substantial facility. The back corners of the house connected to a tall fence that squared up into a quarter-acre observation and holding area, gated to let in big trailers. Beyond, subsuming the holding area, was a larger chain-link enclosure around two banks of inward-facing stables with an open alley down the center, anchored at the far end by a large pole barn. Horses nickered and snorted in their stalls, aware of someone at the office. Concentric around the office and stables, Old Friends ran a mile of three-rail white vinyl fence, containing pasture and woodland with riding trails.

Leading with her Mauser, the sheriff sneaked behind the horse trailer and crept through shrubbery along the near side of the building. She ducked beneath one window, then another, only inches separating her from Hoof as he slammed around inside. She eased the framed-fence gate open, wincing as this cast a slow shadow across the back of the office.

She waited.

The sky muttered and seemed to inhale. More snow coming.

Then she crept after the gate shadow, stopping where a sliding glass patio door faced the holding area and gave a clear view inside.

Hoof had turned on a desk lamp. Using something rigid in his right hand, he pried off a locked cabinet door, flung it away, and stood there with his spine slumped and his head jutting forward, panting. He was now shirtless. The sheriff saw how bad her aim had been. The bullet from the Deerslayer had entered behind his left shoulder joint and exited through his armpit. That arm hung dark and bloated, poorly supported by a makeshift sling, probably his shirt. Her round might have blown through his scapula, but obviously she had missed his brachial artery—missed murdering him by centimeters.

She continued to watch. Without the use of his left arm, it seemed she had a decent chance to take him without shots fired. The M16 was strapped across his back. Extra magazines rode both hips in bulky, belted pouches. Once she squared him up with the Mauser, he would have to haul the big gun around while clearing the magazines and without snagging his wounded arm. If he got that far and still wasn't obeying her commands, the Mauser at close range would blow a hole wide through him. All she had to do, she decided, was get out of sight and wait for him to exit the office out the front.

But she lingered at the glass door, somehow fascinated as this monster from her old life pawed through ruptured cabinets until he came out with something. When he held his find under the desk lamp, she recognized the half-gallon plastic jar with the purple silhouette of the horse. He had found phenylbutazone, pain-killing tablets as big as half-dollars.

Did she stop him from overdosing and killing himself?

Or was that perfect?

The question froze her—and she could not stop herself from watching. Desperately he chewed several tablets, white foam forming at the corners of his mouth. Then he went back to busting cabinet doors and ransacking. He swept out a whole shelf of bandages and antiseptics. A power drill clattered to the floor—for drilling pill holes in carrots. Then he made another find. From the blue-swoop graphic on the glass bottle the sheriff recognized Excede, a concentrated antibiotic in sterile suspension, for injection.

As a sudden gust of snow pushed Sheriff Kick in the back, Hoof cracked the cap and drank it.

Then a crash of brilliant lightning lifted her from her skin and shook the Mauser from her grip, stunning Hoof into vivid zombie colors as it etched her staggering shadow across the cabinets he was looking into.

Before she could collect the Mauser, he had let the bottle smash to the floor and yanked the M16 around. He had the pistol grip, the bump stock jamming his ribs. She dove as glass exploded.

He kept shooting as if he couldn't see well and thought she was still there—shooting her *harder*—until she guessed his magazine was empty.

Under the trailing boom of thunder, she crawled back and caught her shotgun by the barrel, pulled it to her, and darted away tight against the building. She knew now that he would not submit. He didn't care if she put a twelve-gauge window through his gut, as long as she suffered in the process. She heard him slur this very point as he kicked through the veterinary supplies he had scattered. The empty M16 magazine clattered to the floor. Should she rush him now? Or maybe she should ambush him. Maybe she should wait where she was and put him down the moment his body mass broke the plane of the shattered door—self-defense—never speak of what happened at the river. She heard the new magazine engage. Into sheets of sudden snow, she dashed for the stables, the M16's wild one-handed scatter chasing but not catching her.

She ducked a gate and peeled left out of Hoof's line of fire into the first stall, finding herself with a distressed old mare, piebald and grayed, blowing and kicking at the sudden intruder.

"Easy, girl," she murmured. "Easy. I'm a friend."

The mare, not eased, was giving her away. She ducked under to the next stall, where a grizzled stallion struggled to his feet.

"Mighty Heidi!" Hoof bellowed sloppily, crossing the holding area toward the stables. Now the stallion began to snort, giving her away. Her mind scrambling for an out, she ducked under to the next stall. A smaller mare wheeled and tried to bite her.

"High-and-Mighty Heidi!"

He was entering the open alley between the stables now, wheezing and spitting, blundering closer. The sheriff clubbed the mare's muzzle with a soft fist. "Easy," she whispered. "I'm not here to hurt you."

But the mare tried to nip again and she had to duck out.

"You shot me, bitch. Not enough you took twelve years of my life. I was gonna help you," he lied to no one, to everyone, to himself, exactly what was going to happen for a real audience when she brought him in, "but no, you put a bullet in my back."

Don't ever change, fucker.

Now she was in the stall of a big gray jenny, the shaggy muscle-bound animal bugling her outrage. The sheriff hustled through, escaping a hoof strike that echoed. In the next stall she squatted behind a massive Clydesdale in too much pain to rise in the commotion. She scratched a patch of mange on his shoulder and murmured comforts. Then she raised the Mauser and waited. Maybe if she let Hoof pass and got behind him . . .

But he stopped. She heard him gasping.

"Come on out . . . High-and-Mighty . . . Heidi."

She stayed down and stroked the big horse's neck. He seemed blind. His name was on his feed bag. *Roscoe.*

"Shhh. Easy, big guy. I know it hurts. You're going to be okay."

Then an M16 burst.

The first mare shrieked in pain, pounded her stall, thumped to the ground, and went quiet.

The sheriff froze, disbelieving.

A peal of laughter.

Then Hoof shot the stallion.

Then the second mare.

Then the jenny.

Then he bellowed, "I'll kill every one of these pieces of shit, Mighty Heidi, if that's what it takes."

She moved the SIG from her hip holster to underneath the back waistband of her jeans. She hurled the Mauser out where he could see it. Just then more lightning tore open the sky.

"I sure know you," he yelled beneath the thunder. "Don't I?"

Snow plunged like wreckage from a bad crash above as Sheriff Kick stepped into the open with her hands high and empty.

CHAPTER 23

Fernanda was stunned that her chance had come so quickly.

Maybe God was hearing her prayers?

Stunned, and glad, and also sick to her stomach as she hustled Hosanna into the peasant dress that the girls wore for choir.

"Comb your hair out, sweetie. Wash your feet. Brush your teeth."

Her silent, obedient child.

Unaware the prophet-father had summoned her as the nubile girl he had seen washing herself in the photos on his laptop. To sing for him, Mother Ruth had said.

Stunned and sick as she was, Fernanda was prepared with a plan. From the empty barrel of a ballpoint pen, she tapped out the Halcion tablets that she had skimmed over the years from the prophet-father's bedside, somehow guided to do this, never able to explain her purpose.

Understanding it now, she crushed six tablets against the bottom of an enamel cup with the back of a spoon. She dumped the powder into a paper cup. On the floor by the door, there to stay cold, was a plastic quart container of the apple cider Hosanna had pressed as a home economics lesson. Fernanda poured cider into the paper cup, swirled it, then poured the contents back into the cider jug. She shook the container, watched the unfiltered apple dust swirl up from the bottom and mix with the drug.

She play-penned the babies—they sensed the mood and were starting to fuss—and dropped in two handfuls of Cheerios. Stepping outside Unit 14, she saw Mother Ruth lit by yard light, shuddering under heavy snow behind brothers Skip and Spooner toward the new chapel. She reached back for her umbrella.

"Let's go, Hosanna. Get under this. Hurry."

▲ ▼ ▲ ▼

Inside his bedroom, the prophet-father's displeasure at seeing Hosanna in the company of her mother showed plainly on his pouched and waxen face.

"I'm just dropping her off," Fernanda tempered him, her skin crawling. If form held, he was nude beneath his white terry-cloth bathrobe. His thin blond-silver hair had been freshly fishtail-braided and there was cologne in the air. To deliver the effect that he was a busy man, not at all thinking about molesting a ten-year-old girl, not at all grooming a new teenage wife, he had arrayed about him on the bed several laptops that flickered with stock tickers, newscasts, spreadsheets—merely interrupted while creating prosperity.

He smiled and spread his arms.

"Ah, well, wonderful. Lucky me. As the Japanese say, Ryō te ni hana. A flower in each hand. Which is prettier?"

He zeroed in on Hosanna, who was clutching the cider jug and a paper cup.

"Child," he said, "have I told you that I love you?"

"As I love you," Hosanna whispered back.

He laughed. He quoted scripture.

"'Her mouth she hath opened in wisdom, and the law of kindness is upon her tongue . . .' What do you have?"

Fernanda nudged her daughter.

Hosanna whispered, "I made apple cider."

"Yes, I see."

"Will you try it? Then my mommy will take it when she goes."

Hosanna came close with the cup that she had poured for him. The girl's prophet-father eagerly took the cup in one hand, and with the other, as if idly, he fingered the hem of her dress.

▲ ▼ ▲ ▼

They turned him on his side, for his apnea.

Hosanna stepped away with the cup and cider container to listen at the door while Fernanda with the ChapStick thumb drive worked fast.

Just as she suspected, a picture of Hosanna nude in the washtub was an open tab, just one layer beneath a spreadsheet.

From there she backtracked to the folder with all the pictures of Hosanna and copied it.

She glanced up at her daughter.

Hosanna shrugged at the silence beyond the door, meaning Mother Ruth had not returned.

Fernanda kept right-clicking folders—*take everything you can get, Mrs. Carpenter*—copying everything she could chug onto the drive.

Within minutes Hosanna waved urgently.

Eject mobile device? Y/N.

Just in time, Fernanda straightened up from the bed with the drive concealed in her fist.

"I don't think he's feeling well," she said as the door opened. The prophet-father's first-wife was wet and clearly anxious. She too had declined quickly these last few months, losing weight, her face sagging, her once-placid smile strained, her treatment of the prophet-father often seeming cold and abrupt.

"He was just tasting Hosanna's cider and he drifted off."

Mother Ruth scowled.

"What is that in your hand?"

Fernanda faked shame.

"I was worrying. You know how sensitive he is. I thought Hosanna's lips might be dry."

She opened her fingers: just ChapStick.

"We'll try another time."

Hustling away with the umbrella held over them, she gripped Hosanna's hand. "No one touches you but you. Is that clear?"

CHAPTER 24

"Don't I? Don't I know you?"

Hoof's braying celebration echoed between the stalls.

"Ha! I know you too good!"

Light from a pole sprayed through snow plummeting about his tilted shape. The M16 was angled her way. She kept her hands high.

"Save the horsies! I know you too good!"

Now he tried a manly strut through the deluge. At least a hundred times, as endangered Heidi White, she had watched this performance, the great Roman Vanderhoof shit-faced out of his mind, trying to walk straight on his broken and repaired legs, convinced he was pulling it off.

Don't ever change, asshole, she growled silently as he closed the distance in erratic strides, baby-stepping between them and just barely avoiding a face-planting plunge. *Don't ever see yourself for who you are.*

"I knew it. The poor horsies. Silly bitch."

As he closed, he kept the M16 aimed vaguely at her chest. With a bump stock, at this range, if he lurched and squeezed his finger, even with her Kevlar on, the M16 could cut her in half. She kept her hands raised, her palms open to the light.

"Don't ever grow up, Dairy Queen."

He stopped over the Mauser in the snow but had no free hand to pick it up. A hundred times she and Missy had held their tongues and watched their man-friend and drug supplier try to think straight, two lost girls dreading the next "great idea" that would spiral them into another long and terrifying night.

"Unload that," he told her, pointing his chin at the Mauser. He backed away from it, raising the M16 barrel to her eye level. "Kneel down and take the shells out."

She did. Heavy flakes melted on her hands.

"Throw them on the roof."

She pitched them underhand and the shells disappeared onto the roof of the stable, over the bleeding body of the piebald mare.

"Stand."

She did, raising her hands again. Would he let her get to the SIG in the waistband of her jeans?

She had to be patient. A hundred times she and Missy had watched him drink from his spit cup, walk into a glass door, fail to see a WRONG WAY interstate sign. This meant there were still a hundred ways she might turn the tables.

"You know," he now slurred conversationally, "what I loved about that time we shared at the river?"

The stallion sputtered and sighed. She smelled blood and fresh manure. Snow slashed between them. She lifted her sweatshirt on the right side to show the empty holster.

"I think I do."

"Yeah. Yeah, I think you do too. I loved how you walked right into the nice slow death that you deserve."

"Sure."

"Karma is a beautiful bitch. I was moved. You had finally killed yourself, which is perfect."

He began to sidestep to go behind her, his every move packed with the latent collision of the OxyContin already in his system with plow-horse dosages of phenylbutazone and equine antibiotic. One slip and she was dead. A different slip and she had him.

"I wasn't going to watch."

You twisted prison rat, don't ever stop believing in your greatness.

He arrived behind her.

"I was being a gentleman. Then you spoiled it."

In a moment more he had arrived back in front of her, staggering a bit past center.

"Unzip."

He had seen the bulge of the SIG in her waistband. She pulled her zipper and her coat halves shed wet lumps, opening on the hoodie's Blackhawks Booster emblem. Squinting at her chest, he staggered closer in wide steps, one inch each. The M16's flash suppressor came almost within reach.

Did she grab for it?

Dive and tackle?

He sensed this and reeled back, still staring at her firm high bust-line.

"That ain't the tidy little rack that I remember," he concluded finally. "You're wearing a fucking vest."

"I'm the sheriff, Hoof."

"Yeah? Let's see how much I care. Take it off. Take that coat off and throw it over there on the ground. Take the vest off."

She wrenched off her coat and threw it.

"Don't be fooled by how much you hate me," she said as she ripped Velcro, shrank her arms through the vest, and pulled it out beneath her sweatshirt. "I'm not just some fucked-up stray girl any-more. I'm a cop now. That's different."

She dropped the vest on the snow.

"Turn around."

She did.

"Pull that gun out of your pants. Drop it. Step sideways. Keep going. Back up. Turn around and face me."

She dropped the SIG and moved as he said.

"You'll always be just some fucked-up stray girl."

"You really want to kill a cop?"

His eyes fluttered. He collapsed to one knee.

Was he bracing to shoot her?

She had to distract him.

"Back to prison forever? I'm worth that? A silly bitch?"

Or was he about to pass out?

"You did your time. You leave me here dead, it starts all over again. And this time it never ends."

No, he was trying to pick up the Sig. He did, with a claw-like stab. He wrenched the M16 around his back.

"Who says I'm leaving you here?" he grunted, hauling himself up and pointing her pistol.

"Turn around. Hands high. Walk slowly."

CHAPTER 25

Feathery new snow swirled about Duke Hashimoto's rented pickup as he eased along U-Stash-It Road. Inside the fence, a Carpenter stood sentry by a barrel fire. The prophet-father's motor coach glowed.

Hashimoto looked toward the golf course. As usual, tiny green-red lights winked deceptively like airplanes high in the sky. Those were the cameras aimed from tall poles on the fairways. At the dead end, as usual, a pickup sat in the dark. Someone always watched the House of Shalah.

Hashimoto killed his lights and cycled through the cul-de-sac. The pickup's windows were steamed and inside the man seemed asleep.

After he had parked with the Ranger aimed back toward the highway and run his window down, Hashimoto heard children singing a hymn. He wrestled himself out and stood still for a moment, listened to the chorus of little voices. The bureau had a deep file on Jerome Pearl, the wandering prosperity preacher who called himself Euodoo Koresh. Having studied the material, Hashimoto found the notion of

Pearl putting down roots—digging a sewer? developing property?—
to be widely out of character. The idea that Pearl wanted to take over
a community, to elect and govern, struck Hashimoto as paranoid and
uninformed local hot air. Pearl's style was to wear out his welcome,
blow town, and caravan a couple states over. Ours was a big country.

Hashimoto popped his club cab. In his heavy-gear suitcase he
had packed a simple thermal camera. Activated and aimed past the
fence, it showed him a yellow-red-orange mass of heat inside Storage
Unit 5. This was the children singing inside the thirty-by-eighty-foot
unit that the Carpenters, per Roy in September, called their "old
chapel."

He panned his camera. The living units were only vaguely warmer
than the outside air. Some contained adult bodies. The mobile coach
was a solid brick of orange with two blobs of igneous red. A few hot
sparks moved with purpose near the back fence, where Roy had said
the Carpenters were building their new chapel.

Hashimoto lowered the camera. The new chapel looked like a
steel pole barn. Beside it was what he guessed was a mountainous
heap of snow-covered dirt. That should have been a red flag for him
back in September, he decided. Pearl had never built anything. Something new was taking place.

Thunder?

Wasn't it too cold for thunder?

A new hymn started: "How Great Thou Art."

Hashimoto hung the heat camera around his neck. He went into
his gear supply again and put night-vision binocs to his face. Out of
the new chapel, sure enough, came a man carrying two five-gallon
buckets and dumping what appeared to be dirt and rocks on the pile.

Dirt from where?

Inside a building?

But at the moment, he was interested in Pearl's project on the
property he had bought outside the U-Stash-It fence. He retrieved his

9mm Glock and his flashlight. Muted by his sleeve and aimed down at the snow, the flashlight threw a yellow dot inside a halo.

His first stop was the open pit halfway across the snowfield, two eight-foot lengths of sewer pipe yet to be laid, a backhoe, an unconnected junction box down in the pit. On inspection, he found the pipe lengths to be elliptical concrete of a diameter nearly equal to his arm span, wide enough to crawl through. His hunch: these pipes were twice as big as they needed to be for a residential storm sewer. As he digested this, Hashimoto uprooted a survey stick and measured depth to the top of the pipe already buried, concluding less than four feet. Another hunch: Was this deep enough for a northern Zone 5 climate? He thought not.

Now he launched himself farther afield, needing a geometrical perspective on the mystery. He prodded and progressed a hundred yards until he reached a stand of half-grown evergreens that had been planted in a grid. On a swath cut through these for an extension of Tee Road, he detected beneath the snow a freshly poured curb, new asphalt, and a manhole.

He squared himself. He was looking back in a straight line that traveled from the manhole to the unfinished junction, and from there across open space and under the fence to the rear bumper of the prophet-father's mobile coach. From the bumper of the mobile coach, continuing the same straight sight line led his eyes to three portable toilets. Straight beyond those was the new chapel under construction, where men were hauling out buckets of dirt.

Dot-to-dot-to-dot, straight as an arrow.

Fourth observation: likely not a sewer. For a group under constant surveillance, more likely this was an access tunnel, a way to come and go without detection.

Why?

Smuggling?

Hashimoto had become well acquainted with smugglers' tunnels on the Mexico border during the gunwalking debacles. Some of those tunnels were architectural wonders, monuments to criminal talent and ambition. One, lighted and paved, traveled for a quarter mile before it came up inside a mini-storage facility. Another had busted into and incorporated a municipal storm sewer line. Yet another had been disguised, like this one, as a development project.

But even a fake sewer had to point somewhere real.

Hashimoto poked his way across the cleared ground to the tree line, stumbling among snow-hidden rocks and brush. Here, over a ravine and obviously coming south from the golf course, was a grated storm sewer outlet that dribbled muddy runoff into the ravine. This was real. He looked back. The real and the fake sewers had to intersect. Did the House of Shalah tunnel begin at the manhole out on Tee Road, travel beneath the snowfield and intersect the real sewer, then continue beneath the U-Stash-It fence and come up somewhere inside the House of Shalah?

Except smuggling was no more Pearl's style than developing property and taking over school boards. Aside from the operational cash he collected from his Carpenters, Pearl stole money electronically and hid it in digital accounts. So why a tunnel? Had he caught Roy setting him up for the feds? Was Fernanda not the only Carpenter pushing back? Did the scammer feel his time was up? But why not just leave out the gate? Well, for one thing, the Kill-the-Cult people watched him. But why not fake a trip to Walmart and never come back? Did Pearl have some special problem—or some special plan— that required the illusion he was still inside the fence? Still inside his mobile coach?

Probing along the back fence, Hashimoto came close enough to hear the children singing again, and close enough that his thermal camera picked up a linear stream of thin yellow heat heading underground from the new chapel, out beneath the portable toilets, past the mobile coach, under the fence, and toward the open trench and beyond to the manhole. A few red spots moved like ants along the yellow stream: men with buckets.

The door of the mobile coach opened. Hashimoto raised his night-vision binocs. The woman they called Mother Ruth held the door. Fernanda Carpenter and a shoulder-high girl with her mother's hair descended the steps and hurried away.

The children's voices swelled to a climax—*how great thou art!*— then diffused into the rumbling sky.

Hashimoto shuddered, guessing that child porn would soon be the least of Fernanda Carpenter's worries.

This was an escape tunnel. Pearl had finally decided he was under too much scrutiny.

Any day now, Fernanda's prophet-father was going to pull the plug and boogie.

CHAPTER 26

Hoof rode behind her in the Ram's club cab with the M16 across his knees and the SIG touching her skull. As the sheriff followed his commands, steering northwest on unplowed back roads, it occurred to her that he would be proud of Missy's bridge-jump suicide.

"Turn left," he rasped.

Thunder grumbled over the truck engine. The deluge shifted texture, pelting down in wet white globs. The turn onto Sumac Ridge Road elevated them out of the wide Ocooch bog, and now the truck toiled up untracked switchbacks, the gravel feeling greasy under the snow. Missy wouldn't be Hoof's first suicide, not in his mind. As the sheriff skimmed his face in the mirror, she began a grim tally of the girls she knew about. Shelby Mattix. Kassidy Wengert. Tatum Bonjour. The self-inflicted death of Missy Grooms would be at least Hoof's fourth example of how intensely he was loved and feared. Suicide, she recalled, had struck him as the ultimate compliment.

"Right on County H."

As she made the turn and they tilted onto high ground, her phone in the drink cup chimed and lit up with notification of another text. Seeing it was from Deputy Luck and reaching, she felt the SIG against the bone behind her ear.

"Don't touch it."

A snowplow had just cleared County H. In its path the sheriff drove smoothly east toward Farmstead. Hoof had boasted of the others, older girls ahead of her, mythic names and stories she had heard. Their love for Hoof had been so great that it had killed them—it was overdoses, actually—and the pitch to the next pain-dumb girl—say, a devastated ex–Dairy Queen—was how much love she would feel, and how long she could stand it.

She glanced in the mirror again. As if he believed he was immortal, he was chewing more horse pills. A new urgency, spun from threads of past and current dread, suddenly knit together. The House of Shalah . . . the Carpenters . . . would they die for their beloved father figure? Like so many disciples before them, did the Carpenters have a suicide pact? Were the current pressures driving them in that direction?

"Lights off. Turn in."

At the private road into the property of Ernhardt Pig Feeder, Hoof tried to growl. But it was more of a gasp.

She turned in. Five hundred yards ahead, the Ernhardt office and barns pushed up a dome of incandescence against the shedding sky. On the sheriff's left, snow fell upon an expanse of shredded soybean stems about to disappear. Opposite the soybean field rose the tall earthen berm that walled-in Ernhardt's three-acre lagoon containing several million gallons of swine manure.

"Take a right."

The heavy Ram fishtailed onto an access lane marked by two muddy tire ruts filling with fresh snow. The berm loomed like a moonscape. After a hundred yards, the lane cornered left and threaded a narrow space between the lagoon and a snow-clogged wasteland forest that reached out with claws and raked the crawling truck.

"Stop right here," Hoof panted at the back of her head as they reached a dead end.

"Kill it."

She shut down the truck.

He wheezed against her neck.

"Out. Hands on the hood."

She complied while he struggled from the club cab, aimed his hurt arm through the strap, and re-slung the M16 across his back.

"Up."

He meant a stairway chunked into the berm, just-visible snow depressions that ascended to a shack where a motor chugged.

She began, letting him keep contact. She would never die for him, back then. She understood suddenly that this compounded the rage that drove him then, and still drove him now, as he climbed raggedly behind her, jamming the pistol into her sacrum.

As they reached the berm's narrow, slippery peak, she saw that the shack was a pump house for the agitator that stirred the lagoon.

Snow touched down and disappeared upon the gleaming, luridly pinkish expanse. Liquid pig shit, half the size of Lake Susan, where Win Carpenter had slid out of the dam spout. The agitator burbled like a fat toad in the middle. Beyond the lagoon's far coastline, pole lights shone on a parking area with just one vehicle, a small red sedan. From here she had a view of the dark-windowed office, the equipment sheds and feed bins, the great gouts of snow-specked steam rising from the two main barns, three thousand hogs in each.

Hoof pressed the SIG against her skull.

"Stand out on that platform."

He meant the grate that extended from the pump shack and out over the slop, access to the air hose and power source.

He prodded her to the edge of the grate.

So this was how he would hide her body.

A bullet to the brain and she would fall right in.

Be digested.

Disappear.

She guessed suddenly that Hoof had *not* killed Win Carpenter—the runaway undertaker, Darwin Fuss. A killer mistaking Lake Susan as a place to make a body disappear was likely someone with no knowledge of the Bad Axe. Hoof would have done a better job. Was this why Deputy Mikayla Stonebreaker had to step in, deposit a backpack with drug paraphernalia that was unrelated to the crime? But if Deputy Stonebreaker had done this . . . on behalf of what outsider? And if Hoof wasn't the killer, why was an undertaker's tool kit at Missy's house?

"Can you give me a minute? To pray for my husband and my children?"

He repeated what he had told her at the river yesterday: "Knock yourself out."

She hadn't been able to pray then either. What she needed now was a minute to slow her breathing and recognize the exact lake of shit that she and Hoof had returned to—and hear what this could tell her.

Look at us, she thought. In Hoof's pack of mutts, she had been his purebred prize, his best victim ever. For a year or so, with poor Missy scuffling along, Hoof and his deposed Dairy Queen had been dive-bar royalty. Hadn't this fed her ruined sense of self? Hadn't this kept her head up, provided she could stay buzzed enough? She had needed to belong to whatever that was. But she would never die for him.

And now she remembered the moment. On the occasion of her grief-addled nineteenth birthday, the man she counted as her rich and handsome older boyfriend had proudly shared that he was also fucking their third wheel, Missy. Hoof had thought this would be news to her. He had expected her to be devastated and he had casually given her enough barbiturates to put herself to sleep forever. But she had laughed in his face and thrown the pills out the window. Not much later, Hoof had thrown *her* out a window.

She stared out over the liquid manure, calculating the agitator to be about twenty strokes away.

"Okay," she said. "Prayer over. I'm good."

She bent her knees and plugged her nose. She popped her rear end into Hoof and jarred him off balance.

The SIG fired skyward as she exploded into a dive.

CHAPTER 27

You should write a book . . .

As for Chapter Four, when Belle Kick reaches twelve years old, her stepfather, Gentleman Jim, makes his move, and afterward he explains that she has given him no choice, she was ready, and other men would have hurt her. Instead, he has protected her, as he will continue to do.

She remembers how at the moment she is unable to think or speak, even to see. Parts of her separate and after that the pieces can't reconnect or belong as they are. Gentleman Jim palms her hot little head and makes her nod. *Say you understand.*

"Call me back," she rasps in a phone message. "I need to talk."

She waits.

Smoking. Shivering.

Nothing.

A door opens.

"What is the difference"—Heidi's dispatcher pal, Denise Halverson, has come out to her porch as if Belle needs rescue—"between a gorilla and a boyfriend?"

Belle blows smoke. He said whenever, anytime she needs an ear. She believed him.

"Pants."

More smoke. "Ha."

At Belle's back, inside Denise's snug little home, yet another family has coalesced easily and warmly with Belle on the outside. Her twin grandsons slumber entwined under a throw in the jumbo vinyl recliner that in Belle's life would usually contain a drunken man sleeping off his promises. Her granddaughter reads above-grade in a beanbag chair. Harley and Denise, friends since fourth grade, snuggle chastely on a scratchy old plaid sofa that reminds Belle of the scratchy old plaid sofa where—but that's where Chapter Four starts—and starts—and starts—like she has fallen into it and can't get out.

Anytime you need, lady love.

But he won't answer.

CHAPTER 28

Hoof would empty the SIG without hitting her.

This was her gamble.

He would not connect. Not while firing a kicky short-barreled pistol one-handed through a curtain of snow, not while fucked up on horse medication, and not with her swimming hard in the dark.

The liquid pig shit was warm and slippery and dense. She came up eyes closed, tasting it, and blew out, whipped her hair once to each side, gathered all the air she could, sealed her lips, and began to stroke overhand toward the chugging sound of the agitator, feeling nothing as the SIG popped behind her.

A hundred times she and Missy had exchanged smirks while Hoof had bounced darts off tavern walls, rolled gutter balls at bowling alleys, went zero-for-everything in his skeet-shooting league. Even not-drunk, Hoof had always been a first-rate overcompensating klutz. Hence easy targets. A bump-stocked M16 was exactly his kind of tool.

She was right. Two more errant pops from the SIG and he gave it up. In the next few seconds, while he yanked the M16 around, she churned into the middle of the pit. By the time he began to strafe the lagoon, she had thrashed behind the agitator. She hung on, first catching her breath, then wrestling off her hooded sweatshirt as rounds pinged off the metal dome.

His magazine would run out.

Then it did. While reloading distracted him, she threw the sweatshirt as far as she could across the surface. She waited for him to see the orange word BOOSTER sinking slowly through the scum. He was pumping sixty rounds a minute at the sweatshirt as she dog-paddled discreetly in the opposite direction and crawled ashore.

Inside the near hog barn, the squealing scrambled her brain. The stench watered her eyes. One man in yellow rubber coveralls worked at the far end. His back was turned, his head down. She staggered past a door that said OFFICE, ducked into a plexiglass enclosure with a desk and a phone.

"Rhino, I need help."

"Sheriff, where are you?"

"Ernhardt Pig Feeder. I need backup."

"Stonebreaker is at that Mill Coulee Road address, the Melissa Grooms place. She's closest. Hang on."

"No, Rhino, not her—"

As the shock caught up, she sank to the floor beside the desk, staring at her manure-plastered chest, heaving, her manure-plastered legs, shaking, a beige plastic phone receiver in her shit-wet hand. Her heart had jumped into her ears. Her vision had blurred.

"Help is coming," Rhino said. "Can you stay on the line? Sheriff?"

Outside, Hoof was still pumping holes in her sweatshirt. She stared up at a clock on the wall until she could read it. How was it midnight already?

"Sheriff?"

"I'm here."

"So . . . um, while Deputy Stonebreaker is coming, there's some stuff you might want to be aware of. You said you didn't know Melissa Grooms, but the purse Deputy Luck found had a picture of you and your family. Taylor and Dylan, their birthday, which was only three weeks ago, because we all remember you brought cupcakes to the office. Seems like you gave that picture to Melissa Grooms, right? But then you said you didn't know her."

Fuck.

Was this what Lindsey Luck had been trying to tell her?

"Deputy Stonebreaker is saying you lied," Rhino continued. "She's saying you obstructed an investigation. Because apparently Ms. Grooms told her—"

"Rhino, stop. Missy isn't dead?"

He paused as if confused. "Missy?"

"Melissa Grooms."

Her dispatcher stayed quiet.

"Yes, Rhino, I know her. I lied about it. But not to obstruct an investigation."

Still quiet.

"Rhino . . . how is Melissa Grooms alive?"

"The river is way low this year, Sheriff. We found her right underneath the bridge. She broke some bones on a mud spit. Her pelvis maybe even. It's serious. She's in surgery. But she was never close to dying."

Poor Missy can't even kill herself successfully.

"She told Stonebreaker what?"

"She was real high on something, feeling no pain, and when they brought her up she was running full-speed at the mouth. You shot somebody. An ex-boyfriend, she said. You shot him in the back."

Fuck, fuck, fuck.

The sheriff rose to her knees and collapsed into the desk chair, spinning it to look outside toward the lagoon. Okay, Missy was alive.

That was a good thing on every level. And now, seeing the Ram's headlights round the berm and point toward the road, she knew that Hoof was leaving her for dead.

That was good too.

She turned back, noting a cell phone and keys atop a duty check-list on the desk.

"Sheriff?"

"Still here."

"You have a grudge, I guess, is what Ms. Grooms told Stone-breaker. You lured him and Ms. Grooms out to go hunting yesterday, and you shot the boyfriend in the back. And then, Sheriff, Stone-breaker said—"

"Call her off, Rhino. No Ernhardt Pig Feeder."

"What?"

"I'm not there anymore."

She hung up and called her own number: the phone in the cup holder in her dad's truck. Hoof answered. "We're sorry," he slurred giddily, "the bitch you have dialed is no longer available."

"Oh, yes, she is."

She took the cell phone and keys off the desk, the ratty jacket off the back of the chair. The man in yellow coveralls never saw her try to roll manure off in the snow before she took his little red car too.

CHAPTER 29

"Rhino, it's me again."

She was just inside the Village of Farmstead limits, pushing through the storm past the Ease Inn at eleven percent battery on the stolen cell. THIS LAND IS OUR LAND and KILL THE CULT, announced signs in the tavern window. It was bad weather on Thanksgiving night, but several plus-sized trucks crowded the closest parking spaces. Unmissable was Dennis Stonebreaker's full-ton diesel dually with its jacked chassis, four rear wheels, and rooftop bar of amber cab lights.

"I'm calling back from a different phone. I gotta be quick."

"Okay, but, um, Sheriff," Rhino said, "I need to tell you a couple more things."

"Quickly."

"Well, first, there was this incident at Old Friends Farm. That nursing home for horses?"

"And?"

"Your basic break-in for drugs, it looks like, but things got crazy. They shot horses. Four dead. And Ms. Grooms's car was there."

"I see."

"And, um, there was a Traeger's Café napkin folded up in the glove box. Somebody wrote a phone number on it. Chief Deputy Stonebreaker called the number. You answered."

"I answered?"

"The machine on your landline at the farm."

"Hmm."

"Then just one minute ago I took a 911"—Rhino paused, his beard rubbing the headset—"about a hit-and-run on Kickapoo Street here in town. Somebody piled a Ram 1500 into that brick house on the curve and ran. Totaled the truck. Major damage to the house. Schwem found the registration and it turns out to be your truck. Blood inside. Driver on the run."

Somewhere nearby, Hoof, with new injuries, was on the run. To where?

"So, you know, Sheriff, as the officer in charge, Chief Deputy Stonebreaker really wants to talk to you."

"I'll call her," she lied.

Now she was rolling the stolen red car down Main Street, where two of the three taverns were also open on Thanksgiving night. Drunken smokers struggled to stay lit on the sidewalks, dimly watching her pass.

"Meantime, Rhino, a few things I need from you. First, I need you to go into the evidence box for the Win Carpenter homicide and get out the backpack Stonebreaker claims she retrieved from the crime scene at Lake Susan. Get a good look at it, and inventory what's inside."

"Sheriff, she's calling you a person of interest."

"Don't worry. I'm going to fix that. Then, Rhino, I need you to go back at least three years looking at drug busts. Did we confiscate a backpack that fits the same description, with the same stuff inside, and store it in the evidence room?"

"Sheriff—"

"The next question: Is that backpack still where it should be? I'm going to guess it's in the Win Carpenter evidence box, with a little mud on it from the banks of Lake Susan. When you get that far, lock everything down and call me at this number. I don't know whose phone it is. I borrowed it."

"Sheriff, Stonebreaker is already talking about obstruction charges with the district attorney—"

She killed the call and turned into the parking lot of the other motel in Farmstead, at the north end of town, the Red Barn. With Missy in surgery, Stonebreaker bearing down, and Hoof on the run, it was time to follow up her dark new hunch about the House of Shalah.

▲ ▼ ▲ ▼

"Holy shit, Sheriff," said a startled Markus Sullivan, the *New York Times* reporter.

"Can we talk outside?" she asked.

"Am I right? That's shit?"

"It's pig shit."

"What about a shower?"

He was serious, stepping aside to invite her inside as a smaller man appeared behind holding a green beer bottle. A laptop screen glowed on the motel desk.

"Kevin and I can just take a little walk in the snow."

"No, thanks."

She felt the motel breezeway pitching like the deck of a ship.

"Then can I make you some coffee?"

She took slow, mind-racing breaths until the reporter reappeared with a foam cup. She felt the warm liquid trail down her esophagus and spread around the lining of her stomach. She and Sullivan stood quietly under the eave outside his door.

"Obviously, you have sources," she began.

"Which I don't have to reveal," he answered. "Not that I automatically won't reveal them."

"The questions you were asking me yesterday morning—it seems like you've been talking to somebody who knows what it's like inside the House of Shalah."

"I have been."

"I think it's true that felons are involved."

"That is my assessment too."

"But involved in what?"

"That I can't tell you."

"You mean you won't tell me?"

"I can't, Sheriff. I don't know. My source doesn't know."

Her mind reeled to the new worry that had struck her on the road to the manure pit. "Do the Carpenters have a suicide pact?"

"My source says so."

"What triggers it?"

"The end of the world, what else?"

"And what does the end of their world look like?"

The reporter shrugged, but on her mind were the constant pressure and surveillance by Kill the Cult, the eviction notice and the deadline, the blitzing onset of a Wisconsin winter, the murder of a Carpenter that had gone unsolved . . . and she said, "Life inside that fence could be much worse than it looks."

"I think so too," Sullivan said.

She felt their eyes share a backward glance: the government loses patience, Sherman tanks blast tear-gas bombs through the walls, the complex explodes, forensics finds the charred bones of children curled inside the charred bones of their mothers.

Suddenly Sheriff Kick was so empty and exhausted that the coffee, weak as it was, made her ears ring.

She told Sullivan, "You mentioned Waco."

"And you said never here," he said. "I sure hope not."

She stared at him.

"Then help me. Give me a name. Somebody I can talk to."

▲ ▼ ▲ ▼

At the address on Black Bottom Road, Town of Jonstad, several signs told her to go away, and the pit bull puppy charging on a chain from under the house would have killed her if it could grow up fast enough. She got out but stayed beside her stolen car, shielding her face with one hand as she waved at a young man looking out the window at a shit-covered stranger under pelting snow. She put her pinkie near her lips and her thumb near her ear—phone—trying to tell him she was the one Sullivan had just called him about.

Nineteen-year-old Timothy Dekker opened his door warily, showing her his hundred-dollar Walmart shotgun.

"You're the sheriff?"

"I am."

"Seriously? Sheriff Kick?"

"That's me. Can I ask you some questions?"

He lowered the shotgun.

"Yeah. Yeah, sure."

▲ ▼ ▲ ▼

She was relieved to find the home clean and tidy, then worried that it seemed almost barren. Too wet and shitty to sit, she stayed on his doormat while Timothy Dekker stood beside his kitchen table, where it seemed he had been drinking a soda and reading his Bible.

"So you joined the House of Shalah? Then you left?"

"Well, my dad joined us up in May. Right away there was a problem, but he didn't see it. Or maybe he saw the problem and he liked it. Not me. I left around the first of September."

"What made you want to leave?"

"God is the author and giver of life, Sheriff."

He awaited her reply with heartbreaking earnestness.

"Okay," she said. "Right. Meaning?"

"Glorify God in your body and your spirit, which are His. Ye are the temple of God."

Again he waited.

"I'm sorry," she admitted. "I'm a little rusty on the Bible. Can you help me out?"

"This means it's a mortal sin to kill yourself."

"Ah. Suicide is a sin."

"A mortal sin. You go to hell."

"Sure. Right."

"Because God is inside you."

"Yes."

Now she waited. But it seemed he was done explaining.

"You mean the Carpenters have a suicide pact?"

He nodded.

"And you're not okay with that?"

"God is not okay with that. The Bible says so."

"But your dad . . ."

"I guess he doesn't care. He has a liver disease. And dementia. We lost my mom, and those Carpenter women are nice to him. He wouldn't leave with me."

"You must worry."

"I do."

"Can you explain how the suicide pact works?"

His shrug and look of disgust seemed to express that aside from its obvious sinfulness, the topic was hardly worth discussion.

"Standard TV-movie cult crap," he said. "Everybody takes drugs and sings kumbaya. Everybody dies. Even the little kids, who have no idea what's going on. And that's not suicide, it's murder."

That had been the outrage at Waco. Those children were murdered. The argument was over who did it.

"When . . . or why," she asked, "would this happen?"

Again he looked disgusted. He replied as if by rote, in a tone without conviction.

"If the prophet-father dies before he can give out the prosperity the Carpenters have earned, then their reward awaits them in heaven, and they are commanded to follow him."

She ran it back in her mind. "An IOU in the afterlife?"

"Which is such obvious bullshit."

"What do you mean?"

He waved at his Bible. "Luke 18:25."

"Well, there I go again," she said after a pause, "having a mental block on my Bible quotes."

" 'For it is easier for a camel to go through the eye of a needle than for a rich man to enter the kingdom of God.' "

"Right. Of course. Luke 18:25."

"Damn straight."

His tone was changing. He was relaxing. He seemed relieved to have her ear.

"That dude ain't going to heaven, Sheriff."

"Got it."

"And he knows it. He's got other plans."

"Like what?"

"I don't know, but one guy died, right? They found Brother Win with his throat slit in a lake? And another guy disappeared? Brother Roy?"

"Who is Brother Roy?"

He shrugged. "Brother Roy," he said.

She made a mental note: *Brother Roy disappeared.*

"That's why I got the gun and the dog. When I left, I was sure they'd come after me."

"Who is they?"

"Out of nowhere the prophet-father had a security team. This was like August. He gave them all wives, these four guys trying to pretend they loved God and believed the prosperity gospel and weren't just ex-cons running some kind of hustle."

"Do you have names?"

▲ ▼ ▲ ▼

On the ridge back to Farmstead, the sheriff texted *this is heidi* and then called Denise on the last eight percent of her stolen cell phone. She spoke before Denise could say hello.

"Is my family okay?"

"Heidi, you don't sound right. Is—"

"Denise, tell me, is my family okay?"

"Yes. Fine. They're all asleep except your mother-in-law. I gave her my room, and she's in there leaving messages for Leo—"

"Messages for who?"

"You didn't know about Belle's new boyfriend?"

"Not much. But anyway—"

"We had girl talk, hon. Leo is his name. He's new in town. A gentleman, she said. Religious. Coming into some wealth. I said, 'Does your gentleman friend Leo have a gentleman friend for Aunt Denise?' "

"Damn it, Denise, *please*."

She waited, her eyes watering, throat stinging. A door shut.

"I'm sorry, Heidi. What is it?"

"I need you to flesh out some bad guys for me, recently released from prison. I only have first names or nicknames. But you have a friend in admin at the prison, right? These are four ex-cons who wormed their way inside the House of Shalah. One goes by Milk, one goes by Peep, one goes by Skip, and one goes by Spooner."

She was reapproaching town, the hospital ahead. A pickup with a blade peeled snow from the outer parking lot. She steered around a limb that had split and fallen onto the road.

"Hang on a second, Heidi. I can hear your mother-in-law dropping a pretty heavy voice mail on Leo right now. Hang on. I'm going to eavesdrop better."

After a short pause, Denise continued, "Okay. She's telling Leo that you and Harley think you own her, and you think you can tell her what to do. But you don't own her, and you can't tell her what to do, and you don't understand *anything*. She's mad to tears, and she sounds about twelve years old. Do you want to talk to her?"

"Not now. I'm guessing these four knew each other and all got out of prison around the same time. I'm guessing one of them is Roman Vanderhoof."

"Shit."

"Yeah."

"I'm on it."

The sheriff hung up and called the hospital.

Melissa Grooms was out of surgery.

CHAPTER 30

Fernanda, sidesaddle on her pallet bed in the chilly pitch-black, her face phone-lit, was just about to send the text—*I have the files*—when the door to Unit 14 racketed up, silhouetting a bent shape against the slashing snow.

Hosanna snapped out of sleep and clenched herself into a ball. Fernanda hid her phone.

One arm hung stiffly from his lowered shoulder as he staggered two steps in and flailed the other arm to yank the light cord. From this small effort he had to catch his rasping breath while the babies mewled awake and the bulb warmed.

"Shut them fuckers up."

In five more seconds, her new husband was lit with hideous clarity. His right palm, both knees, and both boots were caked with mud. His shirtless torso was freshly bruised and lacerated, his swollen lips were stuck shut by white crusts in the corners, his smashed nose dripped blood. Fernanda flinched—he looked like he had been in a car crash—but as she kept looking, she saw it was more than that. His left arm had been cocked into a sling made from his shirt. The pockets of his bloody pants bulged with pill bottles, plus a cell phone that wasn't his. Hung by a strap around his wilting neck was a military-style gun, not one she recognized from the arsenal but no doubt the one that was missing. His spindly legs barely held him up as he lurched in another step. He swung the gun at the babies as they rose to grip the mesh, howling and grasping at their mother.

"Shut those fuckers up before I do."

Finally Fernanda could move. She scooped the babies into her arms and retreated beside Hosanna on her pallet.

"Husband, maybe we should pray."

She sounded absurd to herself. He let the gun hang while he upended the plastic basket where she kept her thermometer, Tylenol, rubbing alcohol, and Band-Aids.

"Please? Let's pray."

Her instincts were wrong. He stripped her purse from its hook on the wall, snapping off the strap. He turned it out and pawed through her personal things until he had a tampon. He knocked over another of her baskets. Scissors.

"Get over here. Cut this off."

He meant the sling, shirtsleeves crudely knotted around the far side of his neck, his injured arm wrenched up and away from his body. She passed the babies to Hosanna.

"Husband, maybe we should take you to a hospital."

"Cut it off."

Warily, she scissored off a sleeve and peeled the shirt away. His arm remained stuck in place. Hidden by the sling, what looked like a purple-black worm now dangled from a spot inside his armpit. He pulled and the worm came . . . and came . . . unwinding . . . three feet long, Fernanda's stomach rolling . . . until he dropped it on the floor and she saw it was a gore-soaked shoelace that he had crammed into the exit wound of a gunshot.

"Someone shot you? You're infected."

"Soak it. Shove it in there."

He meant the tampon. She dipped it, applicator and all, into the bottle of rubbing alcohol. She ground her teeth as the gooey wound resisted.

"Goddamn it, push."

She shucked the applicator. The string hung.

"Get me a shirt."

One of Roy's, he meant. But Roy was smaller. He set the weapon on the bed while she draped him with one of Roy's plaid flannel long-sleeves, able to fasten only one button midway down his chest. He wore it like a cape.

"We should get you to a doctor."

"Gimme a coat."

"Sister Florence was a nurse—"

"Put me in a fucking coat. And a hat."

He was going somewhere, Fernanda understood as she hung him with Roy's McKormick's Farm Supply windbreaker. He was clumsily thumbing letters into a phone that didn't belong to him. Fastening the jacket's zipper at the bottom, Fernanda glimpsed his search term: *Heidi Kick adress*. Who was that? She balanced Roy's threadbare old Reno Aces cap on his head. He looked even more frightening. Then he hung that dangerous gun back around his neck.

"Go and borrow Sister Cornelia's car."

She did this sometimes, running errands for her prophet-father. "It's the middle of the night."

"Go."

"I don't know what I'd tell her—"

"Bitch, move."

He retrieved the big gun and pointed it at Hosanna and the babies. Fernanda was just touching the door when she heard, "Yo. The fuck you been, bro?" and it jerked up from the outside.

She retreated. Brother Skip's smirking face appeared as he deliberately raised the door—*clack-clack-click!*—the last few inches to the end of its track. His eyes skimmed Fernanda and the children. Then he studied the mess of his brother.

"Wassup, Milk?"

His reflexes slow, Fernanda's husband lowered the phone.

"Nothing's up."

Brother Skip, with his chin ticking up and his hand collecting his dick, showed he disagreed.

"Ain't nothing nothing. Why you come sneaking back in underground? Why you ain't just use the gate? The fuck you been at? The fuck you going now? Whose phone you got?"

Just then Brother Peep and Brother Spooner caught up. "Iss all good," their Brother Milk assured them absurdly as they inspected his injuries, his misfitting clothes, his obvious deep intoxication. Fernanda glared off Brother Peep's eyes when they slid to Hosanna.

"Juss taking care of some business, is all."

"Ain't no business some business." Brother Skip gave himself a tug. "It all, all of us business."

"Iss . . ."

Losing his train of thought, he dumped pills into his mouth and chewed. He looked blurrily into the phone in his hand.

"Iss all good, brothers."

Brother Spooner's small head, bald and wrinkled, appeared briefly as he upended snow from the gutter of his hat brim. He said, "Like hell it's all good. The brother asked where you been. Seems like you don't have an answer. Seems like you have business you can't share. Meanwhile, the outside is coming in, brother. The prophet-father is melting. The mother is freaked. We're not paid yet. And you're going off the script and playing games."

He sent Fernanda a dry smile and she froze.

"Something about the señora's husbands, it seems, so maybe the señora is the problem."

Then, with a movement so quick Fernanda hardly saw it, Brother Spooner snatched the phone from her husband's hand. He looked at it, turned it over, looked at the back. As he did this, his other hand rose slowly from his suit coat pocket. Then in a second sudden motion he swung something hard inside a white tube sock and clocked his Brother Milk on the side of his skull, collapsing him to the floor.

"Property of Bad Axe County Sheriff's Department," Brother Spooner said, showing the others the phone before he dropped it in his pocket. He leaned and stripped the gun.

"Get him the fuck out of here."

His brothers carried him off like a dead man.

Fernanda returned to task. She sent Duke Hashimoto the text: *I have the files.*

▲ ▼ ▲ ▼

There was only one chair in his motel room, so after Fernanda Carpenter had dried herself off with his spare bath towel, Duke Hashimoto situated her on the bed, his laptop between them.

"Okay?"

"Yes."

"No one saw you sneaking over the fence?"

"He came back. He was shot. They were distracted."

"He . . . is?"

"My husband after Roy. I don't know his name."

"Shot by?"

"I don't know."

"Your kids are okay?"

"My daughter's watching the little ones. We need to hurry."

Hashimoto let it go for now. He plugged in the ChapStick drive and the file-explorer window filled with folders. He told his laptop to copy all and let it work. He tested the first folder, unnamed, with his right-cursor arrow, worried it would be encrypted.

No. The folder opened like a blunt assault, Hashimoto recoiling from several dozen photos of the Carpenter girl nude or in stages of undress. He scrolled to gauge the volume of the crime and quickly closed the folder.

"There's an FBI Child Exploitation and Human Trafficking Task Force," he began as an offering to the trembling mother. "They take on this sort of thing."

But his stomach churned with the knowledge that weeks or even months of interagency wrangling—basically the definition of "task force"—would be required to get this on CEHTTF's radar. And meanwhile . . .

"Do you know how these were taken?"

"Holes in the walls of my storage unit."

"Do you know who?"

"I'm sure it's the one they call Brother Peep."

Hashimoto felt sick. "Peep?"

"That's what they call him. We call him."

"He's another one of the new Carpenters?"

"Yes."

"Any others?"

"A Brother Spooner and a Brother Skip. And my husband after Roy, Brother Milk."

"And who sent these to you?"

"My guess was my neighbor, Sister Maryellen, wife of Brother Peep. She's my friend and she would tell me. But she denied knowing anything about it."

Hashimoto moved on, convinced by the escape tunnel that photographs of her child were no longer Fernanda Carpenter's primary problem. He guessed there was more.

There was. The next folder, bluntly named *Accounts*, contained the trove of financial data that his gun-assembly plot with Roy had been designed to leverage into the hands of the IRS. He would pass it on. But that was the old more. There had to be a new more.

Alphabetically next, the folder labeled *Acquire* contained several dozen inmate profiles downloaded from a site called meet-an-inmate.com. Some release dates were highlighted, and features of some profiles.

The next folder, named *BR*, opened to photographs of landscapes and parking lots—and Hashimoto's heart sank as he skimmed and recognized the blue Dodge Laramie that he had rented for his last trip to Bad Axe County. In several photos, pulled up beside the blue Laramie was the heavy gray utility truck that *BR*, Brother Roy, had driven to their meetings, property of the implement dealer he had worked for.

"Mrs. Carpenter, I'm so sorry. Someone found out. Someone was watching him."

Her eyes crossed his with a hot, resentful look that said, *You got him killed.*

But not exactly. Royland Rogers had been wanted on tax evasion charges of his own, stemming from the sale of a failing auto body shop that he had owned in Reno. He had slipped away into the House of Shalah, tithing his untaxed profits to Jerome Pearl in exchange for a hiding place and a promise of future prosperity. But after three years as a Carpenter, basically an honorable man gripped by conscience and wanting to pay his back taxes, Roy had asked for a withdrawal from his prosperity account. For this he had received concrete threats that had made him suspicious. He had "called the feds," as they say, and step-by-step over the summer Roy and the feds had worked out a confidential-informant deal that turned out to involve Hashimoto and the illegally modified assault weapon.

"I'm so sorry, Mrs. Carpenter."

A sub-folder inside *BR* was named *Find Someone* and opened on close-ups of tattoos. On a white man's hands, the artist had inked square-headed nails trailing drops of blood, like the hands of Jesus nailed to the cross. On one forearm, a dove flew pinching an olive branch in its beak. On the other forearm, two hands paired themselves in prayer. On a shoulder and neck, the face of Jesus exuded rays of light, the portrait inset with numbers suggesting a Bible verse.

"Are these Roy's tattoos?"

"Roy didn't have tattoos. Those are the prophet-father's."

"Can you guess why?"

"I don't know."

"But you've seen these tattoos on him?"

"Those are the tattoos that anyone can see."

"Every Carpenter knows these?"

"Yes."

He put the curser on the numbers below Jesus's neck.

"This is a Bible reference?"

" 'He who trusts in the Lord shall prosper.' Proverbs 28:25."

"Who could have taken these pictures?"

"Any of the wives. Or Mother Ruth."

The next group of photos showed someone's hair: long silver locks in a uniquely patterned braid that hung between weak white shoulders.

"Is this the prophet-father's hair?"

"That's the fishtail braid that Sister Celia gives the prophet-father."

"Are these his eyes?"

Pale blue yolks afloat in veiny white.

"Yes."

"Any idea why?"

"I don't know."

The next sub-folder inside *BR* was named with a phone number and contained a single photograph of a small, junk-surrounded house.

"Do you recognize this place?"

"No."

Hashimoto studied it. Square and colorless, the house squatted alone in its own shadow close by a crumbling road that passed between fields of brown October corn. The towers and cables of a high-voltage power line bisected the sky above like strings of a distant puppeteer. Far across the field in the background showed the close-set silver domes of three silos.

Fernanda Carpenter looked away and sniffled now, as if the emptiness in this photograph had triggered her tears.

Why this house? Hashimoto could guess. Some of the places where he had met Roy were not on any map, and the burner phone Roy used could not use GPS. Instead, Hashimoto had provided general directions, distances, road names, then guided Roy to the precise spot using photographs: a certain train-crossing sign along the Mississippi, the realtor's sign on a tract of hunting land for sale.

Roy was wary—but was this how he had disappeared? Had Pearl or someone working for Pearl tricked Roy into visiting this house? Texted him this photograph at the number that labeled the folder? Hashimoto had turned in his bureau phone at retirement. But he guessed so. He guessed someone in the House of Shalah had fooled Brother Roy into thinking he and Hashimoto had a meeting at this house, and they had been waiting.

So they know who you are too, Hashimoto informed himself.

He studied the power lines over the house, the shadows it cast, the silos behind it. Using plat maps, power-grid diagrams, Google Earth . . . he could he find it.

He clicked quickly through the rest of the folders and files, noting what to study later. In addition to a tunnel out through a fake sewer, Jerome Pearl's basic idea was obvious enough. A folder labeled *Klearflow* led Hashimoto to account numbers, routing numbers, passwords, wire transfer codes, dozens of line entries for sums just below the legal threshold of ten thousand dollars. He needed Wikipedia to tell him that Klearflow was a German banking service operating in unregulated jurisdictions such as Switzerland, the Cayman Islands, Belize—and Andorra, where the file detailed contact information for a brokerage.

With Mrs. Carpenter waiting tensely on the bed, he checked Wikipedia again. Andorra was a sovereign microstate on the France-Spain border.

The folder labeled *Transportation* was a cache of links to flight schedules, livery and courier services, comparison prices for helicopter rental, compilations of updated travel rules and restrictions, and a link that Hashimoto followed into the dark web to a site selling passport forgeries.

The Pearls were cashing in and bolting on the House of Shalah.

To deal with the increased scrutiny—one of theirs talking to the feds, Kill the Cult watching day and night—they had hired a team of ex-cons to help them escape.

But what about the rest of the Carpenters?

A folder labeled *XYZ* contained a single document with a link to a medscape.com page that listed dosages for estazolam, flurazepam, quazepam, temazepam, triazolam, zolpidem. The document included a dark web link to a chemical supplier that sold bulk chloral hydrate. And a link to another dealer that wholesaled powdered phenobarbital.

It was not enough to threaten children with another Waco, Hashimoto thought. Add deadly drugs, and here was the outline of another Heaven's Gate, another Jonestown Kool-Aid party . . .

Suddenly and urgently, Fernanda Carpenter gripped his arm. Wide-eyed with dread, she spoke a painful truth about cults and followers.

"I have to get back inside!"

CHAPTER 31

Dr. Alka Patel surprised Sheriff Kick at the emergency room entrance.

"How very nice to see you again, Sheriff."

The doctor was even more carefully polite than she had been at noon, when she had told the sheriff's family to watch for signs of mental impairment.

"Though to say that perhaps you haven't followed your discharge instructions, would such a statement be possibly correct?"

"Where is Melissa Grooms?"

"Please follow me."

Dr. Patel led her briskly down an administrative corridor and closed a door behind them. This was an office. No Missy.

"Sheriff," the doctor began, now sternly, "I have three problems with you being here. First, Ms. Grooms has already been questioned extensively by Chief Deputy Stonebreaker, before her surgery and against my better judgment. At this time, she is still under the effects of both our medications and her own."

"I understand. I have different questions." As the doctor inspected her, she added, "Ms. Grooms is a person of interest in an attempted homicide."

Nodding, Dr. Patel lifted a Bad Axe County Sheriff's Department card from the pocket of her examination coat.

"Second, Chief Deputy Stonebreaker said you might show up here. She gave me her card and asked me to call her right away."

"Have you?"

"Not yet."

"Thank you."

"However, Deputy Stonebreaker gave out many cards, down to the parking lot guy. 'Call right away if you see Sheriff Kick.' In her story, *you* are the person of interest in an attempted homicide."

"Someone lied to her."

The doctor frowned.

"I'm in a bind here, Sheriff Kick. I trust you."

"And likewise."

"I wish I could say that Chief Deputy Stonebreaker inspired the same confidence. The woman does not."

"Your usual good judgment."

The doctor crossed her thin arms and sighed.

"Sheriff, less than twenty-four hours after discharge for hypothermia, your eyes are red, your fingers are white, your voice is hoarse, you're filthy, and you smell like sewage—and my third problem is that in this condition you have walked into a hospital, indicating to me that possibly you are mentally impaired."

"I understand. It's important."

"I'm going to take your pulse and temperature and ask you some basic questions. Then you will either be readmitted and put on IV antibiotics, or you are going to shower, dress cleanly, and mask up before you get anywhere close to Ms. Grooms."

▲ ▼ ▲ ▼

A confused and slurry whisper: "Heidi?"

"Yes, it's me."

Whatever low-water sand spit Missy had landed on under the bridge had probably saved her from drowning but had also injured her badly. Rocks. Driftwood snags. Her handsome face was bloated and her dark eyes had sunken deep into her skull. Her dense black hair was half shaved off and she was stitched from her right eyebrow to her right ear. A traction weight pulled up and back beneath her arms, and her left leg was cast to the hip. Monitor leads and IV tubes trailed to the various machines and supply bags surrounding her bed.

"Oh . . ." She leaked tears. "Oh, my God, Heidi . . ."

"Yeah. How about that? We're both alive. Still."

"Heidi, I swear, I promise you . . ."

Her usual beginning. This time she couldn't finish.

"We're both still surviving him."

Missy at last said weakly, "He just said he wanted to talk to you alone."

"With an assault rifle?"

"I was high on crystal. He said keep the car warm and when he was done talking, we'd go get more."

"You haven't changed."

"Heidi . . . I can't change."

"You kept the car warm."

"I was really high."

"What did he say when he came back?"

Missy seemed to drift. The sheriff imagined her waiting in her car, buzzed and jittery and guilty, the snowstorm swirling prettily while Hoof tracked her ex–best friend a half mile away. Had she felt anything at all? Had she heard the gunshots?

"What did Hoof say when he came back to your car?"

"He was bleeding, Heidi, and he was really, really mad. He said you and him argued and he walked away and you shot him in the back. That's what he said."

"He's a liar."

"I know."

"But I did shoot him."

"You should have killed him."

"Did you go get more meth?"

"I took him home and kind of tried to help him. He passed out all night until this afternoon. Then he said you were going to die and so was I, if I warned you, and then he said he just might kill me anyway, I deserved it, and I just . . ."

"He took you to the bridge?"

She tried to shake her head no. "I got high and I walked."

"Five miles in the snow?"

"Was it?"

The sheriff moved on.

"I went looking for him at your place. I saw your pay stub on the kitchen table. I caught up with him at Old Friends Farm. He took your car and your key to the building. He was stealing meds. He shot four of those old horses, two mares and one stallion, and a beautiful old jenny."

Missy burst out, "Oh, no!" and began to weep silently.

"He left me for dead twice, Missy. Once in the Bad Axe River. Once in the Ernhardt Farms manure pit. He hates me more every time I survive. He won't give up. I'm worried that if he can't get me, he'll come for my family. Besides your place, where would he go?"

Missy wept even harder. The sheriff went to the window. A hospital security officer circled the stolen red car where she had left it in emergency parking. He cleared snow from the windshield with his forearm and shone his flashlight inside.

"Why is there an undertaker's tool kit at your place?"

"I don't know."

"Missy . . ."

"I don't know!"

"Did you know the undertaker?"

"He came over once. Hoof told me to get lost. I never knew his name."

The security officer backed under the ER awning and began poking at his cell phone. Calling Mikayla Stonebreaker. The sheriff turned back to Missy.

"Did Hoof join the House of Shalah?"

She looked blank.

"That's the name of the cult."

"Oh. Yes. They recruited him. Online."

"Who did?"

"Whoever in the cult. While he was in prison. Email."

Missy lost focus for a moment, maybe feeling pain. The sheriff thought: *Same way Deputy Luck is contacting inmates.* She needed records from the prison email system, and the new connection to a criminal like Hoof inside the House of Shalah should finally convince the judge.

"The cult-leader guy and his wife, I remember they said," Missy went on, "started writing to guys who were just about to get out, offered them, you know, shelter, women, save their souls, whatever, come join. Hoof was putting in a sewer system like he used to do for developments. But those guys are playing something, Heidi."

"Which guys? Playing what?"

"I don't know. Three other guys with Hoof. When they're not at the cult they hang out at my place to talk about stuff. They call Hoof 'Brother Milk' and laugh because it pisses him off. They're working for the cult people, Father and Mother whatever, doing what they want."

"Names."

Missy put the same names with "Brother Milk" as Timothy Dekker had: Brother Peep, Brother Skip, Brother Spooner. The only real name she knew was Hoof's.

"Why do they call him 'Brother Milk'?"

"I think you."

"What?"

"Sent to prison by the Dairy Queen. He hates it."

"He hates me. Anyone else?"

Missy had recovered to sniffling and now seemed to drift out of focus machine. Machine beeps marked the passing seconds as the sheriff waited in fear of the unholy mess if Stonebreaker caught her now—a break for Hoof, a boost for Kill the Cult, a feather in Stonebreaker's cap—a potential disaster for innocent Carpenters and for the whole Bad Axe.

"Missy . . . is there anyone else involved?"

"Oh . . ." She sighed, making the sad, bewildered face the sheriff had seen a thousand times when her friend looked back on something she had done.

"I feel bad that I got Raven Furtzig involved. Remember Raven from high school?"

"My Sadie Hawkins date."

"He does tattoos now. Hoof asked me who does tattoos. I said this guy Raven. Then Raven showed up at the same time as the undertaker guy and Hoof told me get the fuck out of my own house. He gave me a thousand bucks and sent me all the way to west Davenport to pick up a bag of junk . . ."

As some sharp pain broke through her medicated haze, Missy had to stop and swallow several times. Meanwhile, the window glass began to transmit flickers of red and blue light. At least one deputy had arrived.

". . . and when I got home, nobody was around and it kind of smelled weird in the house, but I'm high as fuck for the next week easy, so let the good times roll, who cares? Next thing I know, Hoof is telling me, 'Why don't you hang out with Mighty Heidi? Old times. Text her. Go on. Text Heidi. Do it.' But Heidi, honestly, yesterday, in my heart I was trying to help you."

"Help me how?"

"Because those guys left some photos at my house. I knew you'd want to see them. I had brought them in my purse to give to you yesterday. But then I didn't see you."

"Photos of what?"

"A woman in bra and panties. Posing. Self-touching. Bathroom mirror selfies. And she's one of your deputies."

Shit. Lyndsey Luck.

"These photos came from Hoof and the others?"

"Yes."

"How did they get them?"

"What I heard is she was sending them to just this one guy at the Boscobel prison and he was trading them for canteen and whatever, and one of these guys, Peep, I think, ended up with a whole collection. And that's what I mean about playing. I think they were using the photos against your deputy. Getting her to do stuff."

"And you for sure saw these photos? This is not just their talk? You saw my deputy?"

"Heidi, I *snagged* those photos. I had them in my purse to give to you yesterday. I really thought you and I were going to drink ketchup."

"Where are the photos now?"

"I left my purse on the bridge. Except . . ."

Blue-and-red flickered in a more complex rhythm. Another deputy had arrived.

"Except I gave some to Raven Furtzig," Missy went on, "because I heard those guys laughing about how they never paid Raven for doing tattoos. I thought he could get those assholes back somehow. I gave him six photos. The rest were in my purse on the bridge . . ."

"What did the woman in the photos look like? Round face, dimples, short brown hair?"

"No head."

"Then how did you know she was my deputy?"

"I heard them say she was a deputy."

She sheriff kept describing Lyndsey Luck. "Young body, thick but in good shape? Small in the chest and freckles all over?"

Missy shook her head so hard she winced in pain.

"Oh, God, no! I mean, I don't know your deputies, but she's a big woman, six-feet-plus, pale as a ghost, D cups, pierced navel, wedding ring . . ."

Stonebreaker!

The recovery room door opened. Dr. Patel went quickly to the window, then turned to the sheriff, frowning intensely as she extended a car-key fob.

"I think you want to leave right now, Sheriff. My car is the white Honda Pilot in staff parking. There's a phone in it. Please let me show you how to exit out the rear of the building."

Sheriff Kick looked back from the doorway.

"Missy . . ."

What she felt surprised her and filled her weary heart.

"I'll always love you."

CHAPTER 32

Fernanda shivered as Duke Hashimoto put out his headlights and crept his truck along a road blanketed with untouched snow getting deeper. Soon the road parted from the margin of the golf course—escaped the view of the golf course cameras, she guessed—and curved through storm-laden evergreens along the boundary of the two-acre lot where she had believed her prophet-father was building her a house.

Hashimoto stopped his truck with its wipers moving, giving her a two-hundred-yard view across the lot to the fence beside her prophet-father's glowing coach. Beyond the coach she could see the rows of storage units where Hosanna in Unit 14 waited with the babies.

Even through her pounding dread, Fernanda looked across this blank snowfield feeling stubborn shreds of hope and desire. A kitchen. A washing machine. Her own toilet. Hosanna with her own room. Grass where the babies could play. But this was only a mind-scape now, a dream frozen into swirls and waves. Beside a machine and an open hole, two unburied pipe lengths broke the snowfield like humps of a creature writhing below.

Hashimoto saw where she was looking. "My guess, that open spot is where their plans say they attach laterals. Except they don't really plan to do that because it's not really a sewer."

He put her window down.

"It comes out about ten feet from where you're sitting."

She stared at the snow-buried road, unsure where he meant, unsure if she should trust him. But what choice did she have now? The messy return of her new husband had triggered a fresh urgency. The bobbing beam of a flashlight told her Brother Skip was out limping the perimeter. Looking for her? The lights inside the mobile coach told her the prophet-father wasn't sleeping. Getting ready to desert them? On U-Stash-It Road, a sheriff's car turned in the dead end and pulled up alongside the pickup truck where a Kill-the-Culter always watched. Windows came down so they could talk.

She had to get back in. Now.

▲ ▼ ▲ ▼

Hashimoto replaced the manhole cover and watched fresh snow cover it in seconds.

Back inside his rental truck, he stacked and restacked his magnetic pebbles, his anxious brain falling into old habit, recycling pain from the past.

At Waco, unfounded rumors, lazy assumptions, and willful ignorance had driven the disaster. All the weapons and weapon parts inside that compound had been legal. The bureau had lied about it later, but at the time of the disastrous first siege, no legitimate evidence suggested that Koresh possessed an arsenal any different than could be found inside a thousand other homes in gun-happy Texas. Grenades? They were inert hulls that Koresh's people mounted on plaques engraved with patriotic slogans, items that they sold at gun shows to raise money. Koresh possessed black powder? So did a hundred thousand other Texans.

Hashimoto stacked and restacked his pebbles.

Child abuse? The state of Texas had found no cause to act upon those allegations. But after the blundering first assault in February cost the lives of four special agents, ATF and FBI had deliberately amplified concerns about the Davidian children, then triggered the death of every single child who by April still remained inside the compound.

What kind of government did that? Then the bureau's big brass blew smoke on TV and in Congress? And expected all its "special" agents to toe the line, talk the talk, or else?

Twenty-seven dead children had tilted the axis of Hashimoto's existence. Twenty-seven dead had triggered his drinking, ended his engagement, tainted his faith in God and country, made his career a trap and a torment and an endless empty quest for redemption.

Except maybe now . . .

He stared across the snowfield, his fingers busy with the silver magnets on his dash.

The Sai no Kawara myth uses the pebbles, he thought, *because our powers are tiny, yet in limitless supply.*

The myth uses the river to hell because without the river's relentless grind—the friction, the stress, the resistance against evil—there are no broken bits of goodness, no pebbles to stack.

The myth uses lost children because we all begin in innocence and never find our way back.

And the ogres?

Fuck the ogres, he thought, shoving the Ranger into gear.

Kill them.

Flush them down the river.

That house in the prophet-father's photograph? That was their house, and after Fernanda made it back inside, he would find it.

▲ ▼ ▲ ▼

She crawled through the pipe, following a headlamp beam, stiff with fear, her palms and knees quickly raw on the rough concrete, segment to segment, the black circle ahead seeming without end.

What if they had found her missing already?

Had they rounded up Hosanna, Rachel, and Josiah?

Made them suffer?

Lord God of protection, I thank You for Your hand upon my children's lives . . .

She reached the unfinished segment of the escape tunnel. She squatted to rest. Fresh air swirled above. Snowflakes melted in her hair. Brother Skip's flashlight skimmed above. She took one deep inhale and scrabbled onward through a muddy gap, around a concrete box, across another gap, into the next pipe.

To map it for her, Hashimoto had traced the path of the tunnel with his finger on his dashboard. Now she was reaching the intersection with the other sewer pipe, the real one, that Hashimoto had told her would be traveling left to right and dumping through a grate into the gulch to the south. Arriving, she saw this pipe was broken through on both sides as if by jackhammers or sledgehammers. Straight ahead beyond the breakage was a dirt tunnel, flooded and muddy.

At least the dirt tunnel was taller than the pipe. Fernanda plodded onward hunched at the waist. Soon after the intersecting pipes, Hashimoto had predicted she might see a side tunnel dug to the left, an outlet for the prophet-father and Mother Ruth to sneak out a multi-access storage bay in the back of the mobile coach and enter the main tunnel.

She saw a side tunnel to the left, shovels and buckets still in it.

Don't go there.

She didn't.

Next, she came to a long, deep puddle, and trailing out of the puddle was a green hose with a white stripe. She straddled the hose, crabbing along. In about a hundred feet, Hashimoto had predicted, the tunnel would pass between the trio of portable toilets.

Was there one toilet that nobody could use?

Yes, she had told him. The middle one.

Then we're hoping that middle tunnel is an exit, he had said.

Finally getting there, Fernanda couldn't tell. The hose bent right into a cavity dug into the tunnel wall, and from there it bent again, down through a gasketed opening into something buried, something that gurgled and chugged beneath a muddy plastic lid.

Hashimoto had not predicted this, but it had to be a pump that was dealing with the flooding, the puddle. Straight up from the lid went an electric cord and also a different hose, a black one. The cord and the hose both disappeared into what Fernanda presumed was the tank of the middle porta-potty with its bottom cut open. Exit or not, she decided she could fit up through there.

Her headlamp hit the underside of the seat lid. She pushed it open and cringed at the boomy sounds she made as she climbed through and into the cabinet space. There she untangled herself from the electrical cord as it continued out beneath the door. The hose, she saw, left the cabinet through a hole cut in the back wall. She closed the seat and sat, resting and getting her bearings. The new chapel would be another hundred feet to her right. The gate was about twice that far straight ahead.

Once you get inside the toilet, Hashimoto had instructed her, *text me.*

She did.

I'll make sure everyone inside is looking toward the road. Wait until you hear some excitement.

She waited.

She heard Brother Skip holler. Brother Spooner barked back. The coach door opened and closed. A car alarm erupted.

She cracked the door.

Hashimoto's high beams cast long honeycomb shadows through the fence.

Ducking beneath this eerie brilliance, Fernanda bolted out.

CHAPTER 33

Sniffling in her surgical recovery bed, Missy had asked Sheriff Kick, *Remember Raven from high school?*

Of course she remembered. Raven Furtzig had been her Sadie Hawkins Dance date—meaning the girl asked the boy—a state of "chaos" that had not occurred again until Heidi White, home from rehab, had seen handsome Harley Kick throwing fastballs from a pitcher's mound in Soldiers Grove.

Raven Furtzig's tattoo shop, Raven's Ink Emporium, was on Main Street in Soldiers Grove where the barbershop used to be, where Sheriff Kick's dad used to get his crew cut and his agricultural gossip. Swiggum's Tap House was still next door. The sheriff rolled past both establishments in Dr. Patel's white Pilot.

Park in the alley behind, she was thinking, and gently jimmy in through the old barbershop's flimsy rear exit, see if she could get a read on Raven Furtzig's connection to Hoof and his ex-con brothers. She and Missy had burgled the barbershop twice—petty cash, fists full of licorice strings, hair tonics for Hoof—crimes she hardly remembered except that two fucked-up girls could pull them off and not get caught.

But as the Pilot slipped past the front window of Swiggum's Tap, she recognized her Sadie Hawkins date perched on one of the barstools and hit the brakes. As far as she could tell, Raven Furtzig still had the same ringlet-style mullet, the same wise-guy slump, the same cigarette stashed behind his earringed ear, the same exotic bottle of Heineken. She had been a bold sophomore, not even driving yet, and Raven, a senior, had already been this aging man-of-experience she was seeing again through Swiggum's window. Her parents had flipped out and stayed up waiting. She had come home later than promised—and wiser.

Remembering, the sheriff parked under a streetlamp on the next block, texted, *this is sheriff hk*, to both Denise and Rhino from Dr. Patel's phone, then hurried through pelting snow back to Swiggum's.

As she arrived, the tavern ceiling lights came on. But Raven seemed unaware that it was bar time. His upper arm was in the grip of a stocky, gap-toothed older man who reminded the sheriff of someone. But not quite the man himself, she realized. The familiar thing was the man's undisguised vehemence, matched by his out-of-date traveling sales-man suit, his houndstooth hat, his brow-line bifocal eyeglasses . . . like the man had appeared out of 1965 to crush Raven's upper-arm bone as he leaned in to level antiquated threats. Who was this?

The bottom half of the man's left ear was missing. The sheriff saw this as he turned to growl at the exhausted barkeep when she came to shoo them out. Raven tried to escape off his stool. The man held him down and leaned closer to make some final remark. Raven finished his bottle of beer. The man let him reel away toward the door.

▲ ▼ ▲ ▼

Seeing her on the sidewalk, the sheriff's dance date did a double-take and nearly tipped himself over. She wore what Dr. Patel's nurse had

found for her, the denim-jeans-and-jacket ensemble of a one-way
ER visitor who had burned ash-holes in her clothing as she rocked
out to Nickelback. How much the outfit made the sheriff look like
the ghost of hell-bent Heidi White—the human train wreck that
all of Crawford County had witnessed—showed in Raven Furtzig's
drunken surprise.

"Mighty Heidi?"

"What's up, Raven?"

"Shoo doin' here?"

"I came to visit you."

"Fucking must still be Halloween," he said. "First I get my arm
broke by Vince Lombardi . . ."

This was why she thought she recognized the man: he looked
just like the Green Bay Packers coach her dad revered, whose iconic
photograph used to hang on the barbershop wall, the coach reaming
out a player.

"And now here's the Dairy Queen who fuckin' dumped me."

"We went out one time, Raven. My parents nearly disowned me.
You were handsy like I hoped, but in the end, you were much more
of a gentleman than I deserved. And thank you for that."

He was going to fall down on the sidewalk.

"Shall we go next door and sit down inside your shop?"

▲ ▼ ▲ ▼

A few minutes later, Raven was gelatinous in one of the old barbershop chairs, smoking that cigarette he always found behind his ear
and answering her questions. He was still an uncommonly bright
guy, she was noticing with her adult eyes, and he was still a painful
misfit. Who knew, back in the day? But it seemed obvious now that
as the son of would-be hippies—halfway with their commitment,
drifting into both actual and ideological poverty—Raven had always
been too smart and too rebellious for his circumstances, while at the

same time too damaged and addicted to escape them. As sheriff, she saw so many like him in the coulees these days.

"Hoof and the others, what did they want?"

"They offered me five hundred bucks to tattoo this guy who seemed half dead. Five hundred. So I did it. Some religious shit, on his hands and arms and neck."

He waved the cigarette at the wall behind himself, where dozens of tattoo patterns were taped. She wasn't sure what he wanted her to see, but from the cluttered countertop her eye had sorted out a ratty Bible, open.

She stepped behind him, closer. The print was too small to read but she could see it was the Book of Luke and something on the thin page was circled in pen.

She said, "That explains why you have a Bible? You tattooed a verse from Luke?"

Raven dropped a heel to the floor and spun the heavy chair.

"Luke something, yeah. The dude I was tattooing whispered it to me, told me those numbers. Hoof and those other fuckers didn't know shit about the Bible. This dude was barely breathing but he says to me, *No, it should be 18:25, Luke.* I came home looked it up to see what . . ."

He stopped because he recognized himself in the mirror.

"Shit, I didn't drink that much, Mighty Heidi. I'm fuckin' melting. But I only had three beers."

She sped up.

"Missy referred you to these guys?"

"She ain't changed, has she?"

"Did you get their names?"

"Bullshit prison nicknames. Brother this and Brother that. Fuck. I said five hundred, cash only. I finish the job, the Brothers Whatnot won't pay me. They said the cult had to pay me. The leader guy, not them. I said so lemme talk to the leader guy and they said no you can't talk to the leader guy, you have to send him a bill, so I deliver a bill for five hundred bucks like they promised, I hand it through that storage-thing gate in Farmstead and Brother What-haveyou, the mouthy punk with the limp, he drops it into his barrel fire . . ."

Raven slid down in the barber chair, gripping the arms.

"Whoa. Shit. Maybe it's the turkey. You heard of that? Sleepy stuff in the turkey? I should not be this fucking drunk."

"Did you use any of the tattoo patterns on the wall?"

"The nails," he slurred, "the birds, the ice-cream-lollipop Jesus . . ."

She was losing him. The cigarette was at his knuckles and he wasn't noticing. She killed it in an ashtray shaped like a skull.

"Raven. Stay awake."

He jerked.

"They never paid you?"

"Yeah. No. So anyways, I tell Missy the fuckers won't pay me for the work. So she gives me like a half dozen of these stupid cheesecake pictures, some lady taking selfies in the bathroom mirror, and she says I bet they'll pay for these. Tell 'em you got these. If they want 'em back, they can pay up."

He reached up and felt unsuccessfully around his ear.

"I need a cigarette."

"You just had one."

"You know . . . Brother Lombardi mighta roofied me."

"Are you serious?"

"I should not be this fucked up. So I tell 'em but still they won't pay me. So I dropped them photos off today."

"Raven, you dropped them off where?"

"And now—right?—*now* those assholes are gonna pay . . ."

"Raven—"

"Ya know?" he barely managed.

She did not know. But he was out.

▲ ▼ ▲ ▼

Sheriff Kick had traveled three miles back toward Farmstead when Dr. Patel's phone startled her with a jazzy sitar ringtone.

"Heidi," Denise said, "I've got full jackets on your ex-cons, the guys in the House of Shalah."

"Okay."

"They were all at Boscobel. They all got out this summer."

Denise cracked what was probably a Diet Coke. It was now nearing four A.M.

"Bunch of real winners, for sure. Clever nicknames. Prison clever. Brother Milk, right? Fucked over by the Dairy Queen. His profile focuses on the life you took away from him and how you should pay."

Her stomach twisted.

"Who are the other guys?"

"The one they call 'Peep' is Nelson Abernathy Woods, fifty-one years old, six-foot-three, three hundred pounds, unfit-for-duty military discharge, eighteen years for using hidden cameras at swimming pools to make kiddie porn. He's in the sex-offender registry and wanted for parole violation. 'Brother Peep'—get it? My friend tells me his fellow inmates kicked the shit out of him on pretty much a regular schedule, and the guards let it happen. Probably some brain damage. Larynx crushed beyond use. Profiled himself on meet-an-inmate.com as a photographic artist."

The Pilot skidded, wipers flailing. Where was she even going?

"Robert Henderson, twenty-three, is 'Skip' because he got shot in some kind of gang thing and walks with a limp. He did four years on a combination of drug, assault, and arson charges. He was somebody's tough guy, body man for a white gang leader in a slum of Kansas City, talked big, roughed people up, threw a gas cocktail through the window of a liquor store. My friend says he specialized in starting yard fights. Profile highlights attitude. Also wanted for parole."

Oncoming headlights leveled out of a long curve, pierced the swooping snow, and stung the sheriff's eyes.

"And now get this," Denise went on. "Donald Dortmunder, Spooner, is seventy-three years old. He did fifty years on a single murder charge that he bargained down from multiple life sentences in exchange for saying where bodies could be found. Not that he had put them there, right? Stone-cold killer, according to my source. Everybody knew it and was afraid of him. At one point, speaking of yard fights, a guy bit off half his ear. As payback he tried to behead the guy with a spoon. Believe it or not, Brother Spooner's profile highlights his astrological sign. I see here he's a Leo—"

The sheriff hit the brakes. The heavy Pilot began to fishtail just as the headlights seared past. As the fishtail jolted into a spin, a second set of headlights squared the curve and blinded her. As Denise talked on as if from a dream . . . *half his ear . . . behead the guy with a spoon . . . Leo* . . . lights whirled, a horn blared, and everything the sheriff did to stop the spin had the opposite effect. She saw a passenger's face. Then a mailbox and the ditch. Then the Pilot was still.

"Denise, where is Mom?"

"She's here, Heidi. She's on the back porch talking on her phone."

"Get her inside."

"I will."

▲ ▼ ▲ ▼

Raven Furtzig's body hadn't left the barber's chair where Donald "Spooner" Dortmunder had knifed him.

Retching, the sheriff held herself upright by the doorframe. These were the same gruesome wounds she had seen on Win Carpenter— on Darwin Fuss—the murdered undertaker.

Most of Raven's blood had spread across the floor from a slit across his throat. A second gratuitous slash across his gut had cut him so deeply that the sheriff could see turkey meat.

CHAPTER 34

"Honeybunch—"

"I've been calling you."

"Busy man, princess."

"And calling you."

"You didn't hear me? Busy man."

"You said—"

"I said on Black Friday I'd take you shopping at the sales. It's time."

"It's four A.M. Everybody's sleeping."

"It's four-eighteen, to be exact. Rise and shine, sugarplum. Pick you up in one hour sharp."

"Do you even know where I am?"

"Put your hair in that braid I like. Be out front in an hour."

CHAPTER 35

With Fernanda back inside the House of Shalah, Hashimoto had sped away out U-Stash-It Road, slowed to a safe speed outside Farmstead, then followed his assumptions and his GPS twenty-some miles south. Now he parked his rented Ranger pickup axle-deep in a drift across the quarter mile of field behind the house he had seen in the photograph. The snow had let up. He dismounted into a cold wind that clattered loose tin on one of the silos.

Before him, the landscape appeared quicksilver, without gravity. The tall brown corn in the photograph had been cut, leaving black dots of stubble across open white like disappearing Morse code. He opened his gear case, aimed his night scope across the empty acres. The drab little house gave away nothing. Of ogres he expected no less.

He shed his puffy coat and, working quickly, he strapped on an under-arm holster with a 9mm Glock and a fanny pack with the night scope and his thermal camera.

With the coat back on, he progressed slowly under the bulk,

about two hundred yards across the field until solid ground disappeared without warning. His right leg sank to the hip, his foot hit mush, and icy water filled his shoe. When he yanked up, the shoe came off. Bending and digging to retrieve the shoe, he took on snow in one ear. To return the shoe to the foot, he had to retreat, sit buried to his armpits, and fold himself across his stomach. Regrouped, exhaling plumes of steam, he went on.

Soon, another challenge: within a hundred or so feet, with his eyes fixed upon the house, he intersected barbed wire, tore his coat, made his palms bleed, then dripped blood dots along the fence until it cornered and went to the road.

From the deep ditch, Hashimoto aimed his thermal camera. Uniform gray-yellow disappointed him with the information that the house retained only abstract heat, barely warmer than outside, just one pinprick of orange, no working furnace, no boiler flame making hot water, no living human bodies. But someone had recently come and gone across the backyard. Boot tracks were sharply cut. Snow was swept away from cellar doors.

With his 9mm butt, Hashimoto broke the window in the kitchen door. He reached in and turned the lock, stepped in and switched on his headlamp.

He worked by old instincts now. Room by room he cleared the tiny house. One unhygienic female lived here. Bad diet. Multiple addictions. Male visitors. Some weird tool kit on the kitchen table. Blue ice in the living room. The orange thermal dot was in the woman's bedroom: a heated tank, one hungry betta fish frantic at the glass.

Using a tissue to pick up the shaker, Hashimoto tipped in food grains.

The fish calmed and rose in graceful pulses, nipping.

Roy had been lured here, he felt sure.

He returned to the kitchen and began conducting a deeper pass. This time inside a waffle box in the freezer he found a rusty

.22 pistol with no ammo, two hundred dollars, and a tiny self-sealing plastic bag containing white powder. Standard lowbrow criminal shit.

On this second pass he took more interest in the bathroom, where an act of first aid had left behind bloody washcloths. He sniffed. Not old. Recent. Illicit painkilling had left behind an empty Oxy scrip for *Roscoe*, no last name. His experience told him Roscoe was likely some poor animal missing his meds. The bathtub retained weird stains and a faint chemical smell. Discarded clothing had been trampled on the floor. A gray-blue faintly pin-striped pattern looked familiar. Hashimoto shook open a shirt.

On one breast patch: MCKORMICK'S FARM SUPPLY.

On the other breast patch: ROY.

Hashimoto shivered. Yes, Roy had been here. Now he was probably looking for a body.

From the kitchen he descended broken stairs into a damp, low-beamed cellar.

No.

Touching the wet stone wall, he climbed back up to the kitchen. The hall closet was too shallow, but he inspected briefly: CDs, gutted purses, old cell phones, shitty wristwatches, obsolete radar detectors, an archaeological record of crap stolen from unlocked vehicles going back at least a decade.

Back in the woman's bedroom, where the betta finned for more, he looked in her closet and lifted her mattress.

No and no.

In the master bedroom he waded through garbage. This was rural Wisconsin, no trash pickup, haul it yourself to the dump and pay precious cash, so this woman had used the bedroom for a landfill, covering every inch of floor and even heaping spilled sacks shoulder-deep upon the bed.

He cleared the mattress, lifted it, and recoiled.

Naked Roy, his eyes bulging wide open, stared up from the gutted box spring.

Hashimoto's first jolt of thought—*He looks so lifelike!*—was the kind of thing mourners blurted at funerals.

Then his gorge rose and he turned away, closing his eyes and seeing Roy anyway on the backs of his lids.

He looks so lifelike . . .

Yet Roy had disappeared a month ago. When had he died? How? Why did his body look so . . . what? . . . so not shriveled, not bloated? . . . occupied by a normal volume of fluids?

Hashimoto made himself turn back.

This time Roy's skin looked waxen, almost slick, and he saw it was expertly made-up. Roy's head had been shaved. His jutting, deep-coffee eyes looked hard as marbles. Strangled? Likely. Makeup pasted his neck.

Hashimoto leaned closer, sniffed, and jerked back.

Roy had been embalmed.

And decorated with the prophet-father's tattoos.

On his hands, the square nails dripping blood.

Across one forearm, the dove-with-olive branch flying.

Upon the other forearm, the hands folded in prayer.

On Roy's shoulder and neck, the face of Jesus in rays of light, with the Bible citation 18:25.

But wait. Hashimoto had sent the laptop photos to his phone. In the photograph it was 28:25—not 18:25—that was tattooed on the prophet-father's neck.

According to Fernanda, Proverbs 28:25 read, *He who trusts in the Lord shall prosper.*

So what was 18:25?

Hashimoto aimed his phone and took pictures—then froze as headlights struck the house and vehicle doors slammed.

He killed his headlamp. Listened. Men talking.

He unfroze.

He worked the mattress back over Roy.

He flung a few sacks of garbage on top.

Then he risked a trip to the living room window, where he fingered back a blanket to see out. From the rear doors of a rusted black van, two men lifted out a shirtless third man's stiff and twisted body. As they carried him toward the house, the smaller man limped like a broken rooster. The larger one, clumsy and soft-looking, squeezed out words that popped like bubbles against the thin glass.

"Brother Spooner. Said to. Dump him in the. River."

He fumbled the man's legs and chased them through the snow as the little guy kept churning toward the house, dragging the body by the wrists. He had a barky, street-trash voice, gang-lite.

"Man, fuck Brother Spooner. This motherfucker can die here just as good. We all paid and gone before them bitches drink the Kool-Aid."

They were at the door and Hashimoto had to go. Hurrying through the kitchen, he heard a thud and a groan. Floundering into the backyard, he heard, "The fuck, yo. I piled shit all up on this fucking bed." Light sprayed through the kitchen window. He hurried back into the shadow of the house.

"The fuck. This floor wet. This window bust, bro."

"Let's. Go."

"Where the pictures?"

"She talks. Her husband. Cuts her tits. Off. So she. Won't. Let's go."

From the corner of the house, Hashimoto watched the two men emerge lugging Roy's body, which they loaded through the rear doors of the van. The smaller one, the limper, got behind the wheel and began to turn the van around. Pressed against the house, Hashimoto watched its headlights strike the tracks in snow across the backyard, now including his. The van stopped. A door slammed. The driver said hotly, "Motherfucker!"

Hashimoto heard a magazine snap into place, knew the meaning of the sound. The M16 he gave Roy now was walking . . . and coming for him. He drew the Glock. Using the angle of the house for cover, he bolted at old-man speed until he hit that barbed-wire fence again. After he belly-flopped over the top wire and was searching for the Glock in the snow, they caught him in the van's headlights.

"Motherfucker! Hey!"

The first burst missed Hashimoto. Plunging away, zigging and zagging at a wretchedly slow speed, he feared the bitter justice of the lethal weapon that he had shown Roy how to put together. A brilliant end to a stupidly muddled career. What could go wrong?

The M16 rattled the air behind him. Then stopped. When he looked back, the van was moving.

▲ ▼ ▲ ▼

Across the field, Hashimoto pressed the gas, but the Ranger's buried tires only spun, hurling bits of snow like sparks through the red fan of taillights.

He pressed harder.

The truck moved vaguely side to side as it sank deeper.

He fumbled with his phone, opened his text stream with Fernanda. No time to think of what to say.

Roy disguised. Prophet not dead.

He mashed the gas.

The tires spun shrilly.

You need to

Filling his mirrors, here came the headlights of the van.

CHAPTER 36

Roy disguised. Prophet not dead. You need to.

Fernanda jolted out of half sleep to read Duke Hashimoto's text. She replied, *?*

Then, *???*

He didn't answer.

She eased up the Unit 14 door and stepped into icy predawn, silent except that her across-aisle neighbor, lonely Brother Rasheed, snored though the steel walls of his tiny unit. She rolled the storage door closed. She could see from the lighted bedroom window of the mobile coach that the prophet-father was awake. The barrel fire was out. Brother Skip's van was gone. Brother Spooner's rusty gold sedan idled outside the mobile coach, puttering exhaust. The golf course cameras winked from their tall poles. The watcher's truck had been snowed over. But all this stillness didn't match the message.

Roy disguised? Prophet not dead?

She tried Hashimoto again.

What do you mean?

She gripped herself against the chill and waited without answer. Suddenly she wanted one of the seventeen rifles from the arsenal at the back of the new chapel. Heading that way, she changed her mind. In this exact rare moment, when no one watched, she should hurry back, wake Hosanna now-now-now, and escape with the babies out the tunnel.

But first she should take a rifle.

She started back for the arsenal.

Except—her brother and sister Carpenters—abandon them?— what did Hashimoto mean that the prophet was not dead?—she needed to what?

She was mired halfway across the grounds to the new chapel, shivering and trying to pray—*Dear Lord, I seek Your hand in protection*—when Brother Skip's van turned from the highway and sped inbound on U-Stash-It Road.

This froze her, and she watched.

The van stopped.

Brother Peep shambled out for the gate.

Brother Skip gunned through and braked beside the mobile coach.

Brother Peep closed the gate and followed and pounded on the door of the coach. Brother Spooner opened up. He stepped down to make room in the doorway for Mother Ruth dressed in jeans and moccasins, her braid coiled beneath a knotted scarf, an outfit Fernanda had last seen when the Carpenters caravanned from Colorado to Wisconsin.

Whatever words Mother Ruth and Brother Spooner exchanged with Brother Peep were brief, and Brother Peep conveyed a message to Brother Skip behind the wheel of the van. Mother Ruth handed Brother Spooner something in a plastic sack before she closed herself back inside the coach. Brother Spooner barked at Brother Peep, who once more rolled open the gate. Brother Spooner folded back into his old car and slammed it in reverse onto U-Stash-It Road. As the gate closed, he sped away. Then Brother Skip's van scorched Fernanda with its headlights and eased toward her.

She backed into half shadow with her thumbs moving.

???

call me

What was all the sudden action? What did Hashimoto mean? Roy disguised, prophet not dead? What did she need she do?

I'm calling you

When the van reached the new chapel, Brother Skip Y-turned to back it against the building. Catching up, Brother Peep heaved the side door open. Just as Fernanda touched CALL to reach Hashimoto, Brother Skip joined Brother Peep to drag out a man with tape-bound wrists and hurl him onto the slush. Brother Skip stood over him.

"Believe this shit? Same fucking cop."

In Fernanda's ear her call began to ring. The "same fucking cop" kneed upright on the slush. When he turned his bloodied face, she saw they had caught Hashimoto.

Before she could kill the call, she heard a ringtone.

Brother Skip kicked Hashimoto in the chest, toppling him back onto his face.

Then, showing Fernanda the ringing phone—Hashimoto's phone, her calling—Brother Skip pinched his thing and limped with an ugly gleam of triumph toward her.

CHAPTER 37

When she reached the Bad Axe County Public Service Building, Sheriff Kick left the borrowed Pilot in the front loop beside the flagpoles and blasted inside through the main doors.

"Call in Chief Deputy Stonebreaker."

From his dispatch desk Rhino regarded her with hesitation, watching as she fought the shakes in her dead girl's cigarette-burn denim ensemble and Nickelback T-shirt. Her deputy had not known her in her Missy-and-Hoof days. But Rhino was seeing a return of that keen desperation now whether he knew it or not.

"You're sure you want to do that?"

"Call her in."

She moved down the bright corridor and tried to focus on the items on the squad room table. As she had directed him hours ago, Rhino had laid out two property lists and the contents of two evidence boxes. She only needed ten seconds to see that the list from the 2018 drug bust did not match the contents of the property box. A green North Face backpack, along with its incriminating drug-related contents, was missing from the 2018 box. Recovery of that backpack was now documented on the Win Carpenter/Darwin Fuss property list, and the backpack itself was now in the box for the current homicide case.

She looked up. Rhino had followed her with a worried frown. But with this obvious incongruity now laid out, Stonebreaker could no longer claim that she had found the backpack at Lake Susan. She would have to admit that she had planted evidence to obstruct a homicide investigation. They would go from there to for whom and why and what was going down inside the House of Shalah. With a little force and a little luck, the sheriff's case could start to break. But her dispatcher was raking nervous fingers through his heavy beard.

"What's the problem, Rhino?"

"She's added auto theft, a Ford Focus from Ernhardt Pig Feeder. She made me put you on a five-county BOLO. She's got the DA agreeing to ask for a warrant to search your office and your house. You know the judge. He'll bite. Sheriff, she's really gunning for you."

"Tell her she nailed me. I'm here. I turned myself in."

He nodded, still uncomfortable.

"Ten-four. So, um, then . . ."

"Something else?"

"Crawford County want to talk to you about a homicide at a tattoo parlor in Soldiers Grove."

"I'm right here. Call in Deputy Luck too."

"She's off. I think she—"

"Tell her to bring in the photos she found in the purse that Melissa Grooms left on the bridge."

▲ ▼ ▲ ▼

As the sheriff finished a round of questions from a Crawford County deputy, she hung up her desk phone feeling she might weep from exhaustion. She could now pull warrants to raid the House of Shalah, which harbored parole violators and murder suspects. But after seeing Raven Furtzig's brutalized body in the barber chair, she sensed dangers mounting faster than the process could handle. She had to make Stonebreaker talk. She had to understand the bigger game at play and stop it before more damage was done.

Sparking through the sheriff's fatigue as she headed for the locker room was hot rage at her Police and Fire Commission for appointing a woman who would pose in her underwear for peeping Toms and killers, letting men like that get their hooks into the Bad Axe County Sheriff's Department. And underneath her rage churned dismay, disgust, and pity: the deputy had degraded herself for inmates at the same facility where her husband had been fired for brutality. In a facility where a man tried to behead a fellow inmate with a spoon, where brutality was the very air they all breathed, the violence of Dennis Stonebreaker had stood out as requiring termination. And into this mix, the brutalizer's wife, a sheriff's deputy, sends jerk-off pictures? What kind of sick-on-sick was that?

That was prison, she reminded herself.

Where you might be headed.

Shakily she dressed in a stiff clean uniform. As she strapped on her duty belt with its violent tools, she felt the depression that often flooded in when certain crimes began to clarify, when people's dirty secrets and twisted motives came to light. The mystery, the chase—these were the easy parts. Getting toward the core of a case so often meant a walk through someone else's sad little hell. This time, her own hell too.

Prison.

You shot a man in the back.

At the locker-room mirror she splashed cold water on her stunned, exhausted face.

Rhino tapped on the door.

"Out in a minute."

"Deputy Luck brought some photographs for you. I put them in the interview room. Stonebreaker is just pulling in."

▲ ▼ ▲ ▼

In the corridor, she crossed paths with Deputy Luck.

"We're going to talk."

"I know."

Then she waited in the tiny cell of the interview room.

Later, she told herself, trying to breathe evenly.

Your own stuff later.

Stonebreaker entered on an audible gust of Thunder Queen arrogance and puffed herself up further when she saw the uniformed sheriff in the good-guy chair, the bad-guy chair reserved for her, a neat stack of her bra-and-panty pictures facedown on the table like playing cards. On the back of the top photo was written *For L'Antonio*.

"It's not illegal," Stonebreaker asserted, raising her soft square chin.

"Sit down."

"There's nothing wrong with it."

"There are so many things wrong with it I don't know where to start. Sit down."

She remained puffed up and standing.

"Wrong? How about shooting someone and not reporting it? How about lying that you don't know Melissa Grooms? And stealing a car?"

To compound the surreality of the moment, Stonebreaker reached for her cuffs.

"I'm the officer in charge here," she said. Then she launched: "You have the right to remain silent—"

"Stonebreaker, sit down."

"Oh, hell, no." She pointed at the photos. "That's free speech. I have every right."

Good start, the sheriff thought. *She admits it's her.* "These photos are not the law you broke. We'll get to that. But they do represent all kinds of unfit for duty."

"Unfit for duty?"

"You're bound by a character clause."

"Says a drug addict," Stonebreaker said, a little sniff-and-smile showing she was ready to preen whatever treasures she had assembled of Sheriff Kick's backstory.

She said, "People know about you, Sheriff. The PFC knows."

"I told them when they hired me. I told them everything. They may not exactly like me, but they know who I am."

That slowed Stonebreaker.

"Well," she said less certainly, "they talk about why you can't solve the Win Carpenter murder. They think you're protecting someone you used to run with from your drug days."

It was a perfect lead-in.

"If you want to talk about Win Carpenter," the sheriff said, "we have his name now, his background. The facts are bad luck for you and whoever *you're* running with."

The sheriff pressed the intercom. "Rhino, get the evidence lists and the boxes."

She touched the stack of photographs. "And speaking of the PFC, what do you think they'll talk about when they see these?"

"I'll sue this county to hell."

"What for?"

Stonebreaker twisted toward the door as Rhino filled it with his three hundred pounds, a cardboard box beneath each arm.

"Those are the lists and evidence boxes of two cases that seem to have gotten mixed up, along with the custody logs showing exactly who mixed them up and when. That backpack disappeared from its proper box on Halloween. It was checked back into the Win Carpenter box the day after. In a homicide case, obstruction at that level is a felony."

The deputy slumped glowering into the interview chair. The sheriff turned the top photo over: Stonebreaker's eyes were above the frame, but her tongue was out, and one hand crushed a heavy white breast inside its heavy black bra cup.

"So let's get at why you obstructed the investigation."

"I never said those picture were me."

"But you did."

"That's not me."

Desperation had leaked into her voice. After all, she was the wife of Dennis Stonebreaker, who had once run her over with his truck in public, who had been terminated for brutality . . . *in a prison.*

"And there's nothing wrong with doing that, whoever that woman is. You can't prove anything."

"Too late, Deputy. We've been asking for prison email records, and now I'm sure we'll get them Monday morning. So walk me through planting the backpack and then pointing fingers at Alexis Schmidt and me, every step. Then we'll work backward until we learn why you made yourself late-night material for convicts, and how they got their hooks into you, and what they're doing inside the House of Shalah. While we're at it, we'll consider whether your husband knows—"

"It's not me."

"A husband would recognize his wife like this, don't you think? Mine would. So we'll consider whether big-bad Dennis knows that while he's whipping up this Kill the Cult stuff, his wife is slutting for the enemy. After that, you're going to tell me what's supposed to happen next inside that fence—what's going on with the Carpenters—so that I can safely stop it."

Stonebreaker crossed her thick arms. "I want a lawyer."

"What you want is a therapist. Just talk."

"Not without a lawyer."

"I can have Rhino call Dennis. If I remember right, he considers himself a lawyer."

Her face froze. Then she scowled. "Don't call Dennis."

"Why not?"

Rhino still filled the doorway with the boxes. Stonebreaker looked into her lap.

"Okay, I planted the backpack," she muttered. "Please do not call Dennis. I planted the backpack. Nothing more without a lawyer."

The sheriff flipped another photo to face Stonebreaker, flinching as she saw it for the first time herself. In this print, her deputy faced away from the mirror, bent forward, and aimed the phone back between her parted legs. Her face was in shadow. Her hair hung to the floor. Her panties, black, said PINK.

"I'm giving you a chance to take this in another direction," the sheriff said, her head now aching dully. "There are ex-cons mixed up with innocent people inside that fence. You lawyer up while shit goes south for those people, you'll end up with every charge I can throw at you. Dennis will know everything. So just talk. Help yourself. Help the real Carpenters, not the criminals."

"Help them?"

Stonebreaker suddenly had her sass back.

"Help a bunch of leeches and losers? They're going to take us over."

"Really?"

"Roadkill eaters. Child fuckers. They shoot horses."

"Really? People like that are going to take us over? Then who are we?"

The sheriff let the question land. Stonebreaker tried to land the answer.

"Who are we? We're a bunch of idiots who elected a snowflake for sheriff."

"Ah."

She turned over another photo.

"This takes a lot of practice, I'd say. I'm terrible at selfies. But you've really got it down. Plus you seem to know exactly where the prison censor draws the line."

"Fuck you," she muttered.

"Deputy, the last time anyone called me Sheriff Snowflake, it turned out some homegrown neo-Nazis tried to bomb our holiday parade in defense of white heritage. It's funny how Dennis never formed a group to stop *them*. But anyway, how'd that go? Remember? They're all dead or in prison. That's what happened the last time someone tried to take over the Bad Axe."

Bracing for disgust, the sheriff spread out the rest of the cheese-cake photographs that Missy had meant to give her, counting ten and remembering that Raven Furtzig, angry over getting stiffed for tattoo work, had given six more to someone. *Now those assholes are gonna pay* . . . But instead of disgust as she saw the photos, the feeling that arrived was more like pity, with a twinge of solidarity for a woman who felt so awful about herself that she would do this. The sheriff's head pounded, and she sighed.

"Deputy, right now I'm giving you a chance to talk your way out of whatever this is, to be someone who didn't mean for all of this bad shit to happen. I'm giving you a chance to be a decent person who made a mistake."

Stonebreaker stared silently at her posing self.

"You could maybe be a woman who is going through some tough times," the sheriff suggested. "You could be a woman who is struggling with some issues, dealing with an injury to her self-esteem, a woman who made some unwise but understandable choices and now she needs to get some help."

Listening, Stonebreaker scowled. Then one by one the sheriff flipped the photos facedown. All the photos were inscribed *For L'Antonio*. She saw now that all the *o*'s were hearts.

The sheriff said, "It seems this was all about one special guy. Am I right? But I guess that special guy traded them for cigarettes?

And someone else collected them? It seems like you didn't mean to become prison currency. Right? Everybody's jack book? You didn't mean to get yourself extorted into a crime and right out of your career. Am I right? These were just for L'Antonio? You're not as bad as this makes you look?"

"Fuck you," she muttered again.

"So you *are* as bad as this looks?"

"Go fuck yourself."

"Tell me why your convict friends killed Win Carpenter."

"I have no idea."

"What are they planning?"

"I don't know."

"What about your husband? What is he planning?"

"I don't know."

"Then what was last night's meeting about?"

"What meeting?"

"The back room at the Ease Inn."

"I wasn't at any meeting."

"Rhino GPS'd your cruiser. Nine P.M. The gas station has cameras. Dennis's dually was there. The bartender told Rhino the banquet room was full of Kill the Cult folks. You were there."

"I changed my mind and left."

"Something's building here, Deputy. Plans on both sides. Be one of the good guys. Tell me."

"You know Melissa Grooms," she countered, trying to regain the swagger she had brought to the interview. "You shot your old fuck-buddy Roman Vanderhoof in the back. Don't tell me about good guys. It'll all come out. You'll pay the price. Your husband—"

Her face stiffened, then crumpled.

"Sheriff," she said weakly, "we're both in trouble here. Maybe we could make a deal?"

The sheriff collected the photos and stood.

"Your weapon, keys, and badge right here on the table, please. Rhino, lock the stuff up while I walk her to the locker room. She'll leave her uniform in there, the vest, the belt, anything that's Bad Axe County property. Then she'll clear personal property out of her cruiser. Do not leave Bad Axe County, Stonebreaker. You'll be charged and notified of arraignment. Rhino, call Dennis. His wife is going to need a ride home."

"Don't call Dennis!" she blurted.

Her face had seized in anguish.

"Please don't call Dennis!"

CHAPTER 38

Duke Hashimoto lay bound in muddy slush, lost in time and space and heart, in beginnings and ends.

Nearly three decades ago, his ATF colleague Robert Rodriguez had bolted from the Mount Carmel compound, terrified that one of David Koresh's followers would shoot him in the back. Special Agent Rodriguez had big news. He was desperate to deliver it in time.

For weeks, Rodriguez had been posing as an acolyte to Koresh, gathering information as prelude to an ATF raid scheduled to begin within hours. But the Davidians had been tipped off. Instead of coming as a surprise, the raid would signal the launch of Armageddon, and the well-armed and well-trained Davidians were unafraid to die.

Safely a half mile away, Rodriguez had begged his superiors to call off the operation.

Ignored, he had broken down and sobbed.

Duke Hashimoto had watched this drama without knowing yet how it would shape his life. He had been with fellow agents, loading weapons. Commanded to proceed, they all piled into cattle trucks with tarps pulled over. The first rounds fired at Mount Carmel came from ATF agents shooting all the dogs. Then two horses.

In just minutes, four ATF agents and at least seven Davidians were dead. Hashimoto helped lay a slain friend on the tailgate of a truck. Six hours later, EMS assisted the injured and dying Davidians.

By nightfall, the federal government was spinning events and bent on revenge. In the coming days, the FBI and the U.S. military took over what media called "the siege." Rumors, omissions, distortions . . . Clinton and Reno on roller skates . . . Sherman tanks crushing outbuildings and vehicles . . . speakers blasting dying rabbits and pornographic soundtracks . . . a then-unknown U.S. Army veteran named Timothy McVeigh selling anti-ATF T-shirts and ball caps . . . sniper teams, elite hostage rescue units, helicopter gunships . . . until two months later, on the gusty morning of April 19, those Sherman tanks again, armed with CS gas bombs—

A squeal. The House of Shalah gate. Hashimoto squirmed around to once more witness a beginning.

A blocky man in a dated brown suit and checked Trilby hat climbed back behind the wheel of a rusty gold sedan, pulled the car through, and got out again to close the gate. But before he could return to the car, a rough old woman bailed from the passenger seat—skinny, long gray braid—and confronted him, squawking and waving her arms. The man in the hat did not hesitate. He struck her one blunt blow in the face and tossed her over his shoulder.

As this happened, the coach door opened on Ruth Pearl dressed in jeans and a scarf as if she meant to clean house. Hashimoto sensed scramble mode as the prophet's wife exchanged words with the man in the hat before he recovered a sack from his car and carried the old woman toward Hashimoto outside the new chapel. Hashimoto watched Mother Ruth close herself inside the coach, then quickly reappear with a small black cortege flag that she stuck into a bracket beside the door before she closed it.

As the man in the hat splattered past Hashimoto, the woman on his shoulder snarled, "My son knows where I am!"

The man took her inside—must have dumped her—then came back after Hashimoto.

"Get up, cop. You came back one too many times. You're done fucking with us."

He jerked Hashimoto to his feet and shoved him staggering in the direction of the old chapel.

"You're going to kill me?"

"Don't need to. You just joined a suicide cult."

Hashimoto got his balance.

"You ever heard of a Jizo? They're stone. They don't die."

"You'll die."

"They protect children."

It felt like helpless blather. The man shoved him forward. The coach door snapped shut. Hashimoto had missed something. On the top step beneath the limp black flag someone had set out an insulated jug, white with a red lid.

Richard Rodriguez had wept. Hashimoto gritted his teeth.

"You think you can make me drink the Kool-Aid?"

"I'm gonna find a funnel."

CHAPTER 39

Mikayla Stonebreaker looked clumsy and forlorn stripped of her uniform, gripping too much stuff to shut the trunk of her cruiser smoothly. She dropped a boot, lost her thermos when she bent to pick the boot up.

The parking lot was cleanly plowed and salted, slickly black, and the thermos rolled away. Stonebreaker followed it, then changed her mind and went back to the cruiser to shut the trunk and unload her stuff on top of it. But with her hands full she couldn't generate enough force to make the trunk latch. The lid kept popping up.

She turned around, backed up, raised one big hip, and sat. The trunk latched beneath her. She rested there, her mouth moving vaguely while she stared at the runaway thermos.

The sheriff touched Line 1.

"Rhino, can you get Stonebreaker a tote?"

"I'm already heading out there."

Rhino retrieved Stonebreaker's thermos and patiently helped her load a blue plastic tote. Her thermos. Her boots. Spare clothes.

Phone charger. Cosmetic pouch. Kotex box. Photographs of a different kind, of her nieces and nephews, and of her former junior high gym classes, if the sheriff remembered correctly. When they were finished, Rhino gestured: Didn't she want to wait inside?

Stay warm?

No?

Moments later, Rhino hustled past the sheriff's doorway. "Go fuck myself, she told me." His non-emergency line was ringing. "And same to you, boss."

Now into the lot roared Dennis Stonebreaker in his six-wheeled dually with its stack pipes spewing black smoke. The sheriff tensed in her chair. Then, deciding she couldn't bear to watch the scene, she spun the chair and saw her blinking phone console. The scrolling banner said the caller was *Blackhawk Pines Golf Course*.

She picked up.

"This is Sheriff Kick."

She winced at the raised voices leaking through the glass behind her. The Stonebreaker marriage was none of her business now. She tried to shut it out.

"This is Roger at the golf course," she heard through the phone. "I'm in here on a security alert, and on my screens I see all these ATVs and snowcats gathering on the sixth fairway. Must be ten or fifteen of them . . ."

From the dispatch room, Rhino bellowed, "Shit! Sheriff!"

"Roger, hang on—"

". . . and more coming. Then I notice they have guns. I swear to God, it looks like someone lined them up to attack—"

As Rhino stormed past, a blast spun her back to the window. For a moment her view was eclipsed by a volunteer charging out from the fire department garage. Then a second blast—and she saw.

Out in the parking lot, Mikayla Stonebreaker sprawled on her back amid her strewn items, blood spreading beneath her, Rhino and EMT Greg Jokurst rushing to her side as Dennis Stonebreaker stood over her, red-faced and gasping like a fish, his shotgun still in shooting position.

As the sheriff bolted toward the exit with her service weapon drawn, she knew what Raven Furtzig had done with the remaining photographs when the ex-convict Carpenters wouldn't pay for his tattoo work. By the time she reached the parking lot, Dennis Stonebreaker had backed off Rhino and Jokurst. He stood over his shotgunned wife, dealing out photos like playing cards. As the last one left his hand, he looked the sheriff squarely in the eyes with the glazed rage of a man letting go of his future.

"Bring it on, Sheriff."

"Drop the gun. On your knees, hands on your head."

"You can't have it that easy. I made my people ready. We're gonna clean house, and those jail-ponies are gonna pay."

He panted through his nose, backing away. Raven Furtzig had known whose wife the convicts had been using. But hadn't understood what the photos would trigger. Stonebreaker tossed his shotgun through his open door and climbed aboard, bulled his truck around, and gunned it toward the road. A sign filled his rear window: KILL THE CULT.

"No!" she barked at Rhino, who was lumbering toward a cruiser to pursue.

"No," she said. "We're not going to chase a man with nothing left to lose. We're going to protect the rest of us that do."

▲ ▼ ▲ ▼

Rhino waited with his message until Greg Jokurst had told the sheriff that Mikayla Stonebreaker's heart had stopped and there was nothing he could do to save her.

"Just before the gunshot," Rhino said, "your husband called."

When Harley answered, his voice was too high.

"Leo picked her up!"

"What?"

"Her friend Leo. Picked Mom up. We were all sleeping here at Denise's. I heard voices. She was outside talking and then she got inside this old gold car. Denise said that's the guy she thinks is Leo. Ten minutes later she texts, *help me*. Then she doesn't answer."

"Bring me your phone, Harley. We put an app on it."

"Heidi, the app shows he took Mom inside the cult."

BLACK
FRIDAY

Donald Gary Dortmunder #547061

Wisconsin Secure Program Facility

A blessed day in the Lord's love to you madam. My name is Donald G. Dortmunder.

You may have already looked at my birthdate, but I assure you that love is infinite and age is just a number. The most important thing to see in my numbers is that I am a Leo, meaning my key strengths are generosity and big-heartedness, kindness, and natural leadership.

In the spirit of honesty I will tell you that I am doing time for protecting many fine ladies just like you from the evils of this world, because, as you know, Leo is the lion.

I treat all ladies as angels who deserve heaven and I have been told many times that I am the ultimate gentleman. But you decide.

Race: White

Date of Birth: 7/27/1947

Height: 5' 7"

Earliest Release Date: March 2005

Maximum Release Date: March 2020

Would you like letters from both sexes? Women only

Education: College degree

Occupation before prison: Accounting, finance, deacon

Activities in prison: Sudoku, prayer

Can you receive and send emails? Yes, also calls/texts/letter/photos

meet-an-inmate.com posted 6/1/2014

last jpay.com reply record 10/13/2019

After he picks her up, Belle Kick's Gentleman Leo turns in the wrong direction for any Black Friday sales, barks at her to shut up about it, then drives her through the cult gate, punches her in the face, and hauls her off like a cave woman . . .

Now she comes halfway back to her senses on a dirt floor as over her head he shakes out the contents of a plastic sack.

"Put that shit on."

From under gauzy blue fabrics, Belle clears her throat of the blood trickling down it and informs him, "My son knows where I am."

"The flag is out," she hears him tell someone else. "They know. They're going to practice their funeral songs and head over here for the Kool-Aid."

"My son is married to the sheriff."

"Put it on."

"They can tell where I'm at by my phone."

The moment Belle says this, she understands one thing from

Blackout Wednesday. While she was blacked out and losing her bra, her Gentleman Leo was linking his phone to her phone, using the whatever-app-thing Harley and Heidi use to keep tabs on her. He had known exactly where she was every moment since then. Her phone . . . no, she doesn't have her phone anymore.

Belle crawls to the nearest wall. Sitting up against it, she looks at what she is supposed to put on. Some kind of gown-like dress and a veil.

Then she looks at who's there. It's Leo and two others. One limps, likes to grab his dick and talk street. The other is pink and fat with crushed features, buried eyes, and a tiny voice she can barely hear. They talk with Gentleman Leo, who faces them with the kind of military-style gun that people use these days to shoot up schools and shopping malls.

"Who wants to put her down?"

Her Gentleman Leo asks this. For a moment Belle is stuck staring at his half ear. A donkey bit the rest off when he was ten, he has told her, while he was at a church camp.

Expertly now, he punches in the curved metal case that feeds bullets into the gun. Belle looks to see where inside the cult she is. It's a pole barn, new, nothing hardly in it except about twenty feet to her right is a homemade double-wide pine box up on several sawhorses. On the tips of the sawhorses burn smutty votive candles. Slowly she stands up to see inside.

"Fuck you goin', bitch?"

That one, from the street, limping at her with his fist on his weenie.

"Nowhere."

"Amen, bitch. You ain't goin' nowhere."

"A lady's gotta stand to put a dress on."

She keeps drifting toward the box. Inside is a dead guy.

The fat one squeals, "Then put! It on!"

Belle threads her legs through the gown, which fits well. While the three men watch her shift around and smooth the gown out and try to reach the zipper in the back, she reminds herself that men have tried to kill her before.

And look who's still here.

"Who wants to put her down?" her Gentleman Leo asks again. "Brother Skip?"

"Oh, hell, no. Ain't Skip do some old stray cat. Any bitch Skip do gotta be fine."

He says this and looks at the fat one.

"Do your thing, Peep. Surf and turf, bro. Stuff it and snuff it."

The one called Peep looks offended and squeals some objection and Gentleman Leo laughs dryly.

"Fucking jitterbugs."

He swings that military gun around his back. Out of an inner suit coat pocket he takes a sheath. Out of the sheath he draws a short knife curved like a claw. When he twirls the knife by its finger-loop grip and saunters toward Belle, this upsets Skip.

"Brother! We ain't make our coin bitch all bloody!"

Then Peep, something wrong with his voice.

"We won't! Get paid! No blood!"

Leo just grins and advances. When he is just a few steps away, Belle hears another groan and thinks it comes from the box. She glances at the dead man's stiff lips, holds the glance until she hears the groan again. Not him. The groaning comes from behind a door behind the box, she thinks. Or it comes from the wide hole in the dirt floor, dug between the door and the box.

"Need a zip, sugarplum?"

Gentleman Leo stops the spin of his knife inches from her chest. The grip fits neatly in his fist, the silver claw curving out like it grew there.

"Turn around."

Belle does, and as Leo works the zipper on the gown, she hears a louder, higher-pitched *unnh!* and decides what she is hearing is a woman, from behind the door, gagged.

"Turn back around."

The way Skip and Peep protest about blood, Belle figures she will now pivot through Leo's blade and her throat will open.

But her chin passes just over the blade. His other hand is out, palm open.

"Take these."

She leans back and squints: four green tablets.

"Roofies?"

"Take 'em."

"That explains how you got into my pants and into my phone. Now you'll overdose me?"

"Take 'em, swallow 'em."

As if, Belle tells him silently. *As if I've never been to rehab.*

She pops the tablets and with a nifty move tongues them up into the pouch behind her top lip, two on each side of the thin flesh partition. She pumps her throat for effect.

"Relax," Leo tells her gently then. "Don't be scared."

"I'm not scared."

"Climb into the box."

"I am climbing."

The woman growls like a sick cat behind the door.

"Don't worry about her."

"I'm not worrying about her."

"Lay down."

"I am laying down."

It's a tight fit beside the dead guy.

"Don't mind him."

"I'm not minding."

"Perfect," Leo says and pulls the veil across her face.

▲ ▼ ▲ ▼

She can't tell how long later she teeters on the bright-dark edge of blackout, pinching her stomach hard beneath the gown and trying to keep from tipping in.

She hears the grim and hurried voice of an older woman like herself.

"Help me up. Take this. This orange jug is the right jug. Give the other jug to me. Here, these are the cups. Here is your money. Father and I are leaving soon. Give us ten minutes."

Then the voice is gone. Belle feels her body getting swallowed into darkness, but then Skip erupts and pulls her back.

"Yo, yo, yo! You ain't give Skip ass only ten!"

Belle sees dim blue light and feels the scratchy weight of the veil on the tip of her nose. She catches hold of her stomach skin again and pinches until her fingers touch and she comprehends that Skip is upset about money.

"It ain't thirty. It's forty, bust by three. Milk gone, we split Milk share."

"You unhappy?" Leo asks him.

"Motherfucker, you ain't give me only—"

A burst of gunfire cuts him off and Belle drops back into herself, feeling her heart pound, smelling the blood.

"Fucking dick-grabber," Leo mutters.

Belle keeps pinching. Peep babbles pointlessly.

"I'd be! Just fine! With ten! If you—"

Another burst of gunfire. One small squeal.

"Fucking chomo," Leo growls.

▲ ▼ ▲ ▼

Time floats, and then Belle, feeling helplessly mellow, thinks, *It's just the two of us now.*

A song starts in her head.

Just the two of us,
Building castles in the sky . . .

She can now see lovely gradations of blue light through the veil, can follow the soft clouds of Leo's movement, can block out the woman yowling behind the door.

It's just the two of them now. Belle plays this one on the juke at the Ease Inn, at Mudcat's, wherever she can find it.

We can make it if we try,
Just the two of us, you and I.

She drifts through an empty patch with the song playing. Minutes? Hours? She has ridden the slowly melting roofies into the same timeless space where on a good day alcohol can take her. This is a delicate, fleeting, precarious place, full of snags and booby traps and monsters, but the chance of just getting here for a few moments is what keeps her drinking. No past. The idea that the future could be different. She craves this feeling. It never lasts, it makes her sick, but she will take the punishment over and over for these moments where she becomes one real woman who belongs right where she is.

Then Leo says sweetly, "Princess?"

Though she can't speak yet, Belle feels warm surprise and the weight of her body returning. She has never stopped imagining that someday the words would be real.

"Darling?"

Yes?

"Wake up, my love."

I am awake.

"It's me, sweet lady. It's Leo."

I know it's you.

"Rise and shine, honeybunch. Your favorite gentleman wants to take you to the Black Friday sales. Listen, though. I'm sorry . . ."

I know you're sorry. We all make mistakes. It's okay.

". . . but you'll have to drive."

What?

Now Belle struggles on the light-dark edge, tilting, falling, some stubborn muscle inside her stiffening and holding on. Living angry, fighting, this is how she does it.

"You'll have to pick me up."

But we're both right here.

"Sugarplum, no, it's not too early. Where? Where I showed you, behind the golf course. Damn it, *listen*. Where I showed you."

It strikes Belle like a punch to her battered heart.

Sugarplum.

Honeybunch.

Princess, sweet lady, Black Friday sales.

Damn it, listen.

She peels the veil off, spits the pills out, and sits up to punch back. She screeches at the other woman through the phone in Leo's fist, "Don't believe that fuckstick!"

He snaps his phone shut. Belle starts, "Listen? You listen, fuckstick—"

She ducks a burst from his big gun, box splinters flying. Then Leo is a blur going down that dirt hole like the rat he is. He tugs a cord and the sheet of plywood whumps down over.

▲ ▼ ▲ ▼

Later—maybe?—or soon?—strangely she senses she has sobbed a bit—Belle climbs out as if from a great height. Clumsily she shucks the gown, then steps wobbly-legged over Skip's and Peep's limp, bleeding bodies. She keeps wobbling across the plywood, the lid over the hole where Leo went. She opens the door.

Like people say about the cult, they have rifles.

But a motley selection, old and not that many, and a mishmash of mostly empty ammunition boxes.

A yowl leads her deeper into the room.

"Hon," she says, peeling duct tape from the mouth and wrists and ankles of the pretty black-haired young woman she finds behind boxes, "I don't know who you are, but I gotta guess you're one of the good girls."

Belle snatches the best-looking rifle, loads it expertly, and follows Gentleman Leo down the hole.

CHAPTER 41

The usual Kill the Cult watcher was gone, but Dancing Jesus was already flailing in the low sky when Sheriff Kick's Bad Axe County team arrived in riot gear on U-Stash-It Road. She led the convoy of mismatched cruisers through the cul-de-sac beneath the golf course cameras, watching in her rearview until each vehicle had rolled one-eighty and spaced itself along the road facing back out to the high-way. Over the radio, she said, "Good job," and realized she meant driving their individual cruisers in riot gear, for which there had been no rehearsal. At Waco, if she recalled, the feds had come pouring out of tarped-over cattle trucks into Davidian gunfire.

She stepped from her cruiser in a glaze of anxious disbelief. Riot gear. In the Bad Axe. But, yes, this was happening. Yes, a phone app showed her kidnapped mother-in-law was inside there. Yes, Kill the Cult was assembled distantly across the golf course, waiting for Dennis Stonebreaker, she guessed, and unaware, she guessed, that Stonebreaker had killed his wife right in front of her and Rhino and launched his own personal apocalypse.

She touched the handset on her shoulder.

"We're going to space out along the north and west sides of the fence. Move slowly. Weapons down. Face shields up. Look calm, be calm. We're a buffer here, facing out. We are not attacking. If we get fired on from inside, we retreat immediately."

Inside the fence, the House of Shalah seemed to be in full choir. As was their practice, the oddly assorted Dancing Jesus people tried to sing over them. This was halfway working. Hymns rose from both sides of the fence and made turbulence with one another in the newly warming air.

The sheriff watched her deputies finalizing their riot outfits and had a flashing memory of her almost-Halloween—how she had helped the kids design costumes—then had never seen them finished because Darwin Fuss aka Win Carpenter had been found in Lake Susan with his throat slit—and if she went to prison would she ever see Dylan and Taylor and Opie in costumes again before they were too old for Halloween?

She looked away over the golf course, noting how fast the Thanksgiving snowstorm had lost its puffy beauty. In just minutes under warmer air and breaking sun the trees had shed all decoration. Yesterday's fluff now squatted like white mud on the fairways. Distantly through the reflecting glare the sheriff could make out what Roger from the golf course had seen on his security feed: a phalanx of off-road vehicles at the margin of the sixth fairway, where in golf season the rough elided into soybeans. They could be here in less than one minute.

"Rhino?"

"Copy."

"Any leads on where Dennis Stonebreaker went?"

"After he left here, he ripped through town and out to the south. That's all I have. For sure, those are his people on the golf course. When Roger went out there to chase them off what he gathered was that Stonebreaker flipped out in the middle of the night—I think he had just seen the photographs—and told them to get ready for assault. Roger said get the hell off my golf course. They said when the cult took over the schools and the government, there would be no golf course. Roger said not a single one of you assholes even plays golf. Bottom line, they were not compliant."

"Tell Roger to go home now and stay there."

"I did," Rhino said. "Also not compliant. He's going to defend the clubhouse."

She let it go. Spotting the *New York Times* guy hurrying toward her away from the House of Shalah gate, she guessed Markus Sullivan had something to tell her. She also guessed he had driven a hundred miles round trip to get a Venti cup of Starbucks. As she watched the reporter approach, she remembered how two days ago the excited Carpenter children had galloped barefoot into fresh snow. Today their little voices were clear in the chorus that leaked plaintively in a slow and solemn hymn. The sheriff tried to shut out the Dancing Jesus people and hear the words.

The darkness deepens; Lord with me abide.
When other helpers fail and comforts flee,
Help of the helpless, O abide with me.

It was the funeral hymn sung at the graveyard when her mom and dad were buried, the day she began her spiral down to meet Roman Vanderhoof.

She put her fingers to her teeth and whistled.

"Luck!"

Deputy Luck trotted across Sullivan's path.

"Clear this road. Everybody out. Then man that gate. Nobody passes either way."

"Ten-four."

"I'm sorry, but this means you," she told Sullivan as he closed in. "You gotta go."

"I understand. But before I do . . ."

The sheriff's eyes had drifted to the mobile coach. From inside, its lights glowed. Its furnace vented steam. A small black flag hung slackly from a bracket by the doorway.

Sullivan nodded that way and continued.

"You probably want to know that Timothy Dekker called me just a minute ago because his dad just called him. The prophet died last night. A few minutes ago his wife joined him. The singing comes before the Carpenters follow to the afterlife. They'll go over to the new building to pay respects to the bodies of Father Euodoo and Mother Ruth. Then they will drink drugged apple cider and follow to their prosperity into heaven. Timothy says they're trained to open fire if anybody tries to stop them."

The sheriff's ear was pulled to the hymn.

I need thy presence, every passing hour.
What but thy grace can foil the tempter's power?

After the burial when she had blacked out upon the hot grass of the cemetery, her next clear memory was sneaking at midnight out the window of the foster home and crossing a cornfield to meet Missy Grooms and her dealer.

What to do with pain? she wondered.

No one seemed to have the answer.

"And there's that." Sullivan brought her back, looking toward the horde across the golf course. His eyes came back to hers.

"Whereas at Waco—"

"Clear the area." She cut him off and turned away.

Deputy Luck was rounding up the Dancing Jesus people, sturdily ignoring their less-than-Christly resistance. The sheriff checked the location app on Harley's phone. The GPS pin was not precise enough to say exactly where Belle was inside the House of Shalah. The activity log said that in the last hour Harley's mom had not moved. But Belle was constant motion. She never went one waking hour without a smoke.

Anything? Harley had texted her.

No.

She jittered the phone back behind her badge.

Sullivan was still there.

"You need to leave."

"First, one other thing I learned."

He pointed beyond the mobile coach at the sewer project.

"The House of Shalah pulled a permit for a sewer, so it has to be inspected eventually. I've been bothering the inspector, saying he should really see it now. He finally came by on his way to inspect something else, just before you got here. He took one look and said wrong pipe, wrong depth, wrong layout. He said the T-in to the existing line from the golf course should not have been buried until it was inspected. He said the permit will be revoked on Monday."

Now Sullivan pointed inside the fence.

"That big dirt pile along the back fence, that people say is from the Carpenters hand-digging a basement under their new chapel because they're too dumb to understand the logic of building construction?"

She waited, watching Luck find the kill switch on Dancing Jesus's generator. The theme of the Carpenters as idiots—imbecilic and insane, yet somehow capable of taking over the Bad Axe—had always been the shabby convenience at the core of Kill the Cult mob mentality. Denial of humanity was the fulcrum of hate. Every Carpenter, angel or monster, came from a life once fully realized in some other place and time, as fully human as anyone in the Bad Axe. Darwin Fuss had been a successful undertaker, for one example, crushed by bad luck and mistakes. Local boy become Carpenter, Roman Vanderhoof, had built neighborhoods once upon a time.

Sullivan's arm was still out, his index finger tracing a visual line from the new chapel to the three portable toilets to the prophet-father's mobile coach.

"That dirt comes from there," he said. "That whole stretch is a tunnel."

"A tunnel?"

"When Timothy Dekker walked away, the new security team had started forcing the Carpenters to dig. They were given the same rationale Koresh gave for his buried school buses at Waco: a place to hide if they were attacked. But last night after you visited at the motel, Sheriff, I came out here to keep my own watch. Somewhere around midnight, a black truck pulled up over there . . ."

He pointed west across the empty ground toward the overgrown Christmas trees alongside the extension of Tee Road.

"I followed it. A woman got out and disappeared underground."

He pointed back inside the compound.

"She came out of that middle porta-potty and ran into the storage units. But I'm sure the tunnel goes all the way to the new chapel. It's a way to come and go without being seen."

"Why?"

"Good question."

She stared at the dirt pile, wishing she could take a few things back. Her faith in humanity, for one thing. Her patience and professional restraint, for another. She could have created some thin pretense and bullied her way inside the House of Shalah, had a look around, taken a few pelts. As she violated the Carpenters' constitutional rights, nobody in the Bad Axe would have blinked an eye. She could have stopped this. Then she might have had the sense, the calm and clarity, to say no to Missy.

The snarl of revving engines began across the golf course.

"Now I'm going," Sullivan said. "Good luck."

The sheriff turned. Several hundred yards away but coming in hot were the dozen or more off-road buggies and snowmobiles, marauding across the fairways and greens, rutting through the sand traps and roughs.

She turned back. Luck had cleared the road. Her other seven deputies had spaced themselves meagerly around the U-Stash-It fence. They were all unrehearsed. Their first cult. Their first vigilante horde. The first view for some of them from behind a helmet and a shield. None of her deputies had ever fired a bean bag or a pepper round at a live target. In their clumsy gear, she couldn't even tell them apart and could only guess who had just stumbled and fallen and was struggling to get up. She didn't know whose name to yell because one of them had spaced himself too far from the others.

She raised her arms and hollered over the approaching din of engines.

"Nobody gets over that fence! Nobody on our side pulls a trigger unless lives are directly in danger!"

She turned and saw the attackers fanning out across the golf course, widening their angle. All around the compound there had to be a quarter mile of fence. Her people could cover one-tenth of it, maybe.

She touched her radio.

"Rhino, where are we on mutual aid?"

"State Patrol is on the way. Crawford and Vernon deputies are on the way. Village cops and constables, also on the way. Some might trickle in any minute. But mostly I'd guess any help is thirty to an hour out."

Just then Stonebreaker's force arrived, dismounting vehicles, brandishing weapons, mouthing off.

"Kill the cult! Kill the cult!"

"You won't protect us"—this directed at her—"so we'll do it ourselves!"

Rhino continued, "I put a BOLO out on Stonebreaker and now we know where he is. He's driving an off-road Caterpillar excavation truck, stolen from the Wedner quarry, one of those beasts that stands twenty feet tall and goes eighty tons empty. He's basically driving a tank, Sheriff, inbound from the south, tearing the highway to shit—"

"Stand back!" bellowed Deputy Luck, and just like that the first scuffle had erupted. A hulking man in homemade riot gear charged Luck and shoved her. Outweighed by a hundred pounds, Luck rebounded off the chain-link gate with her baton drawn. The sheriff's stomach dropped. But instead of attacking again, the man began to stomp and prance like a WWF performer while he launched into some kind of boogaloo oration at the Carpenters that included, "Horse-shooting motherfuckers!"

Once a rumor, now a fact.

Next the sheriff heard Deputy Schwem bellow and she looked west along the fence. His problem was a big woman with a heavy pistol in a thigh holster who dangled sideways on the fence with one leg snagged over the top while she screamed about a takeover of the schools. Her sturdiest, most cautious veteran, Schwem conscientiously helped the woman back to earth, then turned to brace for attack by a man in a Blackhawks football helmet, lumbering in to threaten Schwem with a shotgun as he yelled about poisoned salad bars and stolen elections.

The smell of Mace turned her back. Deputy Luck was squeezing out a second burst to keep her dancing attacker at bay. Now the guy was hollering a different rumor-turned-fact: "You people are criminals!"

This triggered her. *Criminals* was the core problem for both sides. Maybe all she had to do was get inside and jack them out.

Un-fuck this, she thought, before Stonebreaker joined his troops. Could she?

The criminals, not the Carpenters, were the targets of Stonebreaker's newly focused vendetta. Those same criminals were the ones who had maneuvered the Carpenters into their present lethal danger.

Roman Vanderhoof, Nelson Woods, Robert Henderson, and Donald Dortmunder.

Jerome and Ruth Pearl.

The fight collapsed if they were gone.

Could she get in? Ambush them? Come out with their heads on a pike? Protect everybody, both sides?

A tunnel, Sullivan had convinced her.

All the way to the new chapel . . .

She wouldn't be sheriff much longer anyway. She opened the trunk of her cruiser. She still had the crowbar she had taken off Leroy Fanta, former editor of the *Bad Axe Broadcaster,* when he broke into his own office at the defunct newspaper. Before the snow fell, she had seen where the House of Shalah's fake sewer came up, where the manhole cover was. She should have gone inside that fence a month ago, trampled some rights, put some bad people down.

Gone commando.

But better late than never.

CHAPTER 42

Fernanda could not catch her breath as she looked into the box at Roy, his body desecrated to imitate the prophet-father except with worn-out nickels wedged into his eye sockets and the wrong Bible verse tattooed on his neck.

As if he were still trying to convince her that the House was not what she believed.

Outside, a man screamed that they shot horses.

Roy had said, *Fernanda, of course.*

He had reminded her that in Texas they had trained children to be pickpockets. In Nevada they had eaten roadkill, preferring snakes. In Colorado each one of them had sold a kidney as the price of admission.

This was the day he disappeared.

Fernanda, of course. People fear belief. They fear faith and sacrifice and devotion. They sought false witness against Jesus, to put him to death. Of course people fear us. They fear the prophet-father. They fear Mother Ruth. But most of all they fear us because we be-

lieve. But maybe we should fear our father and mother too, and our-selves.

She had been furious.

'Nanda, he had responded, *no one joins a cult.*

She had nearly slapped him for saying the word. She had hated him for smiling sadly when her hand stopped short of his face.

No one starts a cult. And no one joins one either. These are never the intentions. Yet here we are.

Under Fernanda's furious scowl as he buttoned his gray-blue McKormick's Farm Supply shirt, Roy had kissed each one of them—her, Hosanna, Rachel, Josiah—on their foreheads.

He who trusts in the Lord shall prosper, he had said, quoting the verse from Proverbs 28:25 referenced by the prophet-father's neck tattoo.

She stared at his lifeless body in the box. The numbers inked on Roy's neck were not 28:25. The numbers were 18:25. And now she remembered that he had pulled her close and murmured in her ear, *For it is easier for a camel to go through the eye of a needle, Fernanda, than for a rich man to enter the kingdom of God.*

She knew this. Luke 18:25.

Be careful who you follow, Roy had told her.

Then he had kissed them all one more time.

▲ ▼ ▲ ▼

Refocused by the shouting outside, Fernanda stepped over dead Brother Peep and dead Brother Skip—Brother Spooner's work with the big gun—and returned to the arsenal room, where the House kept a seventeen-piece assortment of well-used rifles. Sixteen pieces now.

Two at a time, Fernanda carried the weapons across the dirt floor of the new chapel and out the open side door, where Brother Skip's van had been backed up to unload Roy. She laid the guns on the floor of the van and went back for ammunition.

Mace stung her eyes and as she rolled the van across the grounds. Outside the fence, Kill the Cult people had arrived on snow machines and four-wheelers to wrestle cops in riot gear. A few saw the van and hollered threats her way. But she heard Roy's voice.

But maybe we should fear ourselves.

At the rear of the old chapel, she parked and sat a moment, marveling darkly at the end of life as she knew it. Inside, tricked into grief, her brothers and sisters sang their hearts out with the children.

First, she unbound Duke Hashimoto where he lay in the old chapel's furnace room. "I saw Roy," she told him. When he tried to answer, gummy strands of tape kept his lips stuck together. He was wet, shuddering from cold and pain. Thrown around, kicked—something seemed broken inside him.

"The Bible quote," he managed at last. "On his neck."

"I saw."

"A warning. From Roy."

"I'm going to tell them. Show them."

She helped him sit up. He grunted and winced, gripping his ribs. She watched him a moment, then asked, "Do you think you can get the children out the tunnel?"

He looked past her out the open door at the row of portable toilets—a long stone's throw away. His face relaxed into a faint smile.

"If I have to crawl."

▲ ▼ ▲ ▼

"The prophet-father is not dead."

The Carpenters' funeral hymn trailed away as Fernanda announced this, distributing rifles.

"The flag is false."

The damaged looks on startled faces filled her heart with grief for their betrayal. But when she returned from Brother Skip's van with the hodgepodge of ammunition boxes, she saw that for some of her brothers and sisters, grief had quickly twisted into disbelief, mistrust expressed in fierce glares of suspicion and resentment.

"He is alive," she said, trying to channel Roy's calm certainty. "But he never was a prophet." The clouded faces, no longer familiar, frightened her. "And he never was your father either."

Tears rolling into his beard, Brother Rasheed turned his rifle on her with shaking hands and a desperate grimace like his soul was splitting open.

"Judas . . ."

She passed him an open box of shells.

"I'm sorry, brother. Before you kill me, go to him and look closely at the tattoo on his neck and remember your prosperity gospel. You will know the truth. Mother Ruth is not dead either."

A single heavy explosion sounded outside. Fernanda's fellow Carpenters gripped their assorted rifles. The prophet-father's promise of Armageddon had been grandiose and false too, she understood without surprise. Roy knew. Their fate was always only going to come to this: a local skirmish, nasty and small, without meaning, only one purpose left: survive.

"But now let's be thankful," she told them all, "that our father and mother have trained us to protect ourselves."

CHAPTER 43

"Rhino, we need fire and EMS here. Anyone you can get."

"Already on the way."

But Sheriff Kick couldn't find the manhole. She dragged a boot back and forth, scraping soggy snow off fresh asphalt, splatting it with stomps.

Where was the manhole?

Shattering glass jerked her head up. The windshield was gone from the mobile coach. Deputy Luck's nemesis lobbed a second heavy rock over the western fence. Carpenters with weapons streamed out of their old chapel, splitting to take up positions.

She had to fix this quick.

Where was the goddamn manhole?

Schwem's voice broke from the radio at her shoulder. "He's got a fifty-caliber!"

Her deputy meant Dennis Stonebreaker approaching from the far side of the new chapel, the huge excavation truck leaving a trail of broken pavement as it lumbered off the highway and began to chew its way across the several hundred yards of tree stumps and fill piles toward the compound.

"There she blows!"

Schwem meant the orange streak that hit the side of a storage unit with a flash of flame. An instant later came the thumping report of a big gun. Stonebreaker was firing tracer rounds.

Deputy Luck gasped into her radio, "Now they've got guns behind us! Inside the fence!"

But the sheriff hadn't heard small arms yet. The Carpenters were holding fire.

Where was the fucking manhole? She couldn't sort the voices bursting from her shoulder unit.

"This sonofabitch is kicking me!"

"They're going to start shooting at the people inside!"

"Keep them busy!" the sheriff barked. "Pepper them!"

She stomped backward, watching Stonebreaker's monster truck as it heaved a thunderous groan. The truck's front wheels spun in space. He had hung its undercarriage on a fill pile.

"Jesus Christ"—the panicked voice of part-time Deputy Ron Sunderberg—"there's a sweet-looking lady behind me with an ax!"

Next another voice, too excited to recognize: "I'm pinned! I got crazies front and back!"

"Rhino," the sheriff panted, dragging a boot through the stubborn snow, "where's our aid?"

"I got one state trooper coming through town right now. The Zion town cop actually followed Stonebreaker. He's behind that excavation truck. He wants to know what he should do."

She didn't know. Stonebreaker got traction in reverse. The giant truck hauled itself back, one wheel crushing a stump. Then it paused.

"Tell the Zion guy to sit tight and stay out of the way."

Another orange streak. Another thump. This one hit the pole barn the Carpenters had believed would be their new chapel. After the strike came an ominous pause when she wondered if the tracer round had rebounded off the thin steel wall or had torn through it. Her answer came in ten seconds: flames jumped inside a tiny window at the back of the building.

"Rhino, we've got a fire."

"Farmstead VFD in one minute," he replied.

Here was the manhole.

The sheriff bent and clanged the crowbar through the haul-up hole. But as she lifted, a beat-up sedan rattled up behind her. At the wheel was a fat and blurry-faced woman whose druggy energy reminded her of Missy.

"Whoever you're supposed to pick up," she snapped through the woman's open window, reaching for zip ties on her duty belt, "they're not coming."

"My boyfriend."

"What's his name?"

"Leo."

The sheriff hauled her out. She yanked the woman onto her ass in the slush and fastened her wrists behind her back.

"Stay there."

She reached into the car and took the keys.

"Rhino, the Tee Road extension behind the golf course. I need backup from the Zion guy. Send him to detain the woman here. Put her in the back seat of his vehicle and wait to see who shows up next. I assume someone for the prophet and his wife."

She lifted off the manhole cover and looked in. Beyond the top fuzz of gray daylight, pure black. Drawing her weapon, she descended.

CHAPTER 44

Working his busted mouth, and stupidly, Hashimoto felt, with time draining away, he began, "My name is Duke, and . . ."

The nine Carpenter children teemed like minnows into the farthest corner of the furnace room of the building where they sang choir, Fernanda's big girl toting her baby siblings one on each hip, the other six kids crowding against her.

. . . *and I'm afraid of you too . . .*

"My name is Duke," he began again, "and I'm going to make you safe."

They stared. He stared back. Not in nearly thirty years had he spoken to a child, for fear he would break down like some scary old fool. In these Carpenter kids, equally flinty and innocent, he saw exactly what he feared, and what made the ogres hate them: nine tiny bodies, but nine large and independent souls, each infused with unspoiled spirit.

A large firearm boomed.

Something struck the roof and the children jumped.

Hashimoto smelled CS gas.

The furnace had a pilot light.

"Hosanna," he snapped, startling Fernanda's girl with her name. "Follow me."

▲ ▼ ▲ ▼

Inside the portable toilet, lithe and strong as a cat, Hosanna Carpenter contorted herself through the toilet hole and let herself down through the empty tank into the tunnel. The panicked babies mewled and arched their spines in Hashimoto's arms, one nearly too big for him to constrain. Fearing they would bite, or one of them would lose a limb in his grip, he quickly handed them down to their sister.

The other six children followed.

The toilet shook as something exploded.

Little eyes, becoming teary, looked up at him.

"Watch out. Here I come."

Slowly and grotesquely, falling in stages, tangling in a hose and a cord, he reached the ground among them.

Several had already bolted the wrong way toward the new chapel. Hosanna called them back, made them hold hands in a chain.

Without a light, in a hunching crab-walk, Hashimoto led them into the pitch-black. The map inside his head imagined that in about two hundred feet there would be an outlet to the mobile coach, an escape hatch for Jerome and Ruth Pearl to vanish from the scene of their crimes.

He had seen it right. A dozen steps beyond the long, mud-sucking puddle, he led the children past what he felt certain was this access, a branch of the tunnel heading to the right.

In another dozen steps they had passed beneath the fence that surrounded the House of Shalah. Next, just visible in the gloom, appeared his answer to how the two sewer lines connected: the concrete main from the golf course was hammered into bits so that perpendicular traffic could pass from the dirt tunnel, through the smashed pipe of the real sewer, into the broad new pipe of the fake sewer on the other side, then onward to the manhole on the new road beyond the open field where the Carpenters were supposed to get houses.

Hashimoto paused amid the rubble to rest, the children piling up against him. Water trickled steadily right to left from the golf course through the real sewer pipe. The faint light from the left had to come from that pipe's grated exit over the ravine. The children waited anxiously. He could smell the sweetness of their fear as even underground they could hear the shouting, the sirens, the heavy thuds of whatever gun was launching gas, their small world breaking open.

Even if I have to crawl, Hashimoto remembered.

Hardly rested, he led them on.

He was in fact crawling now, inside the new pipe. At least this shifted the pain from his back and hips to the surfaces of his palms and his knees—and shifted his mind out of worry into something like gratitude. He was saving children. What else did he want?

Now he spoke calmly as he crawled, finding it easy to say over and over, "You're going to be okay. Your mommy and daddy are going to be okay. Everything is going to be okay."

And then it wasn't.

Far ahead, the manhole clanged.

Then from much closer came the scraping sounds of rapid inbound movement along the bottom of the concrete pipe.

The movement stopped. A man's voice hissed, "Pearl, is that you? Somebody's out there on the road. Cops. I heard a radio."

Hashimoto froze. The first kid stumbled over his heels. Hosanna whispered, "Shush," to the babies.

"I said, who's there?" Now the ogre spoke in a growl that whorled down the pipe. "I'll shoot."

Groping in the dark, Hashimoto started turning bodies around.

"Go, go, go," he whispered, pushing, following. They had to get back to the intersection where this pipe smashed into the real sewer.

"Pearl?" the demand echoed. "Answer or I'm shooting fish in a barrel, no more questions asked."

Hashimoto knew by heart the sound of an M16 switched from single-shot to full auto. Then the ogre was cursing and coming faster, his scramble grinding on the bottom of the pipe.

As the children stumbled into rubble, Hashimoto grasped Hosanna. He pulled her head to his. He mouthed the words into her hot ear.

"Turn right into the other pipe. Don't stop. You're going to see daylight. Keep going. There's a grate there. Squeeze everybody through if you can. Then hide. If you can't get through, just stay there and keep everybody quiet."

He raised his voice to cover the departing children. Time to blow some smoke.

"You know me. Same fucking cop."

Tell some lies.

"Agent Hashimoto, ATF. You're surrounded."

Almost funny, saying that to an ogre in a pipe. But slow him just enough.

"Let me hear that magazine released."

Slow him just enough.

"We're behind you."

Someone was. That was all he had. But the kids had made it into the real sewer outlet.

Hashimoto continued noisily another fifteen feet into the flooded dirt tunnel and plunged left into what he had guessed was the Pearls' escape outlet.

To his surprise, a small light winked on.

He looked ahead in dismay at a VIP escape hatch, spaciously dug out and lit by a motion-sensing LED night-light. On a spike in the dirt wall hung a pair of headlamps. On a plastic mat awaited over-shoes, knee pads, and leather gloves. A sawed-off aluminum ladder led up to the hole in the surface, closed by treated plywood. Just beyond this hatch would be the storage bay where the Pearls would crawl unseen from the coach.

He couldn't turn the little light out, too late to smash it with his fist. No doubt seeing the new glow ahead, his pursuer accelerated through the intersection of pipes. A moment later the M16's flash suppresser eased into the light, followed by a face.

"Ah, you again," said the half-eared ogre in the brown suit and Trilby hat, the one who had threatened to pound poison Kool-Aid down Hashimoto's throat through a funnel. But that had never been his rodeo. He was fleeing the scene. He wiggled the gun.

"ATF, huh? Those fools. So I guess this is yours?"

"Yup."

"I love a walking gun. Best kind there is. My new problem, though, is some other fucking cop who's not you, coming in that hole out there. I thought I might have to shoot my way out. But now I have a hostage."

Still faintly hearing the children, Hashimoto said, "I'm not moving."

The statement wrinkled the ogre's face into a gap-toothed grin. He held the M16 inches from Hashimoto's chest.

"You don't think?"

"Try me," Hashimoto said. Then, to string him out: "Meanwhile, style-wise, what happened? The suit, the glasses, the Bear Bryant hat . . . the clothes you got arrested in, right? What, selling Fuller brushes forty years ago?"

His answer: "Ladies love a gentleman."

"And after they survive you," Hashimoto said, "they hope to meet one someday. If they survive."

"Move. Get ahead of me."

"Not a chance."

He looked at Hashimoto thoughtfully for a moment, then flipped the M16 on its strap until the weapon hung across his back. He squatted closer, crowding in on Hashimoto. From inside the suit coat, he withdrew a karambit, its deadly claw-blade gleaming. From deep creases his eyes burned with excitement.

"I'll gladly take pieces, whatever you can still crawl without. Now move, cop."

Hashimoto proceeded with forced calm. "I'm not moving." He straightened his spine and closed his eyes, held them closed for one breath, then challenged himself to open them and stare over the knife, directly and blankly into the ogre's eyes.

"Go ahead."

Distantly a child whimpered. The ogre tipped his half-gone ear and waited keenly for more. Soon there came a muted wail, a desperate shush.

"Ah. Right. Protecting children. They're escaping, they think?"

Another wail and shush.

"Little fuckers," he murmured to himself. "Big mouths."

He wrenched his coiled squat around as if to chase them down and Hashimoto sprang for the M16 across his back. He caught the barrel of the weapon and pulled. The ogre lunged powerfully forward, reined in the strap. Hashimoto, weaker but larger and heavier, hung on, skidding on the tunnel floor. At a stalemate of momentums, he released one hand and reached for the clips that connected the gun to the strap. He got one clip free but now the gun slung loose and the ogre could turn and attack. Hashimoto was hapless in the close-in struggle. The claw-shaped blade passed through his gut just as a Carpenter child cried out, "We made it! We're safe!"

"Children keep thinking that," he gasped as his clutching hands grew wet.

He collapsed to sitting.

"Over and over."

"That so?"

The ogre cocked his elbow, angling his blade for a second swipe.

Then a close-range gunshot blew him into Hashimoto's lap.

CHAPTER 45

"The children thank you," a voice says.

In the lighted side tunnel, a bloody stranger pushes Leo off himself and stiffly sits up cross-legged.

"They thank you for their safety."

Belle Kick doesn't know what this means. Exhausted, confused, she dissolves to her knees. The rifle drops on blood-sticky dirt. Her hands still jitter around its empty shape.

"But they'll need us again. And again."

Belle has no idea what he means, this bloody Oriental-looking stranger whom Leo has slashed deeply through the gut. She watches blood wick across his Packers jersey, blacken the crotch of his gray knit slacks, pool on the mat beneath his muddy loafers.

Belle doesn't know what she has done—no, she doesn't know *how*, with no hesitation, with absolute certainty—except that for a moment she was transported back in time, down that tilting hallway, behind that closed door where her mother is in bed and her father is dead on the floor, ahead of that moment, all the way back to touch that hot, bright, untouchable beginning—and she had reversed it.

Now her mind has gone blank, as if she's been shut down and needs restarting. As if he knows this, the injured man, sitting completely still, showing no signs of pain, instructs her.

"Drag him out of here. Please."

A clang of iron sounds from somewhere. The man observes this with a nod and calmly repeats himself.

"Someone's coming in from that manhole at the road. Drag him away, please. Take him a ways down the tunnel. Out of sight."

Belle bends and grips Leo's ankles—hard bone under thin white socks—and with unexpected ease she rolls him over. He is not the heavy man he seemed to be. His gentleman's hat drops off his skull and she sees for the first time that his head is small and bald and badly scarred. The exit wound from her rifle shot has opened his throat, making a second mouth that blows bloody bubbles as he still tries to feed her lies. He has fallen on his claw, more blood leaking around its loop-hole handle. She can't understand him, ranting red bubbles. It doesn't matter. She's not listening.

She heaves back, straining until it seems her muscles will pop. She rests, strains, rests again, finally drops his ankles and bends to look closer at the blood-smeared envelope she has watched emerging from an inside pocket of his suit coat. *I'll be coming into money*, he had promised her on Blackout Wednesday, IOUing her for their afternoon rounds.

And he has come into money.

A lot of money.

A minute later, Belle stumbles back into the light with a two-inch brick of cash beneath her shirt. The bloody stranger puts his fingers to his lips and whispers, "I'll take care of this."

He means the rifle she used.

Thank you. He only mouths this. *Now go.*

He touches the rifle all over, then lays it aside and turns around to face a ladder segment at the back of the short tunnel. He sits propped against the dirt wall. He pulls Leo's big mall-shooter gun across his lap and returns to stillness.

She hears faintly, "Go!"

Belle is squatting away into her own thinning shadow when the light behind her goes out. Then suddenly she stumbles over broken concrete and there are different directions she could take. From ahead come grinding footfalls and a noise that grates on her nerves at home: crackling police radio static.

"Who's there?" someone calls.

Freaking Heidi?

Belle spooks left into a narrower pipe just wide enough for crawling. Ahead appears a different light, first just a gray shade but brightening, brightening, until she comes to yet another dead end in her life. She's probably headed for prison next, she thinks, staring at an oval of cloudy sky and shrinking snow through a barred metal grate.

Anyway, she begins to count the cash.

CHAPTER 46

Sheriff Kick emerged on hands and knees from a hole in a dirt floor into smoke and scorch. Directly in her face as she rose was a large wooden box freshly in flames. Nearby on a burning sawhorse steamed an orange Igloo jug, and beside the jug a stack of red Solo cups melted together.

"Dead body in the tunnel, Rhino. Possibly a shooter. Make sure we keep someone at that manhole."

Alongside the burning box sprawled another two bodies on blood-puddled dirt. In the tunnel she had stepped over Donald Dortmunder, an astrological Leo who had tried to behead a man with a spoon. These two would be Nelson Abernathy Woods—Peep, the hidden-camera photographer—and Robert Kenneth Henderson—Skip, the all-purpose gangbanger.

That left Hoof.

And the prophet. And his wife.

If she was going to stop this.

As she paused over the bodies, Harley's phone chimed in her

pocket. *Success!* the app reported cheerily, but it was only telling the sheriff that one of the dead men had Belle's phone.

So where was Belle?

What did they want her for?

And where was Hoof?

As flames jumped up the barn walls around her, searching for more fuel, a young woman with flowing black hair ran past the sheriff to the burning box.

"Ma'am, no! Out!"

Tear-streaked and gasping, the woman paid no attention. She reached through flames into the box and tugged, unable to lift out what was inside. In a desperate surge she bucked her whole weight against the box—the sheriff moving toward her: "Ma'am, you need to get out of here now!"—until the box toppled off the sawhorses and out of it fell another dead body.

This one was bizarre.

Nickels wedged into his eye sockets.

Tattoos curdled weirdly on his hands and neck and arms. In his fall from the box, a long blond-haired wig had come off the man's roughly shaved head. The general wax-museum feel to how the body hit the dirt headfirst and kind of stuck there, unbent, while gravity shed the bottom half of a peasant robe to reveal muscular, black-haired legs—all this told the sheriff this was not the prophet, a tall and feeble-looking man with his own blond-gray hair, supposedly just hours dead.

"My husband!" the black-haired woman shrieked blindly at the sheriff. "They murdered him! Help me!"

Together they carried the body clear of the building just as Stone-breaker's behemoth truck was mashing down the eastern stretch of the fence and coming in. The woman fell wailing to her knees beside the body. The sheriff shook her by the shoulder.

"Have you seen an older woman? Not a Carpenter? Long gray hair?"

"She escaped!"

"Escaped where?"

She pointed into the pole barn they had just evacuated, the new chapel.

"She took a rifle and chased Brother Spooner down that hole! That way!"

Startled, the sheriff followed the woman's pointing finger along the tunnel's aboveground path until a worry coalesced—if Belle went down the tunnel with a rifle, had she shot Dortmunder, Spooner, her boyfriend, Leo?—and then she pushed the problem away.

Right now Stonebreaker's truck mauled across a hundred feet of open ground and rammed the first row of storage units, buckling steel walls, scattering Carpenters. As Stonebreaker backed up to ram again, the sheriff looked the other way and saw that flames now leapt avidly inside the old chapel. Up on the road, the Farmstead VFD milled uncertainly about while deputies skirmished at the fence. Armed Carpenters fled for new outposts as Stonebreaker crushed their storage units. A beanbag gun popped and someone yelped. Smoke and Mace thickened the already dense air. At the eastern edge of the compound, some Bad Axe defender in a welder's helmet and hockey pads had cleared the fence and climbed onto the roof of the mobile coach, where he was jumping up and down and hollering Kill the Cult talking points.

Chaos. Damage. But from the depths of her exhaustion, the sheriff heard a plain voice speak.

Heidi, this is basically over.

Slowing down to survey the whole of it, she felt the inrush of a deeper breath than she had taken in hours. Days. Unfolding before her was the crisis she had feared, the climax that all of this had come to. Wife-killer Dennis Stonebreaker in his self-destroying cuckold rampage . . . the undead prophet and his wife cowering in their luxury coach, caught at whatever they were up to . . . the Kill the Cult people still dancing and sloganeering, but not quite attacking . . . the Carpenters armed, but not quite fighting back . . .

The hard criminals were dead, gone, or hiding. Surrounding the sheriff, on both sides of the conflict, followers were witnessing the true nature of their leaders, and discovering that they had followed too far. In fact, she could sense conviction waning fast. The Carpenters did not really want to die—and Kill the Cult didn't really mean it.

The young black-haired woman rose from her knees beside the body they had dragged out. She faced the mobile coach. "You devils!" she screamed and began to stalk toward it.

The sheriff caught her arm. When the woman fought, she cuffed her. With her free hand she touched her radio.

"Solverson?"

The Farmstead VFW chief answered, "Here."

"How much hose do you have?"

"Five hundred feet, Sheriff. We're on the hydrant."

"Drive Pumper One right through the fence and get to work on the building closest to the gate."

"What if they shoot at us?"

"They won't. Deputy Luck?"

Hearing her name on the radio, a figure in riot gear disengaged and turned.

"Come and get this woman."

When Luck had followed Pumper One across the crushed fence and jogged up, the sheriff said, "Put her in a car. Keep her safe."

Now she started for the excavation truck as it plundered through another row of storage units. Closer, she wondered if Stonebreaker didn't notice she was coming. Then she wondered if he did, but as a doomed man, he didn't care.

Suicide by cop was on her mind as she reached the truck, caught the pull-up grip with her left hand, and swung herself up to the cleated stairway that led to the cab where Stonebreaker ground gears.

The platform bucked and surged, but she hung on, unsnapping her service pistol while the truck shuddered, then roared in reverse to line up another run.

She stepped into the cab and leveled the pistol, center mass.

"Stop."

The big gun Dennis Stonebreaker had used to fire tracer rounds lay across his lap. He wore a pistol on each thigh. He had grenades. But he only stared ahead and kept his hands on the wheel, his shoulders slumped as the truck hauled back, dragging shreds of storage units over the Carpenters' scattered possessions.

She saw the truck was a tractor, basically, and she kicked the gear lever. The differential clashed and shrieked.

She kicked again.

The truck wrenched to a halt.

"Hands on top of your head."

But Stonebreaker's head hung and his hands shook as they went the other way and fell into his lap. He had kept one photograph of his wife, bent in the blueprint clip on the dash. Mikayla's square white chin showed, and the tip of her tongue.

"I said hands on top of your head."

"Just shoot me," he answered.

Schwem was coming, his tactical rifle aimed.

"You wish," she said.

Schwem climbed in.

"You wish it was that easy."

CHAPTER 47

Hashimoto sat perfectly still with the M16 across his blood-sticky lap, feeling colder and stiffer, watching the perfect darkness before him roil with colors and streaks of light and sometimes graphic visions, remembering things that never happened, it seemed, but that perhaps had been possibilities, or dreams, or scenes from a past or future life.

The entangled strata above him had gone mostly quiet.

Below him—was there hell?

Right here, in between, seemed to be where he belonged.

He waited.

Still as stone.

▲ ▼ ▲ ▼

At last he sensed movement above him. He heard muffled clicks and thumps and low, careful voices. Then the plywood lifted and gray daylight poured in through a narrow ellipse of cloudy sky.

The backs of legs came down the ladder.

The motion-sensing light winked on.

Birdy woman's legs, red tendons, moccasins, blue-jeans cuffs snagging on the rim of the hole.

Then, facing the ladder in a crouch, she helped the prophet come down.

He moved unsteadily in travel loafers and wide-bottomed knit pants that from below showed calves like soft-boiled eggs. He reached bottom and lifted down two small bags and sighed.

"I want to see the love."

She answered, "Zip your pants."

He said, "You promised me I'd get to see."

She said, "We'll see it on the news."

He said, "They love me so much."

She said, "Are you going to zip your pants or not?"

They turned and froze, seeing Hashimoto before them on the mat with the weapon.

He focused through the intense strain of keeping his spine straight, his hands still, his face mildly blank, his blurred eyes open.

The final thing he saw was topsy-turvy: two ogres climbing back up to the hell they had created.

CHAPTER 48

Now the prophet.

In a surprise shaft of sunshine, Sheriff Kick gave Stonebreaker to Schwem, who cuffed him and pushed him down the truck steps.

"Rhino, one coming for the jail."

"Ten-four."

She decided she had judged the mood correctly. Kill the Cult had stopped war-dancing and they did not defend their leader, the wife-killer now waddling ahead of Schwem with his head lolling down as if his neck were broken. As for defending the House of Shalah, no Carpenter moved an inch to rescue the prophet as the boogaloo in the welding helmet continued stomping on the mobile coach roof.

"Schwem," she called after him, "when you get off the property, ask a state cop to finish custody to Rhino. Bring me back a bullhorn."

"Copy."

"Solverson," she addressed the VFD chief.

"Yes, Sheriff."

"Can you spare that hose for ten seconds?"

"We need to move it around the other side of the building."

"I'll move it for you."

Solverson dragged his fire hose to her with the head-valve shut. A couple VFD guys got behind her and she led with the nozzle. Around the far side of the old chapel, when she got close enough, she made a wide base with her tired legs, aimed the nozzle, opened the head valve, and blew the boogaloo off the coach roof.

Schwem handed her a bullhorn.

Studying the mobile coach at closer range and thinking of the trajectory of the tunnel, she said, "I gather there's a way to sneak out the back of that thing. Make sure that doesn't happen."

"I'm on it," Schwem said.

"Rhino, my mother-in-law?"

"No sign of her, Sheriff."

"Who do I have out on the road?"

"Now you've got three Crawford deputies, four Vernon deputies, and two smokies, minus the one you just sent with Stonebreaker. You've still got the Zion guy at the manhole. Oh, and Denise just arrived."

"Give me Denise, please."

"Coming!" Denise chimed in.

The sheriff took a moment to look for Carpenters. They had vanished. So had the body she and the Carpenter wife had dragged from the burning new chapel. Were they waiting safely in one of the units Stonebreaker hadn't crushed? Or had she figured them incorrectly and they were headed via apple cider for the afterlife?

She told Rhino, "Have mutual aid take the perimeter. I want all my deputies in a contain around this coach. Shooting positions."

"Ten-four."

She let Rhino distribute the radio commands. Nothing moved at the coach. The curtains remained drawn. The furnace still pushed out steam. Schwem appeared around the rear bumper and signaled her with crossed arms: no action on the backside.

"Sorry, Heidi," Denise panted on arrival. "I had to wait for my girlfriend Tina to come over. She's making waffles for your kiddies. Then I had to get this goddamn riot gear on. I swear it shrank in the laundry. What can I do?"

"Bullhorn."

"Sweet."

"I want them out of there. You know what to say."

"I sure do."

As her fellow deputies moved into position, Denise raised the horn.

"Hey, dipshits!" her voice boomed out.

"Denise—"

"Know the difference between Jesus and a can of Raid?"

"Denise!"

"I got this, Heidi." She said into the horn, "Look out the window. This right here is a can of Raid, and Jesus ain't saving you. Come out that door one at a time and slowly, with your hands out in front. We're going to give you . . ."

She lowered the horn.

"Your call, Sheriff. Maybe two Our Fathers and one Hail Mary? What's that, about sixty seconds?"

"Tell them we're coming through that door in sixty seconds."

Denise raised the horn.

"Two Our Fathers and one Hail Mary. Let me know if I can help you with the words."

"Denise—" the sheriff began.

Then she let it go.

She had a sudden feeling anyway.

▲ ▼ ▲ ▼

She decided to wait five whole minutes for good measure, asking Denise to repeat a standard operational command on the minute. Nothing moved inside the coach.

Around minute four, she called over Deputy Luck.

"Pumper One has a battering ram. Go get it."

Luck hustled away.

She noticed then: the whole scene had gone quiet. When the ram arrived, all eyes were on Luck and Schwem as, swinging together, they needed about ten bone-jarring collisions against the coach door before it collapsed inward.

Inside at the rear of the coach were two aging hustlers with their shoes off lying side by side upon a king-sized bed. An insulated jug, white with a red lid, rested on the floor beside the bed. The paper cup Jerome and Ruth Pearl had shared was tipped upon the prophet's motionless chest, where it had left a brown stain on a white golf shirt.

Behind the sheriff, Denise murmured, "Holy shit. They drank the Kool-Aid."

CHAPTER 49

The sheriff let out a long sigh when Belle appeared on U-Stash-It Road—muddy, wobbly, but no rifle in her hands—and Harley in the Kick family minivan rolled up beside her.

After that, the Carpenters were easy to find once they began to sing inside one of the un-crushed storage units. They were holding a service for the dead man who had been costumed as their prophet. Their firearms were neatly left inside the roll-up door. The sheriff counted heads. Subtracting the four ex-convicts that she knew about, there should have been nineteen adults. She counted fourteen. A brown-skinned woman approached and said placidly in an accent like Dr. Patel's, "The others are bringing back the children. They're out beyond the trees."

Another long sigh. After a weak but steady stretch of sunshine, everything had begun to trickle and drip. It was mop-up now. Put out all the fires. Search all the buildings. Detain any Kill the Cult followers who would not leave immediately. Map and photograph the crime scene. Remove the bodies. Write the reports. Then see what was left of her career.

When the children and their finders appeared out of the ravine behind the southern stretch of the fence, she called over Deputy Luck.

"You can let that woman out of your car."

The Carpenter mother who had approached Heidi seemed to move through the chaotic scene in a dream, or possibly through an afterlife in which everything had become a surreal version of its old self. She passed the sheriff with her eyes fixed on the children in the distance and her hoarse voice saying, "Thank you."

▲ ▼ ▲ ▼

As she worked, Sheriff Kick felt dazed too. She felt unwell and unsettled, shaky on her feet and unclear in her head. She struggled to find herself in time. It was Friday. Black Friday. Thanksgiving was just yesterday. And the afternoon before, she had gone to drink ketchup with Missy. Nearly forty-eight hours in a blink that was also an eternity.

And *later* was upon her.

Maybe she had averted a Waco-style disaster, but she had still shot a man in the back. She would still suffer those consequences. She would still put herself and her family through some kind of wrenching, life-altering passage.

Then again . . . oh, God, she was so exhausted . . . but since Hoof was probably dead . . . and since the Deerslayer could stay unfound at the bottom of the Bad Axe River . . . and since Missy might be convinced to keep her mouth shut . . . And anyway, in the final analysis, didn't she deserve to keep the job? For the most part, weren't the bad people dead, the good people safe, and the in-between people wiser?

But none of this quite felt like the victory she wanted it to be.

▲ ▼ ▲ ▼

She wandered into the barn the Carpenters had called their new chapel. She drifted with a bad feeling into a world of smoke and steam and char and lingering tear gas fumes. Something was unfinished.

Later wasn't quite here yet.

It was still to come.

How this would end.

The makeshift casket smoldered in pieces. The sheriff was staring down into it, watching coals die, when Hoof lunged up from the hole behind and grabbed her.

CHAPTER 50

One arm gripping both ankles from behind, he tugged her feet from under her and dropped her on her face to the dirt with a shock that knocked her breath out.

Then he dragged her into the hole on top of him.

The crown of her skull ground down the side of the hole until her neck was pinned between his muddy knees. He still gripped her legs, somewhere back by his face. She kicked and hit something soft and heard him spitting. He dug with his heels, driving them back together into the tunnel until he had the space to turn her.

Then he was on top. He hissed, "I had you. Bitch, I had you so goddamn easy. I never should have turned my back. Not now, not then. Never. You should be dead."

She wasn't breathing yet. She tried to reach her duty belt, but he crushed her neck with his knees and caught her groping right hand. He held her at the wrist while he released one knee and ripped it forward across her chest and stomach into her crotch, pinned her there, dragged the other knee forward to spread her legs apart. Then he thrashed himself around, twisting her arm until her elbow popped from its joint and his face was in hers, spraying spittle.

"I should have watched you die."

She still couldn't breathe. He let her ruined arm drop. He spread his knees. She squirmed with every muscle as he took hold of her throat.

"Now I will."

As his mad eyes bore into hers, a calm recognition surprised her. *He's still Hoof.* She pulled in a short gasp of air. *This is still Hoof.* This could be just like old times, when his muddled and self-glorifying threats always seemed unfocused, his plans struggling to catch up with his raw need to threaten her.

Heidi, you've been down this road before . . .

Did he want to kill her? Rape her? Was there something better? In the case of both murder and rape, which first? She watched his uncertainty amplify his rage . . . *Hoof is still Hoof.*

In his jerking body language, she watched a new concern develop. With only one usable hand, kill her how? Rape her how? He had tried both before, using both hands, and gotten himself hurt by a girl who rode rodeo and stretched fence and baled hay and carried calves on her shoulders. Missy he could damage with a word or a look. Mighty Heidi required an assault.

A squeak of breath through his fist allowed her thoughts to progress.

This is Hoof, Heidi.

Give him rope.

He will hang himself.

To remove the distraction of his bulging face, she closed her eyes. That helped. Now she saw from inside the situation. Her Mace was in the left-hand holster on her belt. He couldn't crush her throat and stop her left hand from reaching at the same time. He could let go of her throat, or he could get himself Maced. That was one edge she had on him. Another: once he thought to take her weapon, the service pistol on her right hip was opposite his working right arm. To take her gun, he would have to release her throat and reach across himself, giving up his center of gravity, and they both knew she was plenty strong enough to buck him off. As if he too sensed all this, he centered on her, spread his knees inside her legs, gripped her throat harder, and seethed into her face, "Maybe I should let you live so you can go to prison, let you feel my twelve fuckin' years, then kill you the day you get out."

Work him, Heidi.

A bad man always needs to explain himself.

He needs you to understand how you made him act so badly.

With barely air to speak, she pushed out fragments.

"I never. Turned you. In. Hoof."

He gushed rancid breath back into her face.

"You lying bitch."

But she had guessed right. He eased up on her throat so she could speak and he could correct her.

"It wasn't about turning you or anybody in," she said. She had to wait for more air. "Not my agenda. It wasn't about you at all. It was about me facing my problems by telling my truth."

"Fucking all lies."

"No. I was telling my truth. That's all. About myself, to myself, and to anyone else who needed to know."

"Cunt. I spent twelve years in a cell."

"Right. For about ten percent of all the laws you broke and damage you did. If I had told *your* truth, you would have got a hundred years."

"You told them I sold crystal meth to Sherilyn Polk."

As he descended into details, the sheriff eased her left hand toward the Mace holster.

"Well, didn't you sell crystal meth to Sherilyn Polk?"

"It was *regular* meth," he raged through clenched teeth. "I got one year extra right there. Fucking enhancer because you said it was crystal."

"But you bragged to me and Missy that it was crystal. All I told them was what you said. You knew that me and Missy would fuck if we thought you had crystal. So you told us it was crystal. I said that you said that you sold crystal."

Her hand was on the Mace holster now.

"So who lied?" she asked him.

"I caught a statutory too. Sex offender. Because you told them I fucked you when you were seventeen."

"You did. The first few times."

"You told me you were eighteen."

"By the time you asked me, I was."

This seemed to make up his mind. She watched him realize that what he wanted was to *really* rape her—in a dirt tunnel, with one arm, a woman in full law enforcement garb—rape her for real until she saw that *it was all her fault*—and she watched how the complexity of this ambition now distracted him from the sound of the snap of the Mace holster: he flinched, then forgot about it.

Now the cartridge was out. She only had to raise it and squeeze it before he let go of her throat and tried to stop her.

"Fucking lying bitch-cunt-whore. You said—"

She raised the can with the button pressed and the first narrow squirt shot into his open mouth so hard she heard it splat against the back of his throat. An instant later the spray had widened as she raised it to his eyes.

He bellowed in pain and reeled back. With her own eyes pinched shut as she struggled to her knees, she didn't see how his boot caught her face. Stunned, she fell back, holding her breath and groping across her hips to release her pistol left-handed. She heard him scramble. When she opened her eyes he was gone. She could hear him coughing and spitting somewhere down the tunnel.

She took her time now.

She re-closed her eyes and waited for the Mace to settle through the heavy tunnel air. When it had, she blinked tears away and set the pistol down. She unsnapped her Maglite, gripped it in her teeth, dialed it open, and raised her chin to shine the light down the empty tunnel.

She touched her radio shoulder unit. It crackled unpromisingly. She said anyway, "I need backup, Rhino. Tunnel access through the floor in the big new barn. Pursuing a suspect."

Her dispatcher didn't answer.

Then Sheriff Kick went alone, crouch-walking between the dirt walls, pointing her weapon into the brightness she cast ahead. Alone was how she wanted it. Who dug tunnels? Worms. Goblins. Trolls. Prisoners. Some went behind bars and got better. Most sank deeper into the hell of who they were. She shuddered as she inched along, flashlight in her teeth, pistol in her clumsier left hand, her future a mystery. Alone was how she needed this to be.

Soon the tunnel floor turned to mud down the middle, drier at the edges. She widened the base of her crouch and moved on. Coming in, after stepping over Dortmunder's body, she had straddled a long puddle threaded by a green hose with a white stripe. The House of Shalah's bogus storm sewer had leaked into their escape tunnel, which they were trying to drain. Now she saw where the hose emerged from the tip of the puddle, snaked toward her another twenty feet, then bent left into the tunnel wall and disappeared.

Where?

Inbound, she had been moving fast. Now she crept toward the bend in the hose until she could see that it went into a different chamber of the tunnel. Was she now below the portable toilets? Remaining still, she picked out familiar sounds she hadn't stopped to hear before. There had been a sump pump in the fieldstone basement on her family's farm. She guessed that one sound she heard was water trickling from the hose into a sump pump reservoir, raising the float, which wobbled faintly on a loose nut. Then the pump engaged with a gulp and a hum, pulling water up to be expelled.

So this explained the placement of the porta-potties and the purpose of one of them—and where Hoof was likely waiting to ambush her.

When the pump stopped, she heard him sniffling from the Mace. But where exactly would he be? How would he attack?

She inched forward and froze where her beam lit the side chamber—the circumference of an oil drum, a black space above where her light couldn't shine, and below the muddy-footprinted lid of the buried pump. Hoof wasn't in the chamber. Then a drip of mucus fell through her flashlight beam and splatted softly on the lid.

He was above.

He planned to let her pass and drop in from behind.

She tried to imagine more precisely. According to Markus Sullivan, *A woman came out of that middle porta-potty . . .* So the bottom of the toilet tank had to be cut out. She must have hoisted herself up and through, then emerged through the toilet hole itself and out the door. From there, Sullivan had said, she *ran into the storage units.*

The sheriff now visualized Hoof curled inside the empty toilet tank, blinking through Mace tears as her flashlight beam panned the cavity below, trying not to cough and snort as he waited for her to move on.

When he made his move, would he come down feetfirst or headfirst? If he meant to let her pass and take her from behind, it would make sense to ease down feetfirst. With only one arm, that was the smarter choice. He would need to let her get some distance and then land quietly, extract his upper half, and explode out of the darkness behind. In these same moments, she would have to turn her light on him and not miss left-handed with the pistol. If he played it this way, he would have a chance.

But he was Hoof.

Instead of thinking logically, wouldn't he be craving a direct collision with her flesh? Wouldn't he be up there itching to drop headfirst upon her like a beast of prey and in one awesome primal moment destroy her?

This is still Hoof, Heidi.

Just give him a target.

Following her light, she inched into the barrel-shaped space beneath the porta-potty, just far enough that Hoof could look down upon her bent bare neck.

The explosion of his movements in the hollow plastic space above sounded like thunder as he writhed into alignment and launched headfirst.

But she was already out of range, looking in from the tunnel with her pistol raised.

He tried to stop himself . . . spread his legs to hook the hole in the tank . . . tried one-armed to haul himself back up . . . snagged himself in the pump's power cord and hose . . . hung there thrashing and hissing . . . losing strength as he called her all the same tired old names . . .

Who knew that deciding her future could be this easy?

And this hard?

Who knew that what came later would be entirely, and privately, secretly, her choice?

Here it was.

Trembling and dropping to one knee, Sheriff Kick aimed her pistol at his dangling center mass.

EPILOGUE

I

At Roman Vanderhoof's preliminary hearing, the sheriff distracted herself from the sound of his lies by musing on an undecided question that for her summed up the whole House of Shalah experience.

The embalmed body was that of Royland Lee Rogers, age forty-three at time of death, wanted by the IRS for back taxes, last known address in Reno, Nevada. Had Raven Furtzig tattooed the wrong verse number on Royland Rogers's neck?

Or was it the right verse?

Or was the answer "both"?

She massaged her reset elbow and thought about this while Hoof misled the judge and the Bad Axe County Police and Fire Commission about what took place at the river on Thanksgiving eve: he had just turned away to go seek help for the sheriff, he said, when she—over unrequited love, he guessed—had shot him in the back.

As he went on, explaining his religious conversion and his membership in the House of Shalah, his shock and heartbreak at being scammed by Jerome and Ruth Pearl, the sheriff decided it had been exactly the right-wrong verse number: Luke 18:25.

For it is easier for a camel to go through the eye of a needle than for a rich man to enter the kingdom of God.

From there—Hoof still blowing smoke, a lawyer in his ear—Sheriff Kick moved on to muse over brand-new information from the state crime lab. Chemists at the lab had tested the two different jugs of apple cider. The jug recovered from inside the mobile coach—a white Igloo with a red lid—was laced with a lethal level of phenobarbital, consistent with the suicides of the Pearls, who had obviously concluded they were neither headed for Andorra nor for heaven, but for prison. The orange Coleman jug recovered from the "new chapel," misshapen from heat but intact, contained pure apple cider. In her first interview, Fernanda Cervantes, the wife of Royland Rogers before Rogers was murdered and Hoof moved in, told the sheriff that while she was captive she had heard Ruth Pearl arrive through the tunnel and switch jugs. In her second interview with the sheriff—after the lab results—Ms. Cervantes had cried and said at least Mother Ruth had loved them after all.

"Sheriff Kick?"

The judge had interrupted her thoughts.

"We are ready to hear your version of events."

II

The sheriff's answer to the court kicked off an immediate desk suspension, pending a PFC review of conduct, as she knew it would. As this review occurred, her district attorney, Baird Sipple, not exactly an ally, would determine whether there would be criminal charges.

Sheriff Kick directed department business from her office in the Public Service Building. There was much to untangle. It seemed proven by her own experience that Roman Vanderhoof had no involvement in the death of Duke Hashimoto, gutted by Dortmunder with a karambit in the tunnel on Black Friday. Neither had Hoof been present when Nelson "Peep" Woods and Robert "Skip" Henderson had been cut down with the M16—Ms. Cervantes testified this was also Dortmunder—or when Dortmunder had been shot in the back inside the tunnel. The weapon that killed Dortmunder, a Winchester hunting rifle, was found with the M16 alongside the body of Duke Hashimoto. In her interviews, the sheriff's mother-in-law claimed to have ditched that rifle in her escape out of the tunnel, during which she met no one. This could be explored. Or left alone. Belle seemed fragile and almost calm, gentler and more patient with the kids these days.

Meanwhile, Hoof and his lawyer had tried to leverage his relative innocence to propose that he had played no part in any House-of-Shalah-related crimes, a dizzying array that included the murders of Royland Rogers, Darwin Fuss, and Raven Furtzig. On the topic of those three homicides, Hoof's testimony had been that when Brother Roy was discovered snitching to the feds, the prophet-father had seen the end of his House of Shalah scam, the need to escape, and he had orchestrated Roy's death by strangulation—Dortmunder again, Hoof claimed, after Roy was lured to Missy's house—and then Roy's embalming by Brother Win and his tattoo work by Raven Furtzig, making Roy into a body double, after which Dortmunder, to eliminate witnesses, had taken those two with his exotic knife.

Much of this was obviously true. How much was hers to figure out. Presenting himself as a naïve observer of other men's evil deeds, Hoof admitted only that he had broken into Old Friends Farm to steal painkillers—because, again, Sheriff Kick had cruelly shot him in the back—and he was sorry about any poor animals caught in the crossfire when the sheriff had tried to finish him off.

III

Truth and resolution developed slowly, as they will.

"Off the record," the sheriff told Markus Sullivan from the *New York Times* after his paper sent him back to profile her, "and no matter what happens with my job, I won't rest until he's back in prison."

After filing his original story, Sullivan had studied Sheriff Kick's career.

"A rural sex-trafficking ring busted in your first year. Two years ago, you were on the international white-power radar. Then you had the cannibal. This time, wow, seven homicides, and you snatch your community from the brink of a Waco-like disaster. What's going on here?"

"It's the bratwurst," she answered him, almost smiling. "And the polka. See, if you polka too soon after eating a large sausage . . . But that's off the record too."

The sarcastic edge of this left a silence between them.

"We can make fun of ourselves," she said finally. "But it's a whole different thing if you mock us in the *New York Times*."

The reporter nodded solemnly. Then he leaned closer over her desk and looked into her eyes.

"Sheriff, something I never told you. You didn't ask, for obvious reasons. But you might want to know it now. Do you know where Purdy is?"

"Sure. Just north of here in Vernon County. Not even a town. Just a couple houses and a sign, the upper Bad Axe River flowing through."

"Everyone's from somewhere," Sullivan said, "and that's where I'm from. The Sullivans of Purdy."

She sighed. "Okay. I feel better."

He pivoted. "What can you tell me about Duke Hashimoto?"

She sifted through her busy mind. Her dispatcher Denise had made a special project of researching the life of the dead man they had found blocking the Pearls' escape outlet.

"Retired ATF special agent, got his heart broken at Waco. Something of an outcast in the agency because of Senate testimony that ran against the grain, a career of being relegated to small one-man projects. He was here in September using Royland Rogers as an informant, setting up a warrant so the feds could raid the prophet looking for financial crime. Then Rogers went off his radar. We had an election and the ATF got busy. The raid fell through. Hashimoto retired. Then Fernanda Carpenter called him about pornographic pictures of her daughter, and he came back on his own. He nursed Keystone Lights at the Ease Inn, probably faking it. I saw him once at Piggly Wiggly—isn't hindsight great?—and asked myself, *What's a federal cop doing here?*"

"And now?"

"We sent him home to California. He has a sister there. Betty. I Zoomed in to his funeral. Bad Axe County sent flowers."

"And the pictures of the girl?"

"We have them. As far as we know, they went nowhere except between computers inside the group. Not in the cloud. Not in circulation. Probably caught just in time. The email that carried them to Fernanda Carpenter came from an account we've traced to Ruth Pearl. One more piece of evidence to suggest that things had gone too far for Mother Ruth."

"What happens to the Carpenters?"

"I don't know."

"I followed up on 'they shoot horses,'" Sullivan said. "It's an absolutely perfect weapons-grade rumor. The best yet. And with no basis whatsoever in reality until Vanderhoof made it come true. So now, yeah, now people can say, 'They shoot horses.' "

The sheriff had been thinking about this. "The problem in that statement, claim, lie, rumor, whatever it is, is not *shoot horses*. A sheriff can solve *shoot horses*. The problem is *they*. The idea of *they* is where the real trouble starts."

"Interesting."

"If I could solve *they*," she said, "I'd be much more than a sheriff."

"Hmm." He made notes for a few moments. Then he moved on. "The Carpenters gave up every penny they earned coming through that gate. Where is the money?"

"Beyond my resources and talents," she told him. "The feds are working on the whole Pearl pyramid, all the financial stuff. As for resources, right now the community is supporting the Carpenters. Homestays. Donations from civic groups and churches. My department is coordinating the fund drive."

"You think some of them might stay?"

She shrugged, belying a much deeper emotional response.

"We're as good a place as any," she said. "But now I have another funeral to attend."

▲ ▼ ▲ ▼

She stood in uniform with her deputies at Mikayla Stonebreaker's burial. All the snow had melted and the full-on visual drudgery of early December was upon them, all things gray and brown. That had been a beautiful snowfall, soft and fast and heavy, back at Thanksgiving. The Bad Axe had been blessed but unable to enjoy it.

It was a muddled moment now, standing on soft cold ground honoring a deputy who had committed crimes, shamed herself and the department, then been murdered by her husband.

Eight homicides, the sheriff had to remind herself, realizing that Sullivan had miscounted.

Just because one was not a mystery didn't mean it didn't count.

Deputies fired old-school carbines into the woolen sky.

Mikayla Stonebreaker's casket was lowered.

"Deputy Luck?"

"Yes, Sheriff."

"You're riding back with me."

▲ ▼ ▲ ▼

"So this man who hurt you, what is his name?" she asked Deputy Luck three miles toward Farmstead.

"L'Antonio," the young woman said. "Like on the back of the photographs that Deputy Stonebreaker was sending. That's the same L'Antonio. He said he spent the photos like money. He told me who she was and who he sold them to. Those are the inmate profiles I was looking at on the department computer."

"So you're telling me that Deputy Stonebreaker crushed out on the very same guy who sexually assaulted you in high school?"

"It's true. It's not as unlikely as you think."

"Why?"

"On meet-an-inmate.com," Deputy Luck said, "they all put their pictures. You can flip right through them kind of like online dating."

"And?"

"Have you ever heard of 'hot convict'?"

The sheriff had, and she drove a full mile silently.

"Pretty good-looking guy, I guess."

"Burn your eyes, Sheriff. And the mail L'Antonio gets . . ."

"And you were investigating Stonebreaker without telling me . . . because?"

Lyndsey Luck fidgeted, pulling on her seat belt and staring out her window as if muddy cows in muddy fields needed careful study.

The sheriff said, "Blowing smoke right now is not an option."

"Okay, I know. But wouldn't you think that I was weird, like something was really wrong with me, if I was corresponding with a guy who assaulted me? Wouldn't you think I was sick like Stonebreaker? And super-unprofessional?"

"I would. I was worried about exactly that."

"But what happened is L'Antonio wrote to me a year afterward to take responsibility and say he was sorry and hoped that my life was good. That's how this all started. On my end, forgiveness, right? For my sake. It doesn't have to be this wound I carry around forever. I don't have to hurt myself with hate. I have the power to forgive and move on. It's the whole reason I'm sitting here right now, in law enforcement, and I love my job. So I thought, *I'll look into it, and if it's nothing, then I don't have to make myself look stupid. I'll just drop it.*"

The sheriff drove another mile in silence.

"And when," she asked her young deputy finally, but gently, "do you think you might have figured out that it was not nothing?"

▲ ▼ ▲ ▼

A mile later her phone rang.

"Sheriff! Good news!" Rhino gushed.

"I can use some. Go ahead."

"Somebody anonymous just dropped off forty thousand cash for the Carpenters!"

"Wow," she said, stunned. She repeated it. "Somebody gave forty thousand dollars to help the Carpenters."

Deputy Luck cheered from the passenger seat.

Rhino said, "I also need to tell you that the judge is ready to do the prelim for Melissa Grooms."

The sheriff dropped off Luck and drove to the courthouse, took her observer's position, met Missy's eyes, and smiled sadly. She didn't know how it was going to go. She had shared facts and recused herself from decision making in Missy's case. As with her own potential criminal charges, she waited on the sidelines, an anxious and vulnerable bystander.

"Your Honor," District Attorney Baird Sipple said, standing, "we can make this quick. The state declines to press any charges on the condition that the court require Ms. Groom to enter a rehabilitation program."

The sheriff smiled again at Missy. Their old-friend eyes shared two words that contained both futility and hope.

Rehab . . . again . . .

▲ ▼ ▲ ▼

The sheriff's fate began to resolve the next day when District Attorney Sipple decided on attempted manslaughter in the second degree, recommending no prison time, a period of supervised probation only, if she saved the time, expense, and unwanted attention of a trial by pleading guilty.

She did so.

On the afternoon of Christmas Eve, as the Police and Fire Commission met to translate the DA's decision into her professional future, the sheriff was speaking at a memorial service for the mule and three horses that Hoof had killed at Old Friends Farm. She said the names: Lunch Bucket, Boots, Maggie May, and Roscoe. As she read a Mary Oliver poem she loved called "Wild Geese"—crossing species, yes, that was the point, our common trials, the limits of grief and atonement—*Tell me about despair, yours, and I will tell you mine; Meanwhile the world goes on*—she accepted that the PFC's hands were tied.

She was guilty of a crime. Her penalty had yet to be paid. She understood they would be glad to take her badge.

Later, at five P.M. sharp, her siren was on, splitting ridgetop silence as she accelerated. Her red-and-blue flashers swatted back the

too-early darkness. She was in love with her job, tearing up the highway toward Farmstead for a 911 call—a happy-hour fistfight at the
Ease Inn—when the call came. She knew that she was done before
she answered: *Sheriff, we're going to need your resignation . . .*

IV

She searched, days later, on frozen ground through new snow along
the bank of the lower Bad Axe River until she found him. She was
both dismayed and relieved by what little remained of the majestic
old buck she had shot, and chased, and shot again in November. His
brittle bones beneath his shrunken, tattered hide, his antlers gnawed
to nubs by hungry porcupines and mice.

She gave back what she had—she told him—she laid her heart
inside his empty ribs—she paid him back nothing and everything.

This was the mystery.

It always would be.

How the world goes on.